I0650734

Tres Vota

The Echo Chronicles: Book 1

Maryella Cooper

Dedicated to Ayla Cooper

My Daughter, My Inspiration, My Friend

Special Thanks to the wonderful Souls who helped in reviewing and assisting in the creation of this work: Sean Clausen (sorry about that cliffhanger), Kristen Rinaldi, Susan McBride, Abigail Griffin, Joe Beardog and Ryan French. An extra special thanks to Molly May Clifford for you amazing artwork and friendship.

Contents

Chapter 1

"Time flies over us, but leaves its shadow behind"
Nathaniel Hawthorn

Phoebe pushed her long auburn hair out of her eyes as she glanced around at her history team. *How can I be so unlucky!* She watched in annoyance as Chris back flipped off the table while countering a swing from Marcus's newspaper sword. Junior year is tough enough, so why would Miss Brandon think this group project would be so stimulating. *Not the word I would choose*, she thought. *How about aggravating.* She glanced at the clock and sighed.

Meeting after school seemed a better idea then missing lunch to plan out this comprehensive report, but in the last ten minutes Chris and Marcus had been practicing their gladiator skills, while Kristy and Benjamin argued about toga fashions. *Oh, why a report on Julius Caesar?* Jaxom was the only other calm one in the room, which was weird. He sat leaning back in his chair, feet on the table, messing with some metal trinket. *This is going to take forever!*

"Why don't we divide some of this work between us, so we can each start getting something accomplished," Phoebe suggested.

"Chill out Pagan, we got a month before this things' due," Jaxom stated, looking up from his treasure. Phoebe glared at him. Jaxom was the coolest jerk in her class and Phoebe couldn't believe her bad luck at having to be in the same group with him. He would be easier to deal with if she could just stay out of his radar, but he never allowed her this luxury.

Jaxom loved to include her in his antics and just as she began to feel things were ok between them, he would make her the butt of his joke. His newest thing since last year was to refuse to use her name. He had a real talent for nicknames and had thought up dozens of different ones for her. His nicknames rattled her, but she ignored it this time and griped back.

"Have you looked at this assignment? We have to do a five page report, a timeline, a computer presentation, and an additional creative, informative assignment, whatever that means."

"That's what we're doing," Marcus remarked, as he and Chris wandered back towards the table.

"Yea, we thought we'd put on a gladiator show," Chris added. The two, who had been best friends since second grade, seemed to be complete opposites. Chris's light skin, blonde hair and blue eyes are a complete contrast to Marcus's dark complexion, black hair, and brown eyes. Chris was a class clown, while Marcus, who of course laughed at his friends antics, was fairly serious about school. Even their families were opposite with Chris having four sisters and Marcus being a single child.

"I don't think that's what Miss Brandon meant," Phoebe said.

"Oh, come on, it's a great idea," Marcus answered back. "We can stage a big fight and set up a fake coliseum! Caesar paid for many extravagant competitions, you know."

"And we can wear swords and togas to school." Chris added.

"Gladiators didn't wear togas, only Roman citizens were allowed to." Kristy interrupted. Phoebe guessed that Kristy would be her biggest help on this assignment. The two have grown up a block away from each other and used to ride bikes together as kids. The past few years they had grown apart some. This was partly because of Phoebe's summer trips away but also when Kristy's mother became sick and her dad left them, Kristy had just stopped coming over. Phoebe knew it was hard on her friend, but wished that Kristy wouldn't shut her out. *I know what it's like to be raised by a single mom.*

When she looked over at her friend, her hope for help wavered. She and Benjamin were no longer arguing, and now sat close together, legs touching. Kristy's comment was made without even glancing at the others around the table, and she was now giggling about something Benjamin was whispering in her ear.

He seemed an odd choice for Kristy. Benjamin was uptight and usually antisocial. Phoebe had never seen him at any school event and he didn't hang out with anyone she knew. Hopefully, for Kristy sake, this new relationship would draw them both out a bit, though she didn't have high hopes for it working out between them. Looking back at the other boys, Phoebe noticed that she had lost their attention again.

"Did you get it cleaned up yet?" Chris was asking Jaxom.

"Yea, check out these symbols," Jaxom replied. Phoebe leaned over to see what they were so interested in and was amazed to see that Jaxom truly had found a treasure. Jaxom held a beautiful silver ring up to the light. Its wide band was covered with intricate designs and what looked like some kind of foreign writing.

"That's got to be worth a fortune!" Marcus declared as everyone admired the incredible artwork of the piece.

"Do you think that Baker's pawn shop would take it?" Benjamin asked as he and Kristy rejoined the group.

Phoebe laughed, "They'd think it was stolen for sure."

Jaxom glared at her and replied, "Don't worry Hippie, I know the right people."

Those would be the wrong kind of people, Phoebe thought. "Whatever," she said instead, "can we just get back to this report? We need to decide something today."

Kristy looked up from the ring and answered, "Benjamin and I can put together the timeline this weekend, if you want. He's stopping by anyways. This history stuff will be a great excuse for him to stay awhile."

"Bet they don't get much history done." Chris said as he and Marcus laughed. Benjamin started to laugh until he realized Kristy was offended. He then acted as if he was also insulted. *What a fake*, Phoebe thought.

Kristy gave Chris a nasty look and responded, "Not like it's too hard. He conquers Gaul, fights the civil war, and then gets murdered."

Marcus startled at this and responded, "There's a lot more to Julius Caesar then that. He was a brilliant politician, an incredible general and a gracious leader loved by his people!"

"Yea," Chris added, "and all his sexual endeavors could fill walls worth of timelines. That could take you years to finish." Chris started to snigger but Marcus glanced at his friend with a look that quickly cut short Chris's laughter.

Phoebe knew she shouldn't, but couldn't stop herself. "Julius Caesar was a bloodthirsty warmonger, who got just what he deserved. He destroyed countless tribes in Gaul and everywhere else he took his legions. He even marched on Rome itself. What do you think the whole civil war thing was about?"

"He was trying to expand the Roman Empire, that's what all Roman generals did." Marcus responded. "And the civil war was Pompey's fault anyways."

"And the Romans brought trade and built roads wherever they went." Jaxom joined in, "Julius Caesar was one of the greatest rulers Rome ever had. If he had lived, the empire would never have fallen apart like it did."

Phoebe shook her head in disbelief at the boys' elevated opinion of Caesar. "That wasn't until 500 years after he died, Jaxom! There is no way that he could have influenced things that far into the future. He died because he was greedy. He seized too much power from the rest of the Senators, and then his adopted son comes along after him and takes complete control. I think the world is well rid of them all."

Jaxom leaned his chair back down on all four legs and began flipping and catching his ring. "I think he would have done great things if he had lived."

"I'm glad he didn't!" Kristy retorted, looking up from Benjamin's advances for a moment. "Phoebe's right, Caesar was a ruthless Dictator."

"He let captive senators go free over and over again during the civil war," Marcus countered.

"And he killed women and children in his conquering of Gaul," Phoebe's snapped back. Then she told herself to calm down. *This isn't accomplishing anything.* She began to take 3 slow deep breaths like Grandpa always prompted her to do when she felt off balanced by something or someone. She was only on her second inhale when Jaxom spoke and then so much happened so quickly that she forgot about the other breaths.

"I wish Julius Caesar had never been assassinated." Jaxom said, as he caught his strange new silver ring. Then the lights went out, the room began to rock, and someone began to scream.

Chapter 2

"Time moves in one direction, memories in another"
William Gibson

Smoke, screaming, fire! *The library is collapsing! Where's Jessica, Mom! I've got to find them*! Jaxom leapt from the floor and bolted for the door, only to trip over Phoebe who had also been knocked from her chair during the quake.

"Jaxom, get off of me," Phoebe complained. Jaxom quickly got up and looked around, pulling himself back into the present. *There is no fire. That was long ago. Jessica and Mom are gone and there is nothing I can do about it.* Jaxom felt the sharp pain in his heart that he always felt when he thought about his lost family. He tried to push the feeling away but was only partially successful. *Stay in the present, man. Leave the past alone*, he told himself.

"Kristy, will you shut up!" Phoebe snapped and Kristy's wailing diminished into more of a whimper. Jaxom's anxiety lessened as the noise did and he saw that there wasn't even any smoke. It was only papers tossed about during the shaking that were now settling to the floor. Soft moonlight streamed in through the windows, *wait, moonlight! It isn't even four o'clock yet.* Then Jaxom noticed something even stranger. He heard rushing water, like a great river was suddenly flowing past the school.

Jaxom hurried to the window, arriving there at the same time as Phoebe. Instead of seeing the inside of the schoolyard or a giant river, he found himself looking out into a beautiful garden in the height of spring bloom. The garden was enclosed by a tall stone wall and in the garden center was a beautiful woman staring back at them.

A shimmering full moon highlighted her perfect features, tan flawless skin and thick jet-black hair. She was clothed in light purple silken robes highlighted by the sparkle of gems adorning her fingers and armbands. She was rising from a small stone shrine with a look of great surprise on her exquisite face. Excitement and worry spared for Jaxom's attention as the woman turned and yelled toward an alcove that began the entrance into a huge stone structure at the end of the garden.

"We'd better get out there and figure out where we are," Jaxom decided aloud. *She looks like royalty. How did we end up in her garden"?*

"What!" Kristy shrieked from behind him. "What's going on? This can't be real!" Then she broke down into tears once again. *She's not gonna be any help*, Jaxom thought, feeling annoyed at Kristy's outbursts. He was feeling nervous himself, but needed to know what was going on.

"I'll stay with you, while Jaxom checks it out." Benjamin responded as he pulled Kristy into a tight embrace.

Marcus and Chris looked at each other, than together answered, "Works for us."

"Well, I'm not staying in here and placing our fate in his hands." Phoebe snapped. "I'm going to see who she is." With that, she headed out the door without waiting to see if Jaxom followed. *She always needs to be in charge*, he grumbled to himself as he followed her out into the hallway.

Then he noticed that he still held the silver ring. *Strange, I kept hold of it through the quake.* He slipped it onto his finger and called out to Phoebe, "Wait up Witch." Phoebe abruptly stopped and turned sharply around to glare at him.

"My name is Phoebe! Are you too stupid to figure that out or do you just enjoy being such a jerk?" She turned back around and pushed open the school door, stepping into the magnificent garden. Jaxom let a small smile sneak out as he watched her go. *She is so hot when she gets all fired up.* He just couldn't help messing with her. He followed her out the door and saw her looking about in breathless wonder.

The rest of the school was missing as well. The history hall was now surrounded by flowering herbs and bushes of every variety. The night air was filled with their incredible fragrance and the full moon illuminated the view with its soft glow. Jaxom had never smelled anything so lovely and thought Phoebe looked stunning standing there framed by the beautiful scenery. He wasn't about to admit to either thought so instead he said, "Come on, let's figure out what's up."

The two teens walked around the edge of the building, and were startled to see the woman had been joined by half a dozen men dressed in ancient-looking tunics and holding swords. Jaxom felt terror fill his stomach as the troop advanced toward them with swords drawn. He felt Phoebe grab his arm and knew she was scared too.

The lead soldier hollered something at them, but Jaxom couldn't understand the language he spoke. Jaxom put his arm up, hand open and said, "We're unarmed, we mean no harm!" The soldier paused for a moment, the spoke again. Jaxom was at a loss about what to do. He couldn't comprehend anything the man was saying. "I just wish we could understand them," he exclaimed to Phoebe. Then suddenly, they could!

"What language is that which you speak, and how have you brought this structure to Julius Caesar's villa?" the lead soldier demanded. Jaxom startled at this strange development. *Could this really be Julius Caesars home? This doesn't look like Rome.*

"We speak English and I don't know how we got here. We were at school. Please don't kill us!" Jaxom begged. The woman stepped forward and placed her hand on the soldiers arm.

"Mark Anthony, calm yourself." she directed. "These youngsters do not feel too dangerous. Why don't you go and inspect this interesting structure while I speak with our guests." The man gave a slight nod and turned towards the schoolhouse. *This woman must be the one in charge around here, if she can order Mark Anthony around,* Jaxom thought, watching as the lovely lady appraised them with her dark eyes.

"Our four friends are still inside! Please don't hurt them either," Phoebe exclaimed. Jaxom was glad she had thought of the others and felt embarrassed that he had been too scared to think of anyone else right then. *I always think of myself when there's trouble,* Jaxom criticized himself.

"They will not be harmed if everyone cooperates," Mark Anthony retorts as he led his men towards the school building.

"Come and sit with me," the beautiful woman gestured toward the alcove. Jaxom felt his knees go weak at the woman's smile, but somehow managed to follow her and Phoebe up the steps, towards a low table and couches. "I am Cleopatra, Pharaoh of Egypt and beloved of Julius Caesar."

Chapter 3

"Courage is the price that life exacts for granting peace"
Amelia Earhart

Cleopatra's mind was racing as she led the strangers toward the villa. The miraculous appearance of these youths seemed to her as divine intervention. She had come into the garden this evening in search of such assistance. Both she and Calpurnia had been having terrible visions of Julius Caesars' downfall, and this evening she awoke from a dream which included the death of her young son, Ceasarion. How these strangers could help, she was unsure, but she must find a way to keep her loved ones safe.

As they reached the veranda, Cleopatra called out to her handmaid, "Miriam, send a messenger to find Balbus and then bring tea for myself and my guests."

"I have already sent for him, you're Majesty," Miriam answered. *That girl is smart one*, Cleopatra thought as she turned back to this unusual couple and signaled for them to be seated.

As she reclined onto her divan, she wondered about their connection to Julius. *Both are too young and inexperienced to be of much help. In fact they seem terrified by their strange circumstance. Yet some power brought them here for a purpose. Was it Mother Isis?*

"You said that you do not understand your presence here, but will you tell me about yourselves and explain your knowledge of Julius Caesar. Both of you were quite startled when Mark Anthony mentioned his name." Cleopatra gently asked.

The girl answered too quickly, "My name is Phoebe and this is Jaxom. We're in high school history class together and we are doing a report on Julius Caesar. We were arguing and then suddenly an earthquake shook the school and seemed to bring us here. We didn't mean to come."

Cleopatra thought for a moment and replied, "Education is a noble pursuit, but it is strange that some power was not risen by your group. What were you arguing about before the quake?"

The girl, Phoebe, stumbled over her words and her friend, Jaxom came to her rescue, "Just trying to figure out our work. I don't think it had anything to do with this magic." *He seems to be covering for her.* Cleopatra mused. *The girl was embarrassed by something and his statement was at best a half-truth. Perhaps they are not as innocent as I first thought.* But there suddenly was a disturbance out by the school building and all three instantly rose to see what was occurring.

The soldiers were escorting four more teens out of the building. Three were male and struggled against the guards' rough treatment. The last, a young woman, sobbed uncontrollably as she was carried out over Mark Anthony's shoulder.

"Put her down!" Jaxom cried as he sprinted from the patio and headed toward the crowd. Cleopatra followed with Phoebe at a slower pace, smiling over the fearless response of this new acquaintance. Mark Anthony immediately dropped the hysterical girl and drew his sword. Jaxom stopped short and spoke slowly, "You said no one would be hurt."

"I am unused to being questioned," Mark Anthony responded, pointing his sword at Jaxom. Then the Consul returned the sword to its sheath. "As of yet, they are unharmed. Yet they only speak your English to us and would not follow my orders to leave this strange structure." Mark Anthony glared at the building with a look of suspicion.

"Consul," Cleopatra addressed Mark Anthony, reminding him of his position. She didn't need him bullying these young travelers. "Leave them be and let us speak of these matters in private." He ordered his men to release the others but keep watch, as Jaxom and Phoebe rejoined their friends. The Queen gave the youths a friendly smile trying to reassure them, before turning to escort Mark Anthony away.

Cleopatra walked back up the stone steps with Julius's trusted friend. Mark Anthony had supported Julius in many ways. He was a Centurion Julius relied on in battle and this year's Consul in the Senate. He even recently made a public offering of the title of Emperor to Julius. It was a strangely foreign ritual to Cleopatra. Mark Anthony had been running naked around Rome in the Lupercalia at the time. *Perhaps*, Cleopatra thought, *Mark Anthony's Priesthood could work to my advantage in this situation. I needed his support in convincing Julius of the danger awaiting us all.*

"Quite an extraordinary turn of events." Cleopatra began as they reached the patio. "This could be the divine help which I was seeking." She sank into her favorite spot in the corner, watching Mark Anthony intently. He first looked past her, toward the group of foreigners with a frown. Then his face softened as he regarded Cleopatra for a moment.

"My dear Queen of Egypt, you have not convinced me yet of this great danger you foresee." Then Mark Anthony gestured toward the arguing group of newcomers. "But if you are right, this group of children would not give us much advantage. I am troubled by their strange appearance tonight, though."

"I saw Jaxom stand up to you. There is strength in this group." Cleopatra responded. "Look at the big picture here. As a priest of Jupiter, you should recognize magic this unusual as significant." Mark Anthony sat up a little taller at this comment. *Maybe he will listen this time.* She had tried to speak to him about her concerns the other day, but he did not take her seriously. "The dreams both I and Calpurnia have had also match to the Etruscan oracle's reading last fall. She told Julius to beware the Ides of March. Look at the moon,

Anthony. It is quite a coincidence that these foreigners would arrive at this time in such an unusual manner."

A small noise from the house caused both Cleopatra and Mark Anthony to turn. Miriam stepped onto the patio carrying a tray of tea. She was followed by Julius Caesar's closest friend, Cornelius Balbus.

"Come and sit with us Balbus. We are in need of your counsel." Cleopatra called to the old Roman soldier." Cleopatra had only known Balbus for a short time, but had already come to understand Julius's complete trust in the kindly elder. *This is a man who sees everything and always comprehends better than anyone else what's going on in Rome. Perhaps he would listen to me.*

"I am always available for a midnight rendezvous with Julius Caesar's beautiful African jewel. I suppose the large, strange dwelling in your garden accounts for your evening distress." Balbus responded as he lowers himself onto a couch near Cleopatra.

"As do the strangers who arrived within the structure," Mark Anthony responds, pointing at the group arguing in the garden. Then he accepted a cup of tea from Miriam, leaned back and looked at Cleopatra. He seemed content to let her take the conversation.

He looks amused, Cleopatra thought with irritation, also taking a cup. *Now how to explain this to Balbus.* She had not had a chance to speak with him previously about these concerns and was unsure of his reaction.

"Balbus, I believe their strange appearance is connected to frightening dreams I have had about Julius Caesar and my son's lives. I think Julius's life is in peril but I do not know from where the danger will originate."

"I agree with you, my cherished Pharaoh," Balbus surprisingly concurs. "I am gravely concerned about the rumors flowing out of the Senate lately. Julius Caesar's power is cause for great jealousy in some of the influential men of Rome."

"I fail to see the connection between the Senate gossip and these strange foreigners," Mark Anthony declares.

"Let us figure it out then," Balbus responded. "Here comes two of your unexpected guests."

Cleopatra gazed towards the garden to see Phoebe and Jaxom slowly heading towards them. They looked so young and confused, Cleopatra's heart went out to them. *Surely there is a connection, but I do not see it either.*

Chapter 4

"A man's character is his fate"

Heraclitus

As the Queen and her soldier left to talk, Phoebe rushed to where Kristy lay sobbing on the ground. Benjamin was there a moment later as the other boys gathered around Jaxom, throwing out questions to which Jaxom had no answers. Phoebe didn't care about their queries. She was just concerned about Kristy's tears. *She's been through so much the last few years. I hope she can handle this strangeness.*

"Kristy, everything is alright," Phoebe softly said, as she knelt down to comfort her friend. Benjamin sat next to them on the grass, and grabbed hold of Kristy's hand. Phoebe wished he would go away, so she could talk with her friend in private.

"How can this be happening?" Kristy sobbed.

"It must be some kind of magic," Phoebe answered her, gently pushing Kristy's red curls away from her tear streaked face. "We're in ancient Rome. We'll figure this out. We just need to stick together." Phoebe consoled her friend, hoping she was right. *This is way beyond any magic I've ever seen.*

"We just need to figure out how to get home," Benjamin responded angrily. "Whatever voodoo this is, there has to be a way to reverse it."

"But this is amazing!" Jaxom countered as the boys joined them on the lawn. "We are actually in the past. That was Cleopatra, the Queen of Egypt!" Phoebe glanced at them as they sat down. Jaxom and Chris looked completely excited over this unexpected expedition. Marcus looked kind of concerned but not as distraught as Benjamin. *He looks like he's going to have a heart attack.*

"I don't care who she is," Benjamin barked, "this is unnatural!"

"Well, I care," Marcus retorted. "We don't know how we arrived here or how to get home, so maybe we should figure out what's happening now." Marcus looked at Jaxom with suspicion in his eyes. "Are you sure you don't know why you and Phoebe can suddenly speak Latin?"

Phoebe was feeling worried. Their group was not close friends except for Marcus and Chris. Even her and Kristy's relationship was timeworn. The anger and distrust with each other could fracture the group. They might not ever figure out how to get back home.

"We aren't keeping anything from you." Jaxom answered Marcus.

"We'll tell you everything that's going on," Phoebe promised.

"Why is Mark Anthony here?" Chris asked. "I thought he and Cleopatra got together after the assassination."

Phoebe was shocked for a moment, which seemed strange with the other shocking events occurring today. *Cleopatra identified herself as Julius*

Caesars love, yet what if the Queen is already fooling around with Mark Anthony. Of course, Julius Caesar is actually married to Calpurnia. The state of affairs in Rome seems more confusing and scandalous then I'd realized at first.

"You would be the first to notice that," Marcus laughed. The boys were snickering and even Kristy stopped crying to consider the question. *That's better*, Phoebe thought, as she felt some of the tension flow out of the group. *Maybe we can figure this out working together.*

"I think we're here to help stop the assassination," Marcus stated after a few minutes. "Remember Jaxom, that's what you said right before the quake brought us here."

"I remember," Jaxom responded. "Maybe our knowledge about Julius Caesar's death can change events."

Phoebe thought about this for a moment. Her mind flowed back to her Grandpa talking about the changes happening back home. He worked for the National Forest and for several years now, she had stayed with him for the summer.

As they walked the old logging trail around his cabin, he would show her the gradual changes of the forest regenerating itself. *Nature needs time for change,* he would tell her. *Modern society causes such sudden changes with their modern progress that the forests can't keep up.* Grandpa liked to say, *thoughtful observation always should come before action. It seems short-sighted to assume our purpose here, like diving in without checking the depth of the river.*

"I'm not sure if that is such a great idea," Phoebe remarked, expressing her concerns. "We shouldn't assume why we are here and we don't know what changes we might make here or back home."

"What if we don't exist afterwards," Kristy joined in with a shriek. "Remember that movie where the kid caused his parents not to meet, so he didn't exist anymore."

"Oh, come on you two," Jaxom argued, "that was just a movie. Don't be so spineless." Phoebe glared at Jaxom, and was about to comment back about his weak anatomy when Marcus interrupted her.

"I also remember what you said Phoebe," Marcus commented. "You told us that there was no way that Julius Caesar could have influenced things 500 years into the future. So over two thousand years should be relatively safe." Phoebe wasn't sure about this logic. *That's not really what I meant earlier. There's a lot of things that contribute to the fall of Rome.*

"I agree with Marcus and Jaxom," Chris expressed. "Imagine how awesome it would be to go to the Senate house and be the heroes that saved Julius Caesar!"

"That's crazy," Benjamin shouted! "This isn't some game. We need to find a way home!"

"We don't have a way home," Jaxom countered. *Again, we are not getting anywhere*, Phoebe thought.

"We won't figure anything out, sitting here arguing," she said. "Maybe we should talk to Cleopatra again," Phoebe decided aloud as she got up. Jaxom, Chris and Marcus also stood, leaving Kristy and Benjamin sitting on the lawn together, both unwilling to move.

"I think you two should stay here with them," Jaxom told Chris and Marcus. "You can't understand their language and trying to translate while we talk will complicate things. Let Flycatcher and me see what we can find out." *That's a weird request and nickname, but at least he included me,* Phoebe thought.

"We'll be right back," Phoebe promised. The two boys reluctantly agreed and settled back on the grass a ways away from Kristy and Benjamin. Marcus frowned at them with another look of distrust as Phoebe turned away and headed slowly towards the stone patio with Jaxom following close behind.

Chapter 5

"And after all, we're only ordinary men"
Roger Waters

Jaxom's mind was racing. Marcus's comment about when he had wished Julius Caesar would live had caused him to start thinking. *That wish seemed to bring us here. When I wished to understand the soldier, I could and so could Phoebe who was with me. Cleopatra mentioned raising power and it seems that the magic came from me!*

He wanted to find out more from the Queen about this power. That was why he had asked the others to stay behind. *If I have some kind of magic, I don't want everyone to know. What if I could use this magic to go back in time to save my mom and sister?* The thought made his heart feel lighter. He glanced at Phoebe, walking slightly ahead of him. *There was no way I could stop her from staying involved and the language excuse wouldn't work.* That spunk was one of the things he loved about her.

"It looks like the Queen has another guest." Phoebe commented. Jaxom pulled his eyes off of Phoebe, a little difficult to do, and looked at the terrace. He saw an older man had joined Cleopatra and Mark Anthony.

"Doesn't look like the Julius Caesar from our history book," Jaxom remarked. "Let's go find out who he is." The two teens walked up the steps to join the three lounging there.

"Come and join us," Cleopatra called to them, gesturing to a low couch opposite of her. "This is our trusted friend Balbus." Mark Anthony reclined on another couch frowning at them. A short wooden table sat between them on which tea was served.

From this higher viewpoint Jaxom could see over the garden's stone wall to the banks of a large river. This is where the rushing water sounds were coming from. The sound of the river seemed to sing to his hopes. *Maybe this magic can make everything right,* he tried to convince himself. Across the water was other stone buildings though none seemed as impressive as this villa. It was a magnificent sight and Jaxom had to pause for a moment to view it before sitting next to Phoebe.

"That is the river Tiber," Cleopatra told them when she saw his interest. "Only a few miles downstream is the city of Rome."

"Unfortunately, we cannot see her around the bend in the river." Balbus commented. "It is an incredible sight. But Julius Caesar values the seclusion of this place."

"He spends so much time in the public with his duties to Rome that he needs to get away." Cleopatra replied. "I am glad he had the foresight to build such a perfect retreat."

"Your company makes it his paradise," Balbus expresses good-naturedly. The Queen gave the old Roman a radiant smile and turned back to Jaxom and Phoebe.

"How are your friends?" Cleopatra asked.

"Confused, but they're ok, your Majesty," Phoebe answered.

"And have you figured out how you ended up here?" Mark Anthony questioned them.

"We have no idea, sir," Phoebe replied.

"I wanted to talk to your Majesty about that," Jaxom quickly told the Queen. He didn't want Phoebe controlling the whole conversation. *I need to learn about my magic, not get sidetracked by the scenery.*

"Have some tea with us and we shall discuss our unexpected meeting." Cleopatra said as her servant brought out several more cups. As Jaxom accepted the warm drink, Balbus suddenly sat up and stared intently at Jaxom.

"That is an interesting ring you wear, Jaxom," Balbus remarked. "It does not match your attire. I would say it was of Egyptian design."

Jaxom quickly set down the teacup and held his hand up to inspect the unusual ring. He also glanced at his ratty jeans and tee-shirt. *Not the best first impression*, he thought.

"That is Egyptian!" Cleopatra exclaimed. "May I see it?" Cleopatra leaned across the low table towards Jaxom looking intently at his hand which wore the silver ring. She smelled like one of the flowers in her garden and was definitely more beautiful. Her silken robes allowed Jaxom to see more of the Queen than he thought was proper. Jaxom was glad his was sitting since his knees felt weak again.

"Of course," Jaxom said. He quickly pulled the ring from his finger and handed it to the Queen. *She could ask for anything*, Jaxom thought.

"See this Cartouche," the Queen pointed out with great excitement, "it is the sign of Isis, Mother of God!" Cleopatra was pointing to engraved hieroglyphics within a raised rectangle. "It was to Great Isis that I came to the garden to pray tonight. She must have brought you here!"

Jaxom was shocked. *The ring belonged to a Goddess and it held the magical power.* He looked at Phoebe, who seem excited, but not really surprised. *Well, she is pagan,* he thought, wondering for the first time what she knew about magic.

And what is the rest of the writing?" Phoebe inquired.

"The rest of the inscription is written in Latin. It reads, "Three wishes," the Queen translated.

"Strange to find both languages engraved on the same piece," Balbus commented, looking up from the ring to Cleopatra. "It may have come from your treasured Alexandria."

"You are probably right, Balbus," Cleopatra agreed.

Then Balbus looked closely at Jaxom. "What wish did you make, young Jaxom that brought you here?" Balbus questioned. Jaxom startled for a moment, but he already knew it was true. *I brought us to ancient Rome.*

"I wished that Julius Caesar had never been assassinated." Jaxom answered truthfully. *They all need to know what they're up against.* For the first time the scowl left Mark Anthony's face and was replaced with surprise and alarm. Cleopatra leaned back into the divan and stifled a sob. Balbus did not move, but remained looking directly at Jaxom.

Chapter 6

"If we look closely enough at the randomness around us,

patterns will start to emerge"

Aaron Sorkin

Marcus watched Jaxom and Phoebe with distrust as he settled himself next to Chris. Those two were heading back up the stone steps to chat with famous historical figures while he got to sit here in the dark, on wet grass, surrounded by guards, and wait. *Why didn't Jaxom want us to come? It would make more sense for the whole group to stay together.*

"It sure is beautiful," Chris said looking around. Marcus nodded glancing first at the flowers, then shifting his gaze to the architecture. His mother had bought and sold houses for years while his dad fixed up the rough ones. This estate was in another league then where his parents played.

Marble and stone were superbly crafted into traditional Roman architecture. Though it was not exactly what he had expected. Marcus admired the simple design of the Doric columns and arches creating the main structure of the estate. He was surprised to see rich coloring painted onto the raised motifs decorating the surfaces. The roof and stone patio were both tiled in earthen shades of fired brick. As he glanced at the patio, Marcus noticed that Phoebe and Jaxom were being served drinks.

Marcus stopped himself. He didn't want to think about structural design right now. *We're in ancient Rome and Jaxom and Phoebe are representing us!*

Marcus did like both of them, but besides the fact that they could never get along, Phoebe and Jaxom were both ruled by their emotions. *That's one of the reasons they're always hostile towards each other.* Marcus liked to think of himself as good under stress, remembering to be logical and look at things from a detached point of view. He thought over the last half an hour, looking at things logically. He could only come to one conclusion.

"Jaxom is hiding something," he declared to Chris. "His wish brought us here, and he must know why he can suddenly speak Latin."

"So can Phoebe, and I don't think she would lie to us." Chris answered back. "It sure is strange though."

"Everything about this is strange," Marcus responded. "Time travel is not even scientifically possible."

"Since when do scientists know everything," Chris countered. Marcus looked at his friends' devilish grin and had to smile back. He was glad Chris was with him on this strange adventure. Chris had the amazing ability to diffuse his stress with just a few words. *He keeps me from taking life too seriously.*

"This is just another great example of the Chaos theory in action," Chris continued. "Did I ever tell you that Chaos is my favorite science?"

"Didn't you say last summer that Chemistry was your favorite science?" Marcus questioned his friend.

"You saw how those experiments went. They were quite chaotic," Chris said with a laugh.

"And after what you did to the garage, your mom said no more experiments." Marcus chuckled, remembering Chris's difficulties at home. "I've never known anyone else who's been grounded for six months.

"And mom won't let up on me!" Chris complained. "But I don't think it counts when I'm in a different century and country. This is more fun than I've had in months and we haven't done anything yet!"

We need to do something, Marcus thought. He glanced over at Kristy and Benjamin. Kristy was still falling apart and Benjamin was using her tears as an excuse to get closer. *Not gonna get any help from those two.* He looked toward the stone patio to where Jaxom and Phoebe sat. *Those two couldn't even get along most of the time. Why are we letting them make decisions for our whole group?*

"How are we going to stop the assassination?" Marcus asked his friend. "I'm sure that's why we're here. It's the only thing that makes sense." Chris quieted down and gazed at the full moon, looked thoughtful for a moment.

"We can stop Julius Caesar from going to the Senate house and have him arrest the conspirators that we know the names of." Chris suggested.

"Julius Caesar can't arrest anyone legally without a good reason," Marcus countered. "The Roman Republic has a pretty good court system and the other Senators would be furious at him. I think they would just try again another time. The conspirator's need to be caught in the act."

"Where are the rest of Julius Caesar's legions? They could stop the assassination." Chris questioned.

"That's a great question," Marcus replied. "They should be somewhere close by. Maybe the Queen could get a message to their general. But if they marched into Rome, it could cause a lot of confusion with the population."

"Well, then let's call it the Chaos plan." Chris suggested and rolled over in laughter. Marcus rolled his eyes and smiled at his friend. *I guess Chris is done being serious for now.*

Chapter 7

"For most of history, Anonymous was a Woman"
Virginia Wolfe

Now we're sunk! Why did Jaxom have to tell them? Phoebe sort of admired his honesty, but Jaxom would never get high marks for subtlety. She thought the soldier, Mark Anthony looked like he wanted to kill someone, possibly even Jaxom. Cleopatra looked like she was trying not to cry. Balbus's face was unreadable. He was intently studying Jaxom.

"How far into the future do you live?" Balbus continued his questioning. Apparently Balbus understood the implications better than the Queen and Mark Anthony because they each looked at Jaxom in surprise. Cleopatra sat up to hear the answer.

"About two thousand years," Jaxom answered. Phoebe thought Jaxom was about to say way too much again, so she quickly jumped into the conversation.

"We are from the other side of the world also," Phoebe added. Everyone looked at her and then back at Jaxom as Mark Anthony spoke.

"Jaxom, do you know the names of Julius Caesars' attackers? I need to put a watch on each of them," Mark Anthony stated. Phoebe was infuriated. *The men here are just as bad as back home. Mark Anthony is acting like I'm not even here*. Jaxom was telling everyone about the books in the schoolhouse and began describing what they had learned about Julius Caesar's death in class.

Apparently, Jaxom paid more attention than Phoebe had thought. All three of the ancient adults were locked onto Jaxom as he listed the names of half a dozen conspirators and described how the attack took place in the Senate house. He told them about the knives hidden in the stylus pen cases and about how Mark Anthony was kept outside talking by Trebonius.

"You forgot to mention that there are over 60 senators that attack Julius Caesar," Phoebe offered. Mark Anthony looked alarmed at this. *I guess he heard me this time*, she thought.

"When does this attack occur?" Mark Anthony questioned, still looking at Jaxom.

"On March 15th, 44 years before our calendar began," Phoebe quickly answered. "The books call it the Ides of March." That comment got everyone's attention. Cleopatra fell back into the couch again. Mark Anthony jumped out of his seat with a furious scowl.

Even Balbus's face collapsed. He took a sharp breath and whispered, "It will be March 15th when the sun rises in the morning.

"We need to speak to Lepidus immediately," Mark Anthony declared.

"Julius Caesar is dining at his home as we speak. Decimus Brutus is also with them." Balbus stated. It was Phoebe's turn to sit up in alarm. Balbus caught her eye and said, "And he is a traitor."

"Phoebe bring your other friends inside," the Queen quickly told her. "We will find a place for you to rest. Phoebe nodded and reluctantly rose. As she headed towards the steps, Jaxom stood and rushed to her side.

"Please don't tell the others about the ring just yet," he asked her. "Kristy and Benjamin would just want to go home and I've got to follow this through. He smiled at her with excitement bright in his eyes. Jaxom didn't seem to notice her aggravation at being dismissed while he remained to hear their plans.

"I'll keep your secret for now," Phoebe sighed, knowing she was breaking her previous promise. Jaxom drove her crazy most of the time, but he also had an irresistible charm in those chocolate brown eyes. *Those deep eyes and that smile is why I can't just hate him for all his mean comments of the past. That doesn't even make any sense!*

"Thanks, Phoebe," he replied and turned back towards the adults waiting for him. *That is the first time he has used my real name in a year*, she thought as she walked down the steps towards her classmates.

The others stood when they saw her heading towards them. Kristy and Benjamin still looked very upset and Marcus still held suspicion in his gaze. Chris had a goofy grin on his face. *Apparently he's immune to stress*, Phoebe thought.

"Cleopatra has invited us to come inside," Phoebe told the group. "They just realized that the assassination will occur in the morning."

"It's already March 15th!" Marcus reacted with alarm.

"Yea, and I guess they need to get us settled so they can figure out their plan." Phoebe answered.

They all startled for a moment as Mark Anthony's voice roared out towards them. The soldiers immediately left to meet their commander without a second glance at the teens.

"I guess we aren't dangerous anymore," Chris joked as the group headed towards the villa after the men.

Chapter 8

"There's a lot to be said for making people laugh"
Preston Sturges

Jaxom could hardly contain his excitement as he rejoined the ancient adults. Talking with an Egyptian Pharaoh, and the chance to change history, *this is more than I ever believed possible*. He tried to contain his smile as a distressed Cleopatra handed him back his ring.

"Keep that safe and secret," Balbus instructed him. "Many would kill for a chance at its magic." Jaxom nodded, feeling a little sobered by the possibility of violence against himself. He slipped the silver treasure back onto his finger. *Of course the violence will be considerable in only a few hours.* Yet Jaxom still felt excitement over this unusual adventure.

"I must go join the legions," Mark Anthony stated, and he called to his troops who were watching the other teens.

"Julius Caesar will need to make the decisions over his defense in this matter. Do not spread rumors amongst the troops yet." Balbus warned. "I will wait in Rome for Julius to return home from his dinner party. Calpurnia will welcome me. She has also confided in me about strange dangerous dreams. I will return with the Dictator. I'm sure he will want to meet our new guests." With that Balbus rose, bowed to Cleopatra and quickly left.

Mark Anthony remained standing near the Queen and Jaxom, looking tortured, his troops waiting nearby for orders. Cleopatra rose and greeted the others as they joined them.

"Please tell your friends to follow us inside," the Egyptian Pharaoh told Phoebe and Jaxom. She then turned to Mark Anthony placing her hand on his shoulder. "You are welcome to remain until Balbus returns with Julius. They should not be long."

"So, what have you figured out?" Marcus asked Jaxom as he caught up to his friend. The group followed the Queen into the villa, leaving Mark Anthony outside with his legionnaires.

"Cleopatra believes we're here to help Julius Caesar," Jaxom told Marcus and the others as they entered into a spacious room decorated with exquisite statuaries and ceramic pottery. The walls were covered with incredible tapestries with ancient scenes of warfare mixed with beautiful women dancing. Jaxom felt in awe at the treasures throughout the room.

Cleopatra spoke with her handmaid for a moment then gestured to their group to follow her through a doorway of marble columns at the other end of the room. They all followed quickly as the Queen showed them into a room down a dark hallway.

"You can rest in here for the remainder of the evening," Cleopatra told them. "Bedding is there, and Miriam will bring fresh clothes for each of you." Then the Queen turned and left.

The bedding turned out to be bundles of cloth laying rolled on a large shelf leaning against one wall. The cluttered shelf held mostly pottery and wooden storage containers. The tapestries here were simple designs, nothing like the value of those in the front room. Oil lamps, attached to the wall with brackets, had been lit. The only other furniture in the room was an empty long wooden table against the other wall, which Chris immediately parked himself on and laughed.

"She walks us through a palace and then sticks us in the pantry," Chris sniggers. Jaxom looked around the room and chuckled.

"Well, we're not royalty," Jaxom answered as he turned to the group. "Balbus went to find Julius Caesar and is bringing him back here to meet us."

Everyone began to speak at once. Marcus tried to question Jaxom about who Balbus was and Chris cheered about getting to meet Julius Caesar. Kristy and Benjamin began shouting about the horrors of their situation. Phoebe fussed at everyone to quiet down before their hosts thought there was a problem.

"Will you all calm down," Jaxom hollered at the group.

The teens all quieted down and Jaxom began again. "Balbus, who is an old friend of Julius Caesar's, is going to get Caesar for Cleopatra. She knew the assassination was coming but didn't have any proof. She believes her Goddess, Isis brought us here to help. I think Mark Anthony wants to get more soldiers. They need our help to convince Julius Caesar and stop the attack."

"Well, I'm not talking to Julius Caesar or anyone else," Kristy protested. "In fact, I think I will stay right here and sleep." With that, Kristy pushed passed the boys and grabbed a roll of blankets. "Are you coming Benjamin?" she asked and went to set up a spot in the corner. Benjamin glared at the others, grabbed a bedroll and followed without saying a word.

Jaxom turned away from them, so Benjamin couldn't see the amusement on his face. *I bet this is not the first date that he planned to have with Kristy.*

"Sleeping together on a first date," Chris joked about the two.

"Benjamin doesn't look that happy about it," Marcus pointed out with a chuckle.

Kristy hollered at them to shut up. Jaxom joined his friends in laughter over the teasing.

"Let's grow up a little, boys," Phoebe snapped at them, bringing them out of their merriment. "We have an assassination to stop."

"Does that mean you're with us?" Jaxom asked her with surprise.

"We might as well finish what we've started." she answered, still sounding a little reluctant.

A knock on the doorframe was followed by Cleopatra's handmaid, Miriam entering the room. "Pardon me," she said. Her arms were full of clothes and a cloth sack which she set on the table next to Chris, who gave her a dazzling smile. She smiled shyly back and left without another word.

"Not much of a talker, but she is cute," Chris exclaimed, inspecting the contents of the sack. Pulling out a small round loaf of bread, he leaned back against the wall and began to eat.

"She doesn't speak English, dumbass," Marcus laughed.

"There's not much we can do right now," Phoebe declared as she examined the bundle of clothes. "You boys turn around so I can get dressed." Phoebe pulled a garment for herself out of the pile and looked at them waiting. The three grudgingly agreed and turned around. It only took a few minutes until she said she was done.

Jaxom turned around and looked at Phoebe. *What a difference a set of clothes could make.* She had changed into a light blue silky dress trimmed with sparkling beads hanging from the sleeves and skirt hem. Golden thread wove an intricate design across the skirt and neckline. The low cut neckline was emphasized with a band of matching beads Phoebe was fastening around her slight neck. *Phoebe was beautiful before in her jeans and cotton top, but now she looks phenomenal.*

"I wonder if it belongs to the Queen," Phoebe questioned rhetorically, suddenly looking self-conscience with the three boys staring at her.

"You could pass for royalty, now" Chris commented with a smirk.

"You look great, P" Jaxom told her. "Now you turn around. We might as well all get dressed." Phoebe turned and Jaxom dug through the clothes pile, pulling out a dark blue tunic. *It kind of matches her dress*, he thought as he pulled off his shirt and slipped it on over his head. The outfit came down just past his knees, but he felt kind of naked as he pulled off his old jeans.

"How's my dress," Chris joked as he finished fastening his belt. He twirled around on the table in a green tunic and almost fell off. Marcus, now clad in red, laughed at his best friends clowning around.

"Not even close to Phoebe new look," Marcus said. "Why did you have to leave me the brightest ones to choose from? I look ridiculous."

"I'd sleep with ya, but Kristy and Ben already claimed the best corner," Chris joked and Marcus shoved at his legs. Chris lost his balance, landing on his knees on the table.

"You look fine," Phoebe answered, shaking her head at their antics. "It's the first time you have all looked respectable at the same time." Phoebe joined in with their laughter. Jaxom wished he could tell her how beautiful she looked with that smile accompanying the dress, but he held his tongue.

"Will you all shut up?" Kristy yelled again from the corner and they all hushed their laughter into quiet snickering. Marcus had joined Chris on the table, so Jaxom also hopped up and leaned against the wall with his friends.

"Come join us, Fe Fe," Jaxom joked to Phoebe, offering her a loaf of bread. For a moment he thought he had made a mistake as Phoebe's smile fell. Then it reappeared and she hopped up next to him.

"When in Rome," she laughed and took the loaf. All joking aside, the teens got down to the business of eating.

Chapter 9

"*No one is so brave that he is not disturbed by something unexpected*"

Julius Caesar

Julius Caesar, Dictator of Rome, walked alone up the Via Sacra towards his mansion in the Forum. His mind was full of conversations from the evening dinner party. He was planning to leave Rome in a few days in an aggressive campaign against Parthia. Their kingdom had taken advantage during the recent civil war and sent horseman to attack Syria. He, Lepidus and Decimus Brutus spent time discussing the upcoming attacks as well as the possibilities of extending Rome's territory around the Caspian Sea towards the Germanic tribes of the north.

Leaving Rome would be a relief. The politicking was exhausting him, which should not be when one is Dictator. Rumors about his plans flowed through every level of the Roman population, and the quarrels and disputes among the Senators were endless. *Where is the pride and strength of the Roman people? Has the years of war fractured Rome's soul beyond recovery?*

I will miss my dear Cleopatra though. Her arrival in Rome last year had spun the gossip full pace, but gave him sweet relief from the tensions of office. He smiled as he thought of his amazing Queen. *There is one with true courage and strength as well as beauty beyond measure. Let them talk. It is just empty words.*

As Julius Caesar approached his estate, he saw an old friend watching for his arrival. Cornelius Balbus waited patiently underneath the new pediment of Caesar's mansion as the Dictator strolled towards him. Julius Caesar had known Cornelius for many years and trusted his judgment. *The reason for this late night call will be important.*

"Good evening to you, Cornelius," Julius Caesar called to his friend as he approached the mansion. "What has brought you to my door on this late occasion?"

"An incident at your villa," Cornelius Balbus said. Julius Caesar stopped midstride and caught his breath. "Cleopatra and your son remain well," Balbus quickly added to alleviate the Dictator's alarm, "but your Egyptian Queen has asked for you. I've horses waiting for us."

"Let us hurry then, my friend," Julius Caesar quickly answered. *Any threat to Cleopatra, is a threat against me. Everyone in Rome should be aware of this fact.* Julius Caesar quickly followed his friend around the side of the mansion to the stables where two horses were saddled and waiting. The horses snorted and stomped with displeasure of being awoke at this late hour. Next to the horses stood Calpurnia, also looking displeased.

"I must go, Calpurnia," Caesar told his wife, hoping she did not protest. He did not wish to waste time in pointless argument right now.

"I know. I have spoken to Balbus," she answered him. "I wanted to tell you first, that I had another nightmare. That is why I was up when Balbus arrived. Take this threat seriously, my husband. I believe all our lives are at stake."

"I live a dangerous life, Calpurnia. But I will not allow fear to make my decisions for me. Return to bed, and I will be back in the morning." With those few words, Julius Caesar was astride his stallion and galloping through Rome, followed by Cornelius Balbus.

He was aggravated with Calpurnia's issues as well as concerned about what awaited him at the villa. *The women of my life can tug at my heart so easily.* Even though theirs was a political marriage, Calpurnia's worry added to his own. Ever since he had dismissed his personal guard, she had been cross with him. *I do not need two thousand men shadowing my every move. It makes it so impossible to get anything accomplished.*

They rode through the sleeping city and were crossing the Tiber River when he and Balbus began to converse again. Balbus explained that Cleopatra was praying in the garden when a strange structure appeared before her. Within the structure was a group of teens professing to know the future of Rome.

"They announced that you will be assassinated in the morning," Cornelius Balbus told him. Julius Caesar reined his horse in a little and looked peculiarly at his friend.

"That is a bizarre emergency, Balbus," Caesar puzzlingly responded. "If anyone else had summoned me for such a tale, I would question the stability of their judgment.   I'm sure you've seen this structure and spoken to its inhabitants.   What did your intuition tell you when you addressed these foreigners?"

"There is something significant here, my old friend, though I did not look within the structure," Balbus admitted. "Mark Anthony was there with men and secured the area for the Queen."

"Mark Anthony is on duty again tonight?" Caesar questioned Balbus. The Consul had stood watch the previous night as well as having spent much of the day in the Senate house.

"Mark Anthony says he is devoted to Cleopatra's safety, for your sake, my liege," Balbus informed Julius Caesar. "Yet his attention is a bit lavish. He is due for a new posting at the end of the year."

The two friends rode on in silence as Julius Caesar considered this new complication. *Mark Anthony is a fine officer and loyal follower, yet he is also a playboy. I know Cleopatra's love is true, but she does not need the harassment while I'm away.* He pushed the concern aside for now as they arrived at his countryside villa. These strange visitors were his first concern. Julius Caesar leapt instantly from his horse. After handing the reins to an Egyptian eunuch waiting near the stables, he hurried into his villa and into the waiting arms of his queen.

Every embrace from Cleopatra washed through him like a dream he never wanted to wake from. As Julius Caesar passionately kissed Cleopatra he recalled the first time he had seen her, wrapped in a carpet and snuck past her treacherous brother to plead for his help. She was so bold and daring, yet so young and frightened. He had loved her from that moment on. Each time he saw her he felt himself fall deeper in love with this beautiful Pharaoh of Egypt.

At times Julius wished he could just return to Egypt and float down the Nile forever with her. *But a Roman must think of his country over himself, and Rome needs my guidance if she is ever to reclaim its strength and glory. I cannot abandon her to anarchy because I am smitten with this amazing woman.*

"I hear you have more exotic visitors for me to meet," Julius Caesar said as she pulled slowly from his embrace. He wrapped his arm around the smooth curve of her hip as they walked into the front room.

"They rest in the front storage room," Cleopatra told him as she guided him down the hall. "Great Mother Isis has sent them in response to my prayers.

They have come to help save you and Rome." He looked into the room at the sleeping teens wondering if Cleopatra was correct.

"Why do they sleep on the table?" Balbus wondered aloud behind them. Julius Caesar had almost forgotten the presence of his old friend. Cleopatra tended to do that to him.

"I wouldn't know," the Queen answered him. "They are peculiar in some ways, but they are from the future, I'm sure. Mark Anthony waits in the garden for you. He's been exploring their structure and is quite excited about what he has found."

"Let us go speak to the Consul first and see what he has discovered," Julius Caesar decided aloud. "I will interview these youth in the morning." Cleopatra led him and Balbus into the gardens. Some of Mark Anthony's men lay sleeping on the terrace though Julius hardly noticed them. His eyes were captured by the remarkable foreign structure taking up much of the center garden space.

Lanterns had been lit all around the strange building with guards posted at both ends. The soft glow illuminated walls of smooth stone block painted white with stripes of green and blue. The stones were exact cubes just like the structure. Much of the surface was covered with square windows and as they drew closer, he noticed the windows were all filled with sheets of perfectly smooth glass. On the largest of the exterior walls was an unusual art piece. It seemed to be some type of horse wearing human clothing and standing only on his back legs. The structure was not huge, only two story, but it was impressive in the quality of workmanship.

Mark Anthony rushed out to report. He was greatly excited over his finding and quickly escorted everyone inside. A hallway ran the length of the building filled with doors and a large, well-crafted stairway just inside the entrance on the left. The consul led their group down the hallway and into a dimly lit classroom. Chairs, desk and papers were scattered throughout the space. Anthony proceeded quickly to the far side of the room and held up the lantern to illuminate the wall.

First to capture Julius's attention was his own image, fairly well rendered, hanging upon the wall. Then his eyes slid down and he instantly grasped Mark Anthony's excitement. There upon the wall was the most precise map of his world he had ever seen. The whole lands of the Mediterranean Sea and her many cities were laid out, as well as accurate coastlines all the way past the British islands to unknown lands beyond. There was meticulous details of terrain and a great many notations written in a foreign block writing.

"The strategic advantage of this map is priceless," Balbus quickly exclaimed.

"I agree," Mark Anthony responded, "and look at the map over here," he insisted as he moves to the opposite wall, again holding the lantern high.

Before them was a huge map of the world. Julius was stunned. Continents and oceans never explored by Roman legions beckoned to him. *With these maps I can extend Rome's leadership to encompass the entire world!*

Julius regarded the maps with intense interest. He knew of no society in today's world that could produce charts of this quality. Looking around the classroom, the Dictator noticed other indications that these youth came from an advanced and unknown culture. The furniture, while rather unappealing in design, seemed to be duplicated with precise craftsmanship. The flooring was a slick solid sheet of unknown material. He picked up a square text from the floor and perused its contents. The foreign language was written in a similar style to the maps. The writing was so precise, Julius desired to know the method in which it was replicated.

"Bring all the maps inside for closer study," Julius Caesar ordered. "Check these texts too. I think it's about time to speak to our young time travelers."

Chapter 10

"We are all hero's, we are all helpless.

It just depends on the day"

Brad Meltzer

A loud knock on the doorframe woke Jaxom with a start. He had fallen asleep on the wall with Phoebe resting against his shoulder. He gently nudged Phoebe, who rubbed her eyes then pulled away from him in embarrassment. The others on the table were also awakening.

"Julius Caesar requires your presence for an interview," Miriam announced to the groggy teens. Jaxom swiftly jumped from the table and told the others. *The Dictator of Rome requires our presence!* Chris looked as thrilled as he felt, but Marcus and Phoebe wore worried expressions. Benjamin and Kristy did not even move. *It's probably better to leave them behind anyways.*

"Let's go," Chris declared. "It's not wise to keep a Dictator waiting." Jaxom smile grew even wider at his friend's enthusiasm. Then his expression fell over the next words from the handmaid.

"I'm sorry ma'am," Miriam apologized. "They are meeting in Julius Caesars private rooms where only men are allowed. Please wait here." Jaxom looked at Phoebe hoping she would be alright with this restriction. She was obviously not, by the helpless look on her face.

"This culture is much different," Jaxom expressed trying to be kind. "We have to play by its' rules." He hated for her to be alienated from him, when they were finally getting along.

"I know, just go on," Phoebe sighed. As the boys followed the handmaid out, Jaxom looked back at Phoebe feeling guilty. Without looking up at him, she grabbed a blanket and curled up again on the table.

"Come on, Jaxom," Marcus called and he turned to follow his friends. Chris was up ahead chattering to Cleopatra's handmaid, who was looking a bit worried by the attention.

"Chris, she can't understand anything your saying," Marcus hollered at his friend. Jaxom's smile returned as Chris answered.

"Yea, but she can catch that I'm interested." Chris grinned back. "The best relationships aren't usually based on communication skills. All that talking gets in way of what both sides are really after!" Chris's leer at the maid made it clear what he was after at the present moment.

"That's terrible, but probably true sometimes," Marcus answered him, shaking his head at his best friends' shameful behavior.

"Your mom's keeping you locked up too tight, isn't she?" Jaxom laughed.

Their conversation died down as the three teens were escorted though the front room and deeper into the impressive villa. The incredible riches of this

Roman general was apparent throughout the structure as they were ushered into Julius Caesar's private chambers. There before them was Julius Caesar, the Dictator of Rome, and the potential victim to the most famous assassination of all time!

To Jaxom, Julius Caesar looked exactly as he should. The Dictator wore a reddish purple tunic and calf length red boots. He was tall and thin with a receding hairline. *He looks just like the portrait in Mrs. Brandon's' classroom.* Yet the depth in Julius Caesars' dark piercing eyes was a surprise. If Jaxom had not known who Julius Caesar was, it would still be obvious that this was a man of destiny. After just a moment of locking eyes with this leader, Jaxom had to look away. That is when he noticed what Julius Caesar possessed and was intently interested in.

The Dictator stood near a long table, similar to the one which they had left Phoebe sleeping on. Mark Anthony, Balbus and another man stood with him. Spread before them and surrounded by stacks of school books, were the maps from Mrs. Brandon's' classroom. Apparently the Romans had been searching the schoolhouse for anything of value. *It makes sense that the maps would be important to them.*

"Which of you is Jaxom?" Julius Caesar demanded of them.

"I am, sir and this is Marcus and Chris," Jaxom answered the Dictator.

"Can you translate the text written on these maps?" Julius Caesar eagerly questioned him.

"Yes, sir," Jaxom quickly replied. "I can translate anything you need."

"Hold up now, Julius," Balbus laughed. "Give the boys a minute to relax. You haven't even been properly introduced yet." Jaxom was surprised at Balbus's correction of Caesar. Yet the Dictator smiled at his friend and chuckled. Julius Caesars entire face seemed to transform as the intensity slipped away from his eyes. Jaxom now saw the face of the popular man of the people, Julius Caesar was said to be.

"In my excitement, I forget myself," Julius Caesar explained to them still grinning. "I am Roman Dictator, Gaius Julius Caesar. You have already met Cornelius Balbus, my chief engineer and dearest friend, as well as Mark Anthony, current Consul of Rome. This is Marcus Lepidus, my Master of Horses and second in command of the legions."

"Mark Anthony sent for me with your amazing story," Marcus Lepidus told them as he passed around silver goblets. "These maps and your unusual arrival are excellent proof to convince me that you are from the future."

"I agree," Julius Caesar responded grabbing a wine flask and pouring himself a cup. "I have been told of your arrival but I would like to hear your story from you. How have you come to be in Rome?" Julius Caesar past the flask to Jaxom and waited for his response.

Jaxom carefully filled his goblet and passed the flask to Chris who was wearing a devilish grin over the forbidden substance. He paused for a moment to collect his thoughts and try the wine. It was horrible, tasting so watered down that Jaxom could barely taste the alcohol. He glanced at Chris again and saw his friend's face grimace for a moment at the flavor.

"We are high school students living in America about 2000 years from now. We're taking a world history class together," Jaxom began. "We were assigned as a group to complete a report about your life and we met after class today to work on the project." Jaxom noticed that Julius Caesar seemed delighted to be studied so far into the future. "While we were discussing our assignment I made a wish to stop your assassination and suddenly our school building was pulled out of our time and brought here."

Julius Caesar did not look as pleased to hear the assassination part, but did not interrupt. Jaxom wanted him to clearly understand the danger coming but he was beginning to feel self-conscious with everyone watching him so closely. He also didn't want to speak of the magical ring with so many people around. Cornelius Balbus had warned him to keep it secret and he had not let Marcus and Chris in on the secret yet.

"Cleopatra and Mark Anthony met us when we arrived and then Cornelius Balbus showed up. I'm sure you've heard the rest from them," Jaxom concluded quickly. Jaxom took another sip of the horrible liquid and waited for the Dictator's reply.

Julius Caesar regarded Jaxom for a moment then wandered towards couches situated in the corner of the large room. The rest of the group followed the Dictator and settled upon the cushions around the leader.

"Watch what you say," Marcus whispered to him as they followed the Roman men. "Remember who you are talking to." Jaxom shrugged off his friends warning and sat next to Cornelius Balbus across from Julius Caesar. Marcus, looking worried and left out, sat to the side with Chris. *This is incredible*, Jaxom thought. *We are actually being included in a secret counsel with Julius Caesar's top men.*

"So Cassius is to succeed in turning a faction against me," Julius Caesar considers. "I thought him to be too weak to attempt such a thing. That fool would throw Rome into chaos."

"Complete disorder," Jaxom answers truthfully. "It's pretty much the end of the Roman Republic."

"This madness will be stopped," Marcus Lepidus responded confidently. Julius Caesar smiled at his friend, but the intensity had returned to the Dictator's eyes.

"I will do what I must," Julius Caesar told his second in command. "And I have complete confidence in our success. Now, I wish to hear your positions over our strategy. Lepidus, you began." Marcus Lepidus paused for a moment, gathering his thoughts. Jaxom was glad to know that Julius Caesar was the type of leader who listened to his men's advice.

"We will need to bring in men secretly, as to not forewarn the conspirators," Marcus Lepidus began. "It would only take a dozen men to subdue them. Most have never even seen real combat and their lightly armed. After you enter the assembly hall, we would form up and storm the proceedings. I suspect that most senators will flee rather than fight. It should be over in minutes." Caesar considered his second in commands words and then turned to Mark Anthony.

"Consul, do you agree with Lepidus's proposal?" the Dictator asked. Mark Anthony responded immediately.

"Yes, his plan seems successful," Mark Anthony answered confidently. "I would recommend not allowing many assassins to live through the day. We do not need the repeat attempt that might follow." Julius Caesar nodded thoughtfully then turn toward the couch where Jaxom sat with Cornelius Balbus.

Julius Caesar looked intensely at Jaxom for a minute but did not speak. Jaxom couldn't imagine that this great leader of Rome would ever ask for his opinion. Lepidus's comment about the Senators fleeing reminded Jaxom of his own cowardice. He had ran when his sister and mother needed him the most. He felt like the Dictator could see the guilt and betrayal that raged within him.

"Balbus, your wisdom is always welcome," Julius Caesar said, shifting his eyes to his best friend.

"I would have you wear a breast plate under your toga," Cornelius Balbus told his friend. "I also think a few more men would be advisable. Watch how many Senators are killed though. Some are from very prestigious families and we don't need too many blood feuds declared against you." Julius Caesar smiled at that and shrugged.

"I already have a few, don't I?" Julius Caesar responded. The Dictator looked back at Jaxom. Then to Jaxom's amazement, Julius Caesar actually asked for his opinion.

"Jaxom what do you think of this plan? Can you think of any details about the assassination you studied that would help," the Dictator questioned him? Jaxom was shocked and did not know how to respond.

"It sounds like it should work," Jaxom answered the Roman leader. "Our school books say you will be surrounded by about 60 Senators when you arrive in the Senate house. The signal they use to initiate the attack is when Cimber pulls your toga off your shoulder." Jaxom couldn't think of anything else important. Then Marcus called his name and he looked over at his friend.

"Jaxom, remember they are meeting in Pompey assembly hall. Remind them about the threat of the gladiators," his friend advised him. Jaxom turned back to Julius Caesar

"If there are gladiators next door loyal to the conspirators you could have a problem," he informed the Dictator. Then Mark Anthony confirmed the worst.

"Decimus Brutus has thirty gladiators arriving as we speak. He is one of the conspirators you mentioned, Jaxom," the Consul informed them.

"Thank you Jaxom," Julius Caesar said, "and thank you, all. That threat changes things a bit." The Dictator leaned back and contemplated the situation for a few minutes and the men all drank their watery wine. Jaxom mouthed a thank you to Marcus and his friend smiled back, yet the smile did not reach his eyes. *It's probably hard to not understand most everyone in the room*, Jaxom thought. Chris looked cheerful still.

"Lepidus, go to camp and call a meeting of all Centurions," Julius Caesar commanded his second. "Inform them I have called a meeting at my mansion for dispatch orders and instruct the legions to break camp. Mark Anthony, go into the city and casually spread the news that I have decided to leave tomorrow against the Parthians. This will account for military presence in the city and ensure the conspirators will proceed with their plans. They will not want to miss their last opportunity before I leave Rome. Meet us at the mansion when your business is completed." Both men rose, affirmed their orders and loyalty to their leader and left.

"Balbus, will you entertain our guests for a moment," Julius Caesar asked his friend. "I need some time with Cleopatra before we leave." Cornelius Balbus nodded and the Dictator of Rome left to find his Queen.

"Let your friends know what's going on," Cornelius Balbus suggested to Jaxom as he stood. "I'll order us some food." The Roman engineer strolled to the doorway and called for a servant. Jaxom rose and crossed over to where Marcus and Chris sat.

"You might have saved us all with that gladiator warning," he told Marcus, giving him a friendly punch on the shoulder. Marcus gave him a quick smile, then let the worried expression settle back across his face. Chris, still overjoyed to be in Rome, jumped up to question Jaxom.

"So what did they decide?" he began. "Do you know how hard it is to not understand most of the conversation? I heard Caesar asking for your advice, can you believe that!" Jaxom laughed at Chris's enthusiasm and explained Julius Caesar's orders to his friends.

"Marcus, how did you know what Caesar asked me? You had the perfect advice," Jaxom asked his friend.

"Mostly a guess," Marcus answered, "but I am starting to understand a little. Remember, I've been taking Latin for a couple months now."

"I'm taking Spanish," Chris laughed, "but all I can say so far is hola and gracias." Still chuckling, Chris went to check out the tray of food Cornelius Balbus had brought to the table. "So when are we leaving for Rome?"

"Soon," Jaxom answered as he and Marcus moved to couches closer to the food. "Julius Caesar went to see Cleopatra."

"I'm not going," Marcus surprisingly commented. "They have Roman soldiers to protect Caesar. What can we do to help?"

"I'm not missing this for anything," Chris commented between bites. Jaxom grabbed a piece of fruit and sat next to Cornelius Balbus again. He wondered about this old man who Caesar asked for help instead of ordering around like the others.

"May I ask what a chief engineer does in Rome?" Jaxom questioned Cornelius Balbus.

"Mostly, I'm relaxing," Cornelius Balbus laughed. "My real work is in the field. I've designed and built everything from war towers to ships. I even built a bridge once spanning the Rhine River, which Julius tore down a week later." Balbus seemed amused by this memory.

"Is that where you met Julius Caesar, in Gaul?" Jaxom asked.

"No, I've known Julius since his Quaestorship in Spain, about twenty-five years ago. He was deputy to the Governor there, and I was working as an engineer for the mining operations. While he was Consul, he sent for me and I have been by his side ever since."

"And I wouldn't have survived this long without your advice," Julius Caesar said as he entered the room. "Let's go give the Fates another go at us, my friend."

Chapter 11

"It was always burning since the worlds been turning"

Billy Joel

Phoebe tried to get more sleep, but she could not. She tossed and turned trying to get comfortable on the wooden table as her mind raced over the events of the day. Being in ancient Rome was amazing and strange at the same time, but to be left out from Caesars interview had stung. *Men everywhere seemed to view women as ornaments to their success, not realizing that they were leaving half the human race out of the decision making.* Phoebe's mind burned with the inequality of being woman. *Even the women's rights movement had backfired. Women now had the right to act like men, if they wanted to succeed in the modern world.*

Her mind kept jumping to thoughts of Jaxom. She was so mortified over falling asleep leaning on him and didn't know why she promised to keep his secret about the ring. *For seven years now he has tormented me. Yet he flashes me a smile and I forgets my own principles.* These thoughts also burned. *I even agreed to help stop the assassination, which is probably a terrible idea.*

Phoebe thought back to fourth grade when Jaxom had showed up in the middle of the year. He bragged about getting kicked out of wherever he came from, and all the boys thought he was the coolest thing around. Jaxom had sat right next to Phoebe when he arrived and she had tried to be friendly. He had come to live with his Uncle and she just asked if he missed his family. *He was so mean to me that day and almost every day since then. When he found out mom was Wiccan, his teasing got even worse. Why am I thinking about him? Stop worrying about him and try to get more rest.*

The creak of the table woke Phoebe from her troubled sleep. Marcus was sitting on the edge of the table looking depressed. Phoebe looked about and realized he had returned alone. She felt exhausted still, but knew she wasn't going to get any real sleep, so she sat up.

"Where are Jaxom and Chris?" she asked rubbing her eyes.

"On their way to Rome with Caesar," Marcus answered her. Phoebe felt her jaw drop and forced herself to close it. *I was left behind again!*

"Why weren't you invited, because of your color?" Phoebe snapped. Marcus looked shocked and hurt.

"No, I chose not to go. The Roman's aren't racist." he snapped back.

"Just sexist, I guess," Phoebe retorted. Then she felt guilty for offending Marcus. "I'm sorry, Marcus. I'm just mad I was left behind. It's not your fault."

"It's all right. This has been strange for everyone," Marcus answered back. "Do you really want to be involved in stopping an assassination?"

"Yes... well maybe not," Phoebe replied thinking it through for a moment. "Roman's aren't known for their compassion in battle, are they?"

"No, they're pretty vicious," Marcus agreed.

Movement from the corner stopped their conversation for a moment. Benjamin quietly crept away from the still sleeping Kristy. He stretched and came over to join their conversation.

"Where are Jaxom and Chris?" he asked.

"They are on their way to Rome with Caesar," Marcus repeated.

"Great, they're going to get themselves killed!" Benjamin moaned quietly. "We'll have to figure out how to get back home without them."

"What!" Marcus exclaimed. "I'm not abandoning them. Chris is my best friend, and he and Jaxom wouldn't abandon us."

"They left us here, didn't they?" Benjamin retorted. *He has a point,* thought Phoebe. *They had gone to Rome without even telling us.* But still Phoebe agreed with Marcus. *I won't leave ancient Rome without everyone we came here with.*

Jaxom's the one with the magic ring anyways, she thought, remembering that she was the only one here who knew about its power.

Phoebe felt guilty for not letting everyone know about it, but she held her tongue. *Benjamin's attitude is so hostile, I don't know how he'll react.*

"There are clothes for you to change into," Phoebe told Benjamin attempting to change the subject. "It will help you fit in."

"Great," Benjamin grumbled sarcastically, but he went ahead and grabbed the last tunic from the pile. Phoebe turned around so he could change. In a moment Benjamin was dressed in an orange tunic. "Are we really supposed to fit in with these bright colors," he complained comparing his tunic to Marcus's red one.

"They are a bit lively aren't they," Marcus agreed. "But check out Phoebe's new look, and there are a couple more dresses for Kristy to choose from." Phoebe felt herself flush over the compliment. She never wore dresses back home and felt a little conspicuous herself. She smiled at Marcus hoping her discomfort wasn't too obvious.

"Maybe I should wake up Kristy," Phoebe commented to cover her embarrassment. "A lovely dress might improve her mood." Phoebe grabbed the remaining dresses and went to the corner where her friend lay sleeping. She gently nudged Kristy's shoulder. "Kristy, it's morning," she said softly. "They brought us beautiful clothes to change into." Kristy rolled over and slowly sat up. She admired Phoebe's dress for a moment.

"All right, I'll change," Kristy answered her. "I'm still not happy about all this." Kristy looked over the outfits that Phoebe presented to her and chose a lovely green that matched her eyes. The boys all turned towards the door as Kristy changed. As she admired the soft silk gown, a knock at the door caught their attention.

"Queen Cleopatra has breakfast ready for you." A short Egyptian eunuch announced in the doorway. Phoebe, being the only one who understood, told the others and they all followed the servant through the beautiful villa. They trailed the Pharaoh's servant into a glorious dining hall and seated themselves on couches surrounding low tables.

"I guess everyone likes to recline as they eat in Rome," Marcus commented as they filled their plates with an amazing array of fruit, bread and cheese. As they began to eat, Cleopatra joined them.

The Queen was dressed in the finest of Egyptian attire. Stunning purple robes were adorned with sparkling jewels. Her beautiful face was painted with rich colors and her eyes were outlined in the traditional black mascara. She looked exactly like an Egyptian Pharaoh should look except that in her arms she held a squirming toddler.

"Is this Julius Caesars son?" Phoebe asked admiring his adorable dimpled smile. Cleopatra set the child down and settled herself across a red divan. The child toddled to the table and began stuffing his mouth with grapes. The boy had beautifully tanned skin and wore his hair in a traditional Egyptian sidelock.

"This is my son Caesarion. In Egypt we are Matrilineal," the Queen informed her. "But yes, Julius Caesar is his father."

"I thought Egyptian Pharaohs ruled together as husband and wife," Phoebe questioned.

"The Ptolemy's of Greece tried to force that type of control upon my country," Cleopatra said, frowning over the thought of the conquerors of her people who were also her own ancestors. "Others conquerors of our past have as well. Yet the people of Egypt will only follow the rule of their Queen, so the Greeks rulers forced marriage upon the ruling Pharaoh. That is why my brother could not rally enough support to overthrow me during our civil war. Only the Greeks of Alexandria would follow him. The true population of Egypt completely supported me as they once did my sister."

"I never knew you had a sister," Phoebe replied intrigued.

"During my childhood, the people of Egypt revolted against my father and placed my sister on the throne. My father escaped the battle and returned later with Greek troops. He had both my sister and mother executed when he regained control." The Queen looked so saddened over the memory.

"So Caesarion will not be Pharaoh after you?" Phoebe asked trying to turn the conversation away from such sorrow. The history books had never taught her any of this. Of course, history was written by the conquering patriarchs. *They didn't want it known that women were in charge anywhere.*

"He will rule only if I have a daughter that accepts him in marriage," Cleopatra answered smiling at her son, who had moved on to the cheese platter.

"What are you talking about," Marcus asked Phoebe. Phoebe told her classmates what the Queen had said. Kristy smiled for the first time since coming to Rome but the boys reacted shockingly.

"There's no way that is true!" Benjamin hollered. "Pharaoh's have always been male and the sibling marriage thing is disgusting."

"I'm surprised to hear that too," Marcus said, less viciously. "I thought most of the old cultures were ruled by conquering Kings. No one ever mentioned Cleopatra having a sister."

"What is the matter?" Cleopatra asked looking offended and rather angry at her guest's outbursts.

"I'm sorry, you're Majesty," Phoebe quickly apologized with a bow. "Our history books tell of Pharaohs being male. They are just surprised."

"Who wrote these history books?" Cleopatra inquired looking less upset.

"After Julius Caesar's assassination, Roman becomes an empire ruled by a series of conquerors and then defeated by other conquerors," Phoebe revealed to the Queen. She felt her frustration from last night return as she continued. "They take over much of the world and women everywhere are made slaves of their fathers and husbands. Anyone with different beliefs were crushed by their growing power, as well as feeding their slave trade. They took over control of the medical and education systems and spent century's torturing and killing anyone who wouldn't follow their new order." The boys looked upset by Phoebe's explanation but did not interrupt again. *They know it's true*, Phoebe thought.

"I can believe that," the Queen answered thoughtfully. "The women of Rome are already slaves of their men as well as the Greek and Jewish womyn. Slavery is accepted throughout our world." Cleopatra leaned back, nibbling on a piece of fruit, thinking deeply for a few minutes. The teens all ate in silence as they watched the Pharaoh. The only noise was Prince Caesarian who was chatting to the green olives he was fitting onto his fingertips. Finally, Cleopatra sat up and announced, "Finish your meal quickly. I have decided that we are going to Rome."

Chapter 12

"Dauntless"

Veronica Roth

Chris galloped behind Jaxom, Julius Caesar and Cornelius Balbus as they raced towards Rome. For the first time since this adventure began, he was feeling worried. *Terrified might be a better word.* He had ridden a horse once before, actually it was more of a pony, at the state fair a few years before. That equine was half the size and tied to a rotating post. *This experience is completely different,* he thought trying to suppress the fear.

He had followed the Dictator out to the stables with great excitement. He was actually heading to ancient Rome to stop Caesar's assassination. Chris didn't want to appear ignorant and risk being left behind, so he had copied the Romans actions and managed to get himself situated in the saddle with a bit of trouble. Luckily the stallion wanted to follow the others, so he did not have to direct its movements. *Otherwise I would probably never have got this beast to move. Why didn't they use stirrups*? He couldn't figure out what to do with his feet.

Chris wasn't sure if he would make it to Rome alive. The Italian countryside sped past as they rode, dotted with stone farmhouses and fields full of livestock and grain. He hung on tight to the reins, yet felt like he would be thrown off at any minute. His rear end and thighs were already so sore and his hands felt raw. *Oh, I hoped Rome isn't far away.*

"Sit up a little," Jaxom instructed him. "Follow his rhythm."

"What rhythm?" Chris stammered, trying to straighten up a little. "How do you know how to ride anyways?"

"During the summers, I've been staying with my Aunt and cousins out in Tennessee. They have stable full of horses," Jaxom informed him.

Chris had wondered before about Jaxom's disappearance every summer. He had thought Jaxom went back to his family. His friend had always been closed mouth about it and Chris wasn't one to pry.

Jaxom gave him a few other pointers and the ride got a little smoother. By the time Rome appeared across the Tiber River, Chris was starting to feel the rhythm of his steed. *Maybe I'll make it alive after all.* They rode past a series of man-made lakes and Chris imagined the relief he would feel if he stopped and dove in. *I need a different mode of transportation for the return trip. Maybe I can invent the bicycle why I'm here.*

Rome stretched out amongst several tall hills and valleys, and looked much different than Chris had envisioned it. The first thing to surprise him was the thick brown smog that covered the city. *I thought that such pollution was a product of modern society.* The great city of Rome looked crowded and dirty from a distance.

As they approached two well-constructed bridges spanning the Tiber River, the traffic became thicker, though most travelers did not have horses to ride. *Lucky them.* Wagons of varied design crowded the bridges as well as many pedestrians. When Julius Caesar and his party were spotted, everyone crowded out of the way and let them pass, many calling out cheers to their Dictator that Chris wished he understood.

Julius Caesar slowed their pace as they crossed the congested bridge. The Dictator waved and smiled at his people and for some reason it reminded Chris of the beauty pageants his sisters loved to watch. A small herd of pigs were driven out of their way as they entered Rome, adding a foul scent to the filth of the city. Chris scanned the shops as the passed seeing a potter working with clay and weavers at their looms. The ring of a metal smith added to the noise of the city and stray dogs added extra dimensions to the smell.

Chris was surprised at the obvious class distinction to the city. To their right rose a hill of slums. Rickety apartments and crumbling shacks crowded between narrow alleys filled the cramped shantytown. The urban poor were jam-packed into the space in obvious contrast to a hill of brightly colored mansions in front of them. The Roman elite lived in these exclusive villas with beautifully manicured gardens, *probably to the envy of most citizens*, Chris thought.

The only similarity Chris could see between the two social chasms was the lovely temples and shrines that existed everywhere throughout the city. The rich and poor of Rome appeared to be alike in their religious devotion to these carefully tended buildings which continually added sweet smelling incense to the smoggy air.

Between the two dissimilar hills lay the famous Circus Maximus. This incredible stone structure, where Charioteers competed for the glory of Rome, filled the entire valley. It was empty now, but Chris hoped he would be able to view the competitions during his stay in the ancient city. Chris loved sports of every kind.

Chris followed Julius Caesar past the slums, arena and mansions and into the heart of Rome. Here was the famous Roman Forum, where citizens cast their votes for their Senator of chose. The area was cluttered with vendors selling food and crafts and the traffic of the Roman people beginning their day. Shadowing them all was Pompey's great theater and temple, the grandest structure in the entire city.

Their group finally arrived at Julius Caesar's mansion, a magnificent structure in the center of Rome. The beautiful new pediment with its huge marble columns made the mansion look like one of Rome's many temples. As they rode into the Dictators private stables, Marcus Lepidus came out to meet them.

Chris awkwardly dismounted, extremely glad to be off the stallion. Julius Caesar rushed inside, speaking with his second in command presumably about their plans. Chris followed them with Jaxom unsure about what he should be doing. Walking was more painful now then riding had been and he again thought about his Roman bicycle business. *I wonder if I could make it work.*

"What now?" Chris asked Jaxom.

"I don't know," Jaxom admitted, then looked closer at Chris noticing his pained expression. "Are you ok?"

"Well, I won't be dancing anytime soon," Chris joked trying to downplay his pain.

"Just stay close, so we don't miss anything," Jaxom told him. The two friends followed the Romans through a series of exquisite rooms and into Caesars private chambers. The room resembled the same space in his country house with a large meeting table and plush couches. "Caesar has good taste," Jaxom whispered to him as they admired the incredible furnishing and tapestries. They found a couch in the corner where they sat as they waited for the action to begin.

Julius Caesar was soon surrounded by an increasing number of Roman men. Chris assumed these were his loyal legion commanders even though no one was dressed in military attire. He couldn't understand the discussions but it was obvious that the Dictator was giving orders to each group that arrived. Cornelius Balbus stayed by Julius Caesar for a while, then after receiving his instructions wandered over to speak with Jaxom. After speaking with Julius Caesar's friend, Jaxom turned to Chris to let him know what Cornelius Balbus had told him.

"Caesar wants us to go into the Senate house with Balbus," Jaxom told him. "If asked we are to be visiting diplomats representing the British Isles. Balbus says to try not to speak to anyone and stay close."

"Who am I going to speak to," Chris laughed, filled with delight at their adventure, sore legs mostly forgotten for the moment. "You're the only one I can understand." The two boys rose and followed Balbus out of the room into another part of the mansion. Cornelius Balbus spoke briefly to Jaxom, then disappeared into a side room.

"He needs to change," Jaxom told Chris. Feeling impatient, Chris stretched his legs. The friends waited and after a few minutes their escort returned wearing a traditional Roman toga.

"I thought you were an engineer," Jaxom said to Cornelius Balbus. The Roman laughed and responded. Jaxom translated for Chris.

"Julius made me a Senator soon after the war against Pompey," Balbus answered. "He needed Senators he could trust, though the togas not my favorite part of the job."

Chris followed Cornelius Balbus and Jaxom out onto the street and through the Forum. A painful hike up Capitoline Hill brought them to the Campus Martius and Pompey's great theater, built ten years prior. It was the most impressive structure on the campus. Their group made its way to the public portico, surrounded by extensive gardens. Chris took a deep breath of the cleaner air within the space and admired the amazing piece of history.

The theater was immense, built of stone and marble encircling the gladiator theater. Balbus lead them past the arena and temple dedicated to the Goddess Venus. *Caesar's supposed to be related to her*, Chris remembered finding it ironic the structure was built by Caesar's greatest rival.

Cornelius Balbus led them through the impressive structure, then down long lanes of private gardens towards the Assembly hall. *More steps*, Chris moaned to himself as the ascended towards their destination. Senators were starting to fill the space. Their guide led them to a corner where they could watch but stay out of the way.

Chris could hardly contain his excitement. He was in the Roman Senate house surrounded by Rome's elite. It was an impressive room with two large entrance hallways on each side of a curved raised seating platform. In front of this, in the center of the room was a small raised platform containing only two seats. One chair was wooden while the other glimmered of gold. The space reminded Chris of the school's lecture hall, except for the giant statue of Pompey standing near the far doorway. There were several smaller closed doors on the opposite side of the room, one close to where they were standing. He looked around, wondering which senators were part of the assassination but couldn't see a difference between the clusters of men waiting for the meeting to begin.

Then he noticed two men going from group to group. Their shifting eyes and the intense way they spoke to their fellow senators told Chris, *those two are trouble*. He bumped Jaxom's shoulder and discreetly pointed the two out. Jaxom spoke quietly to Cornelius Balbus, then turned back to him with the answer that confirmed their identity.

"That is Cassius Longinus and Decimus Brutus," Jaxom told him. "They are two of the assassinators. Balbus says Cassius has always hated Caesar. He was a soldier of Crassus, then Pompey's. But Decimus Brutus was trained by Caesar in Gaul." Chris watched the two traitors circulate through the Senate house. *Why would one of Caesars own soldiers betray him?*

All eyes turned towards the farther entrance and the air seemed to crackle with increased anticipation. *Julius Caesar must be here*, Chris knew. First to enter was the lictors, the escort of a commanding general. They held out in front of them rods wreathed in fresh laurel branches. Then in strolled Julius Caesar, dressed in his purple toga with a golden wreath crowning his balding head. He walked with such easy confidence, Chris wondered if he was even concerned about the assassination attempt. *Such a dauntless leader.*

The lictors turned to wait outside, leaving the Dictator unprotected. A rush of senators immediately swamped Julius Caesar, as the Dictator made his way to the middle of the room. The Roman elite were calling out to their leader, waving papers towards him, and a few even bent to kiss the hem of his toga. Chris watched with nervous excitement. *Was our advanced warning enough to save Julius Caesar, or is it the Dictator's destiny to die today?*

This commotion only lasted for a few minutes, when Julius Caesar, in the middle of the crowd suddenly screamed, "Invado!" Chris instantly jumped towards the crowd of Senators, sure that Caesar's life would be lost before help arrived. *Why didn't someone give me a blade?* Just as he neared the mass, Mark Anthony stormed into the Senate house followed by dozens of armed centurions. Swords drawn, they slammed into the now panicking Roman leaders.

Stunned and frozen motionless, Chris watch as a handful of Senators were hacked down before they even knew of Mark Anthony's arrival. Their death screams brought complete madness to the remaining men. Many senators fled screaming toward the other entrance, knocking right past Chris without even noticing him.

Absolute Chaos!!! Now he had a clearer view of Julius Caesar, who was catching a double-edged Spanish sword thrown to him by a legionnaire. The Dictator was bleeding from a small slice on his throat, but did not stop to notice. Many of the remaining Senators flung themselves on the floor, *probably begging to be spared*, Chris figured. But twenty or so conspirators remained standing, wielding medium length knives in a desperate attempt to complete the assassination, while another dozen turned to block the legionnaire's path to the Roman leader.

Julius Caesar instantly swung the sword across the crowd of conspirators, beheading the first and catching the shoulder of a second. Covered in the spraying blood of his enemies, Caesar looked completely confident of success. He easily knocked aside a feeble attempt of Cassius Longinus to stab at his chest and ran the leader of the conspirators straight through the gut. He then shoved the dying senator off his sword with his red boot into another attacker.

Chris felt confident too, until he heard Jaxom's scream his name and turned around. Pouring through the small side door was a troop of gladiators from the games next door. *These are the men Marcus warned about*, thought Chris, as he realized the dangerous position he was in. Standing alone in the middle of the Senate house, he was the only one between the gladiators and the fight.

Chris dashed toward Jaxom, who was crouching by the side wall attempting to stay out of the battle. His legs were so sore from the ride into town, but Chris tried to hurry. There just wasn't enough time for him to reach his friend. As the gladiators rushed forward, Chris passed right in front of the leading edge of the warriors. He saw Jaxom catch his breath a moment before searing pain sliced through his back. He looked down and saw the tip of a blade cut through his chest, staining his new tunic red with his blood. He stumbled forward and felt the blade rip out of his body. Then he felt the floor as he crumbled onto it.

Chapter 13

"And Enoch walked with God"

Moses

As the city of Rome came into view, Benjamin scowled with displeasure. The brown cloud of smog over the city matched his mood. *Here is the reality of the Roman conquerors. Peasants and slaves toiling their life away while the rich stand on their backs. Literally on their backs*, he thought as a group of eunuchs carried the carriage he shared with Marcus and Kristy into Rome.

"This city is disgusting," Kristy remarked. She was sitting next to him, holding tightly to his hand. This new relationship was also bugging him. Since they had been in this century, Kristy had jumped between freaking out and ordering him around. *Just another problem to add to this horrible turn of events.*

"What would you expect from such barbarians," Benjamin muttered.

"Oh, come on you two," Marcus responded. "It's an old city, but Rome's awesome. There's the Circus Maximus and up on the hill you can see Romulus and Remus's old home. The Romans have preserved it all these centuries."

"You mean the shack next to all those mansions," Benjamin snapped back. "What I see is the greedy on one hill and the deprived on another." Marcus rolled his eyes and turned back to look out at the sights.

Just as well, Benjamin didn't want to talk about Rome. He just wanted to find a way to get home. He was suspicious of Jaxom and Phoebe's part in this magic, but he had no understanding of the occult. Benjamin wished he was never a part in this vile adventure.

As the group headed towards Julius Caesar's mansion, they watched the bustling citizens go about their day. They could see the Forum now, and Pompey's huge theater. Senators were already heading that way and Benjamin wondered where Jaxom and Chris were right now. *Hopefully they don't get themselves killed in this hare-brained scheme of theirs.*

Then something on the hill past the Forum caught Benjamin's attention. A temple stood out amongst other smaller structures. Its design reminded him of his family's temple back home. He stared at the building for a few minutes to convince himself it was true. *There is a Jewish Synagogue in Rome.*

Benjamin felt excitement wash over his displeasure for the first time since he came to ancient Rome. His mind flowed back to his childhood and the long hours he had spent at the temple back home. His father and grandfather were strict orthodox Jews and insisted on traditional education for their children. While other children played all summer, Benjamin and his sister spent their time learning to read the holy books. This fact usually irritated him, but not now. *The Hebrew language is the same in modern times as it is here. If I can get to that Synagogue, I should be able to speak to the Jews of Rome!*

They soon stopped in front of Julius Caesar's obscenely rich mansion. The newly built pediment made the structure look like a temple. *Julius Caesar the god*, Benjamin thought with disgust. The eunuch slaves carefully settled their transport down. Benjamin quickly jumped out and then turned to give Kristy a hand. He watched as Cleopatra and Phoebe exited the carriage in front of theirs.

An elegant Roman lady emerged from the mansion and stood under the huge Pediment. Benjamin assumed this must be Calpurnia, the wife of Julius Caesar. *She wears as many gems as that female Pharaoh.* As Queen Cleopatra came into view and walked towards her, the woman bowed low and opened her arms in greeting.

Calpurnia greeted the Queen and Cleopatra answered back. Benjamin wished he understood them. It must be strange for these two to talk. Calpurnia then stood and the two women embraced. *How can she stand touching her husband's mistress?* Benjamin cringed, as the ancient women went inside. Benjamin followed the others, Kristy still holding tight to his hand.

The mansion was even more exquisite then Julius Caesar's country villa had been. They were led into a front room filled with seating and low tables which were decorated with elegant ceramic pottery and precious metals shaped in all manner of design. Benjamin knew these ornaments were trophies from the Dictator's conquests. The others were looking around in awe at what

Benjamin just saw as greed. He was ready to leave and find the Synagogue but what would Kristy think of the idea? Benjamin hung back from the others, keeping her with him so they could speak privately.

"Do you really want to stay here?" Benjamin questioned Kristy.

"No, but we don't really have a choice," Kristy answer back.

"There is always a choice," Benjamin countered. "These people don't get to control us. On the way here, I saw a Synagogue and I want to go find it. I can speak to the Jews there and we won't have to put up with these adulterous Roman women. Maybe the Jews would offer us their help."

I don't know," Kristy replied. She glanced over at the others nervously. Cleopatra was talking to Calpurnia and the others were listening attentively. "We don't want to get lost. Maybe we should invite Phoebe and Marcus to join us."

"Alright, but I'm getting tired of Phoebe thinking she's in charge here." Benjamin retorted. They walked over to the others. Marcus just rolled his eyes and ignored them but Phoebe turned to see what they wanted.

"We've decided to leave," Benjamin curtly informed her. Kristy glared at him so he quickly added, "there's a Jewish Synagogue in Rome and I want to check it out."

"You are welcome to come with us," Kristy added.

"I'm staying here," Phoebe answered. "You sure it's safe for you two to wander off? Rome's a big city and you can't understand anyone."

"At the Synagogue, I will be able to," Benjamin snapped. "And didn't Chris and Jaxom head into the most dangerous spot in town? If Julius Caesar dies, so will they and the next place the assassinators will probably head is right here. We're leaving!" With that, Benjamin turned and practically dragged Kristy out the door with him.

"You didn't have to be so rude to her," Kristy commented as they headed down the Via Sacra and through the Forum. "And she's right about us not knowing our way around." Kristy glanced about, looking nervously at the bustling activity of the city around them. Citizens and slaves hurried in every direction and the Synagogue was no longer in view.

"We'll be fine," Benjamin reassured her. "The temple's right this way." He led her around the Forum's open spaces into the crowded streets. The population of Rome pressed around them and Benjamin held tight to Kristy's hand to keep them from getting separated. They wandered through streets filled with stores and workshops bustling with activity. The farther they moved from the heart of Rome, the shabbier the city looked and the worse it smelled.

For almost an hour they crossed through the crowded narrowing streets looking for the Synagogue. Kristy began to grumble about them being lost.

Benjamin was beginning to feel nervous about his idea when they turned the corner and he saw the top of the temple appear above the congested streets.

"There it is," Benjamin told Kristy releasing the breath he didn't realized he was holding. Kristy seemed reassured and the two teens hurried towards the sanctuary finding it only a couple blocks away. As they walked up the marble steps, Benjamin gave a prayer of thanks and allowed some of his anxiety to slip away with it.

"Shalom chaverim," a Jewish priest called out to them. Benjamin smiled, glad that he had been right.

"Boker tov," Benjamin called back wishing the priest good morning in traditional Hebrew. Now he could speak to locals who just might help them in their plight.

The priest invited them inside and introduced himself as Brother Enoch. Benjamin introduced himself and Kristy and let the priest know that only he, not Kristy could speak Hebrew. The Synagogue was beautiful in its simplicity. Simple wooden benches and a common altar decorated the pleasant room. Benjamin was relieved to see this temple believed in minimalism.

Brother Enoch asked how they came to be in Rome. *This will be hard to explain*, Benjamin thought. He couldn't lie to a priest but knew the story of their arrival was too strange to fully share with this holy man.

"We have traveled from across the ocean with friends from a country called America," Benjamin began, continuing to speak in the traditional language. "Our companions wished to visit this city, so we followed them here." Kristy was fidgeting next to him so he gave her a stern look, hoping she would sit still and be quiet. Hopefully she realized that he didn't have time to translate for her.

"You are welcome at our temple. How is it that you speak the holy language so well?" the priest questioned him.

"My great-grandfather traveled overseas as a young man with a group of other Jews to escape persecution. My family takes the duty of instructing their children very serious. We belong to a Synagogue where I spent a lot of time in study."

"I give high praise to your forefathers," Brother Enoch said. "Your use of the language is excellent, though I do not recognize your accent."

"We have traveled quite far. The culture I am from has very little contact with Rome," Benjamin told the priest.

"Then it is an even greater blessing to have you here with us," Brother Enoch kindly proclaimed. "You and your family are unaware of the recent events occurring in Judaea, I presume." Benjamin tried to remember the date of Jerusalem's defeat, but couldn't recall when the Palestine region had come under Roman control.

"I know of the revolt led by Judah the Maccabee to free Jerusalem from the Syrians. We celebrate the rededication of the temple of Jerusalem with the eight holy days of Hanukkah." Benjamin told the elderly priest.

"Do you light the candles each day?" Brother Enoch asked with a joyful smile and Benjamin nodded. "It is superb these traditions are remembered. We are planning a great centennial celebration in honor of this wondrous occasion."

"I recall hearing of Pompey occupying the holy city," Benjamin commented, hoping he remembered his history correctly.

"Yes, in his Proconsul in the East, Pompey the Great occupied Jerusalem," Brother Enoch agreed with him. "He did not pillage or profane the temple apart from entering the inner sanctum for a few moments. He made us a providence of Rome and he left us to conduct our lives in peace. More recent events are quite distressing, though. A decade ago Proconsul Marcus Licinius Crassus plundered the temple of Jerusalem, robbing it of all offering made since the temple was restored to our people."

"That's terrible", Benjamin answered. "Was anything done to recover the offerings?"

"No," Brother Enoch shook his head sadly. "They are Roman plunder. Yet our God would not allow such an act to go unpunished. Within a year of the theft, Crassus and almost all of his seven legions were slaughtered by the Parthians."

"I bet Rome went after the Parthians after that," Benjamin commented.

"Benjamin," Kristy tried to get his attention.

"Not now," he told her, hoping the priest wouldn't be offended by the interruption. *My father would snap over a rude interruption like that.* But Brother Enoch only smiled at Kristy and continued the conversation.

"Actually, the civil war took all of Rome's attention for years," Brother Enoch informed him. "Julius Caesar is currently planning an attack against them. He is to leave in a few days with his legions."

"If he survives todays attack," Benjamin grumbled. Brother Enoch reacted with alarm.

"What attack do you speak of?" the priest asked, a look of distress rising across his face. Benjamin had forgotten that brother Enoch wouldn't know about the assassination. *That was stupid*, Benjamin criticized himself.

"I heard something was happening at the Senate meeting," Benjamin explained. "Julius Caesar was aware and bringing legions in to stop the assault."

"This is grave news," Brother Enoch. "I know the Dictator well and he wouldn't bring in legions without good reason. How did you come by this news?"

"My friends and I are staying with the Dictator," Benjamin admitted.

"Oh, you are acquaintances with Julius Caesar," Brother Enoch said in surprise. "I have known Julius Caesar since he was a young boy. His family home is just down the road from us."

"I didn't know Julius Caesar was from this area," Benjamin remarked. "I've never heard anything about his childhood."

"He was a bright and friendly boy," the priest answered with nostalgia in his voice. "Julius loved to write and always paid attention to everything. And he has never forgotten us. He has granted his protection to the Synagogue. He even stops by now and then." Benjamin was surprised to hear the priest speak so highly of the Dictator. He found himself hoping that Jaxom and Chris actually did stop the assassination. *And then they better find us a way home!*

"Benjamin, I'm ready to leave," Kristy broke into his thoughts. "I want to know what's happening with the others." He looked at his new girlfriend. Seeing resentment and irritation in her eyes, Benjamin decided it was time to go. *I don't need her causing a scene.*

"Brother Enoch, we must leave now, but I thank you for your time," Benjamin express his gratitude to the priest. "I am glad to have meet you. I will return if we have time."

"I am blessed to have met you, young Benjamin," Brother Enoch answered as they walked together out of the Synagogue. "I hope your stay in Rome is enjoyable. We have wonderful services each Saturday and I would love to see your faces in the congregation." Benjamin smiled at the kind man.

"I will try," Benjamin called to the priest as they walked down the steps. *It is good to meet someone who walks with God in this unholy city*, Benjamin reflected. Kristy was sulking again but Benjamin felt better about this trip to Rome. *Who would have thought that Julius Caesar was a friend to the Jews?*

Chapter 14

"People will forget what you said, people will forget what you did, but people will never forget how you made them feel"

Maya Angelou

Jaxom and Chris stood near Cornelius Balbus at the edge of the Senate house. Senators dressed in formal togas were filling the room. Jaxom was wondering why Julius Caesar would leave the huge statue of his rival in the Senate house when Chris bumped his shoulder. His friend looked worried and Jaxom leaned in to hear Chris's question.

"Watch that group of Senators," Chris whispered to him, pointing out a small gathering near the center of the room. "Do you see the two that just split away?" Jaxom nodded and watched the two Roman's move towards another cluster of Senators, looking around suspiciously before joining the group. They talked quietly and intensely for a few minutes and then moved towards another group. Something was going on, and Jaxom knew just what it was.

"I'll ask Balbus about them," Jaxom quietly told his friend. He turned to their escort and pointed out the two obvious conspirators.

"The taller man is Cassius Longinus," Cornelius Balbus informed him. "He's hated the Dictator for years. While Julius Caesar was pacifying Gaul, Cassius served as a quaestor under Crassus. They lost almost all of seven legions to the Parthians and Crassus lost his head. Then Cassius joined Pompey during the civil war and had to receive a pardon from Julius Caesar."

"Shouldn't he be grateful for having his life spared?" Jaxom questioned, still watching the two Senators circulate through the room.

"No Roman likes to owe another that kind of debt," Cornelius Balbus answered him. "He's suffered too much humiliation. Now the other Senator is Decimus Brutus. He was with us in Gaul and was trained by Julius Caesar. He owes his entire career to our Dictator. It surprises me to know he would betray him. I thought him to be a loyal supporter of Julius Caesar."

Jaxom turned back to Chris and translated what Cornelius Balbus had told him. He watched the Senators, wondering ones would betray Julius Caesar. He hoped that none of Caesar's Centurions would betray him to the conspirators. They might not attempt the assassination at all. Then the Dictator arrived, led in by his escort of twenty lictors. *We're about to find out*, Jaxom thought.

Jaxom watched as the conspirators surrounded Julius Caesar. They seemed to have no clue that Julius Caesar knew what was going to happen. The scene looked exactly like the textbook version. Under the shadow of Pompey's great statue, Senators pressed into Julius Caesar from all sides calling out to the general asking for him to pardon some guy named Lucius Tillius. As Julius Caesar was lost in the crowd, his voice suddenly ran out.

"Attack!" screamed the Dictator of Rome, letting his legions know the assassination had begun. Then, for some insane reason, Chris ran straight towards the attack. Jaxom froze, not knowing what to do. Chris stopped as the Centurions poured in through the far corridor, led by Mark Anthony. Then Chris just stood there watching the battle.

Jaxom called out to his friend, but Chris didn't react. Jaxom held his breath as countless Senators fled in terror past Chris. The Senators didn't even see Chris, as they attempted to escape the fight. Jaxom turned for a moment to watch them flee out the hallway near him. Just then legions appeared barring their escape and began cutting down the first deserters. Most of the fleeing men flung themselves down to beg for mercy. The legions stood guard but didn't attack the pleading prostate men. The few who attempted to fight their way through, were quickly slaughtered.

Jaxom turned back towards the battle within the Senate house. Chris still stood in the center of the room, watching Julius Caesar slice through Cassius Longinus stomach. Senators lay dead or dying and most those alive cowered on the floor within the carnage. A handful of conspirators remained standing, defiantly attempting to complete the assassination. The battle seemed about over. Then from a side door near him, gladiators poured in to join the fray. The only one standing between the gladiators and the battle was Chris!

"Chris!" Jaxom screamed to his friend and flung himself onto the floor against the wall. Chris turned and his eyes grew wide with terror. He headed towards Jaxom's safe position against the wall. One of the first gladiators spotted Chris immediately and turned to intercept his escape. He plunged his sword straight through the center of Chris's back, the tip protruding from his dying friend's chest for one moment. The gladiator yanked his sword free and moved to join the attack against Julius Caesar, and Chris fell to the floor.

Jaxom cried out in anguish, crawling toward his friends crumpled body, dimly aware of the ensuing fight. *This is my fault. Easy-going Chris, everyone's friend, dies today because of me. My wishes put Chris in this danger and I stood like a coward against the wall while Chris ran to help. First I killed my mother and sister, and now my friend.* Smothered in guilt and despair, Jaxom reached Chris's bleeding body and pulled his friend into his lap. Chris moaned and looked up at him with pain glazed eyes.

"Did we save Caesar?" Chris whispered and then coughed up blood. Jaxom held tight to his friend and looked to see the state of the battle. Julius Caesar was dispatching gladiators surrounded by his loyal legions. The battle was almost over and Jaxom noticed Cornelius Balbus standing by their side, a look of pity on his weathered face.

"Yes, Chris, we saved him," Jaxom told his dying friend.

"Use the ring, Jaxom," Balbus said. Jaxom startled, realizing Chris would not die today. But then his three wishes would be used. He could not bring them home or try to save his family from their fiery death.

"I wish for you to be healed," Jaxom said through his tears. Chris suddenly gasped and his eyes rolled back. Jaxom thought for a moment that the ring hadn't worked and his friend was dead. But then Chris gasped again and this time sat up quickly. He pulled his blood soaked tunic open to reveal a perfectly healed scar on his chest. Jaxom quickly looked at Chris's back and found a larger scar also healed completely.

"How did you do that, Jaxom?" Chris questioned him.

"It's the ring," Jaxom explained. "It grants wishes." Chris looked at the silver ring fascinated by the magical item that had just saved his life.

"Three wishes," Cornelius Balbus specified.

"What is Tres Vota?" Chris asked, not understanding the old man's Latin.

"Three wishes," Jaxom translated for his friend. "We're probably stuck here now. That was the last, but I had to save you."

"I'm glad you did," Chris said, grabbing his friend in a tight embrace. "Thanks, Jaxom." Then looking around, Chris smiled. "Looks like we have won."

Jaxom grimaced at the scene of carnage around the Senate house. The slaughter was staining the smooth marble floor red with blood. Corpses of Roman elite and their slave entertainers lay crumpled around the Consul seats in the room's center as well as scattered throughout the gory room. The remaining Senators cowered on the floor. Legionnaires guarded every exit and the remainder stood in formation near their victorious leader.

Julius Caesar was moving through the room. As he approached a Senator he ordered the man to rise. When the man did not move, Mark Anthony grabbed him and roughly jerked him to his feet. Julius Caesar searched through the man's toga. Pulling out a long thin box, Julius Caesar opened it and found it to be empty.

"Caius Trebonius, you are found guilty of treason," the general announced, then ran the Senator through with his Spanish sword. Chris stifled a sob. Jaxom looked at his friend with concern. Chris may be healed, but he had still experienced the horrible near-tragedy.

Julius Caesar turned to another cowering Senator, ordering the old man to stand. This time the old Roman quickly jumped to his feet. He then asked to see the man's stylus pen. The Senator meekly pulled out his long case and opened it for the Dictator. Within the case was the man's life saving pen.

"You may leave, Marcus Cicero," Caesar dismissed the Senator, who was quickly escorted out by a legionnaire.

"Can we get out of here?" Jaxom questioned Cornelius Balbus. Between almost losing his friend and the slaughter he had just witnessed, Jaxom was starting to panic. I *need to get away from this carnage!*

"Let me find out," Cornelius Balbus answered, approaching Julius Caesar to ask. The Dictator turned, gesturing for them to join him.

"Jaxom and Chris," Julius Caesar began, "you have helped to save my life and almost lost one of yours. I am grateful. We shall talk more later of your experience." He gave them a look that told Jaxom he knew about the magic ring. Julius Caesar then turned to his legionnaires. "Let it be known that these two are friends of your dictator and are under my protection. Balbus escort them out now." Finished with them, the he turned back to the bloody business at hand.

The boys followed Cornelius Balbus out through the gore of dead and cowering senators and then through the ranks of guarding legionnaires. As they hurried through Pompey's great structure, Jaxom began feeling a little better. *I've slaughtered enemies in video games. It's not that different*, he tried to convince himself.

They emerged onto the public portico. A handful of blood splattered Senators lingered in the shadows. The Senator who had left right before them, approached.

"Cornelius," Cicero called to their guide. "What do you know of this tragedy?"

"I know a great deal, Cicero," Cornelius Balbus answered him. Then he questioned the elderly Senator back, "what do you know of it?"

"I was completely unaware," Cicero responded franticly. "A good thing in this case, though not a position I am used to." Then Cicero noticed Jaxom and Chris. "Who is this accompanying you today?"

"This is Jaxom and Chris." Cornelius Balbus introduced them and Cicero firmly shook each of their hands. "They are friends of Julius Caesar and under his protection. This is Marcus Tullius Cicero, the greatest orator of Rome," he told Jaxom. Chris stood near, pretending he could understand.

"Another secret?" Cicero mused. He seemed quite pleased with Cornelius Balbus's introduction of him. Then his smile quickly dropped as he remembered what had just occurred in the Senate. "How high is the death count? I counted over seventy dead Senators but I couldn't see them all."

"It depends on how many traitors remain," Cornelius Balbus replied. "I would say we lost nearly a hundred Senators today." *Why would the number be so high*, Jaxom wondered? *It was supposed to be only sixty traitors.*

"At least that many," responded another Senator standing close by. Other innocent, blood soaked Senators were congregating around and more continued to join the group as they were released from the Senate house by the Dictator.

"Boys, this is Marcus Junius Brutus," Cicero introduced the young Roman, then turned to question the man. "What do you know of this attack?" Jaxom realized that this was the alleged child of the Dictator. He even looked similar to Caesar. *This man is a traitor! How had he gotten out without being discovered?*

"I had heard rumors, but never thought anyone would attempt it," Brutus casually responded. "How did Julius Caesar know it was coming?"

"That is not your concern, Brutus," Cornelius Balbus snapped at the senator. "Be glad of your relationship to our Dictator. You were allowed to leave without being searched. How do we know you were not involved?"

"That is enough, Balbus," Marcus Cicero said. "Julius Caesar seems to know what's going on. I'm sure that you weren't searched before you left." This elderly Senator seemed bothered to have been put through such humiliation.

He knows where my loyalties lie," Cornelius Balbus responded.

"Blood creates strong ties," Brutus countered.

The conversation ended abruptly as the recent dead began flowing into the Forum, hauled out of the Senate house by Julius Caesar legionnaires. A river of soldier after soldier dragged most of the dead into the center of the Forum, tossing the bodies onto a growing pile of carnage. Strangely, a handful of deceased Senators were carefully placed in a line on the public portico where Chris stood with the others.

The people of Rome began to gather a short distance away, for the first time realizing that something big had just occurred. All other activity in the Forum had ceased by the time a bloodied and bandaged Julius Caesar emerged from Pompey's great structure. Mark Anthony was still at his side. The gruesome pile of dead stood between the growing crowd and the Dictator. The legionnaires clustered around the scene, reforming rank as Julius Caesar stepped forward to address the crowd.

"Citizens and friends of Rome, a grave tragedy has occurred in our great city today," Julius Caesar began. "Traitors in our midst have struck at the very heart of this great city. In a conspiracy to gain political control over the people, the Senate meeting was attacked and even I, your chosen Dictator was assaulted." Jaxom was impressed with Caesar's impromptu speech over this event. *Instead of making it about his own assassination, he is swaying the people to believe it is their own safety that was at stake.*

"Yet this disaster was averted," Julius Caesar continued, "thanks to the loyal Romans who brought me warning and our steadfast legionnaire's quick response to any threat to our noble Roman Republic. Eighty-six traitors within the Senate itself have been caught and executed. The list shall be posted. They are all declared Traitors of Rome. Their property is forfeit. Thirty attacking gladiators were also slain during the attack. They share the fate of their conspiring masters. Let their heads be severed and raised to show where such treachery leads."

The citizens of Rome raised such a cheer that Julius Caesar was forced to pause in his speech. Jaxom could see where the Dictator's man of the people reputation had come from. He wasn't sure about this raising heads thing. *If it was what I think it is, things are about to get even more gruesome.*

"What's he saying?" Chris eagerly asked him. Jaxom had forgot for a moment that Chris couldn't understand anyone else. He quietly told his friend what Julius Caesar had said so far.

"I bet there's a lot of property between those eighty-six Senators." Chris responded. *He's right. Rome just got a lot richer*, Jaxom thought. As the cheering crowd calmed down, Julius Caesar continued his speech. This time, Jaxom remembered to quietly translate for Chris.

"There is greater sadness to this tragedy. Nine of our loyal Senators were also slain today. These men were innocent victims in this horrible conspiracy. Rome shall provide monuments and honors to the victim's families." Jaxom wondered about these honors. *What good would that do for the families? Will it wash away the pain? It won't replace their lost loved ones. Nothing could ever replace my mom and sister.*

Julius Caesar continued his speech, listing the names of the victims, but Cornelius Balbus caught Jaxom's arm and led him back into the shadows of the Public Portico along with Chris. The old engineer looked worried about something. Jaxom glanced around and noticed Cicero and several other Senators watching their withdrawal.

"Your native tongue is completely unknown to Rome and your conversation is drawing attention," Cornelius Balbus warned them. "It might be wise if we retire to the Dictators residence and clean up. Julius Caesar has much to do, but he will meet with you both later." Jaxom and Chris followed Cornelius Balbus away, out of the Forum.

As Jaxom walked towards Julius Caesar's mansion, he felt a pride in himself that he couldn't remember feeling for so long. *We stopped the assassination and I prevented Chris's death. Julius Caesar has even placed us under his protection and called us friends.*

Chapter 15

"*I lived through this horror. I can take the next thing that comes along*"

Eleanor Roosevelt

This is fantastic! Phoebe was riding to Rome with the Queen of Egypt and chatting the whole way as if they were destined to be best friends. Without the others to question or interrupt, they were able to talk openly about all kinds of topics. She had been amazed to find out that Cleopatra was the wonderful seamstress who had made the dress she was wearing. The Queen spoke a dozen languages and knew so much about the many cultures of her world. Cleopatra gave credit for her incredibly knowledge to the libraries of Alexandria where she had studied for much of her life and her skill to her big sister who had shared everything with her until her sister's untimely and unjust death.

Cleopatra asked many questions about the time from which Phoebe came. Phoebe summarized much of the history she could remember for the Queen. She began with the Roman Empire's conquest of Europe and the Middle East. Then told of the Renaissance that began right here in Italy. She skimmed past the 16th and 17th centuries. *I don't want to think about the atrocities of that time right now.*

Phoebe described the colonization of the America's, including the destruction of the native tribes and the increase in the slave trade. She also told Cleopatra about freeing the slaves and the women's liberation movement. Cleopatra was excited for Phoebe over the women's right that had already been gained.

"So women can now vote in your country after generations of servitude," Cleopatra said. "That is a great achievement. So many women in this world have no rights in government."

"Yea, and we can attend any of the schools or try for any career also," Phoebe replied.

"That is how it is in Egypt and we have the best schools in the world," Cleopatra boasted. "Egyptian women have never had all their rights stripped from them like the Roman, Greek, and Jewish women. Do you find that the men of your country are less competitive?"

Phoebe laughed, "Most are as competitive as ever. They channel it into their careers, sports, and military. There are still controlling types around but most Americans support equal rights for everyone."

"And do you have rights over your children?" the Queen asked.

"Some rights, but not enough, and fathers have rights too," Phoebe told her. "There are many old laws and traditions that still need changed."

"With women getting to vote, your people should be able to find a better balance," Cleopatra reassured her.

"Yea, it's slow going, but we're already heading that way," Phoebe replied. The conversation ended since they had arrived at their destination in Rome. Phoebe followed Cleopatra out of the carriage and looked around in wonder at the city of ancient Rome.

They had stopped in front of Julius Caesar's incredible mansion situated right in the middle of the city. Phoebe looked down the Via Sacra into the forum and watched as Senators headed towards their fated meeting. For a moment, Phoebe thought about Jaxom and Chris, hoping they were safe. She sent them a wish of safe return as Cleopatra was greeted by Calpurnia, Julius Caesar's wife.

"Greetings Cleopatra, great Pharaoh of Egypt," Calpurnia said sweeping into a low bow. "Your arrival is unexpected, but you are welcome, as always." Graceful and elegant, Calpurnia was a perfect example of a Roman aristocratic wife. She wore a beautiful red silken gown with matching slippers, accented by fine jewels.

"Your generosity is warmly accepted," the Queen responded. Phoebe wondered, trying to hide her smile, if that included being generous with her man. Then to Phoebe's surprise the two women embraced.

"Come in and tell me all that I have missed," Calpurnia insisted, ushering them between beautiful marble columns into the front room of her amazing home.   Cleopatra began explaining the past nights activities to Calpurnia. Phoebe listened to Cleopatra's reasons for being in the garden with new understanding of their reasons for being here. The Queens nightmares and her pleas to Isis were connected to Jaxom finding the ring. Then Calpurnia spoke of also having terrible dreams. *Divine influence was definitely involved. But why would an Egyptian Goddess want them to stop the assassination of a Roman conqueror?*

Benjamin and Kristy approached her and told her of their plans to visit the Jewish Synagogue in Rome. This didn't seem like a smart idea, but who was she to stop them. As they left she was split between worry for their safety and relief over their departure. Benjamin's attitude was getting on her nerves and she was getting sick of Kristy's fits.

Cleopatra was continuing the narrative, telling about the conversations after their arrival and Phoebe's attention began to wander. Julius Caesar's mansion was the most elaborate home she had ever been inside. The large open room was arranged with several clusters of beautiful couches surrounding low tables. In the center stood a stone pool situated directly below an opening in the tiled roof. The floors were polished marble and elegant tapestries also covered the stone walls here, as they did in the country villa.   Enormous elegantly painted ceramic pottery was placed throughout the room filled with long stem flowers and feathery ferns. *Julius Caesar was said to have exquisite taste.*

Numerous artifacts of the Dictators many travels were on display. As Calpurnia led the group to a seating area, Phoebe admired a silver ship displayed on the table. Its delicate details were beautifully rendered completed with thin sheets of shimmering gold sails. *The wealth in this one room is immense.*

"What are they talking about?" Marcus asked sitting beside Phoebe as she settled herself across from the two ancient womyn. She had forgotten for a minute that Marcus couldn't understand anyone.

"Cleopatra is just filling her in on what's been going on." Phoebe told him.

"It's strange that they get along so well," Marcus commented.

Though the women chattered freely, Phoebe could sense the tension in the air. Both women were frightened for Julius Caesar's safety. In a strange way, it seemed to be something that bonded them. *How different it is in my world*, Phoebe thought. *We would be filled with hatred and jealousy.* When Cleopatra finished, Calpurnia turned to welcome her and Marcus.

"Welcome to Rome, young travelers, I am Calpurnia," the elegant lady greeted them.

'I am Phoebe and this is Marcus," Phoebe introduced them. "He doesn't understand Latin but I can translate for him. We are honored to stay with you. Your home is lovely."

"Thank you, though it belongs to my husband. He inherited this estate many years ago, when he became a High Priest," Calpurnia explained. "I will give you a tour soon. I was blessed by Fortuna to marry such a man." Phoebe thought she saw something pass across Cleopatra's face as she translated the conversation for Marcus, but the expression was gone quickly and the Queen smiled at her friend.

"He provides well for you and I hope that he always will," Cleopatra expressed to Calpurnia. Then Cleopatra changed the subject. "Phoebe has shared much with me about her home. Its political structure is similar to Rome's."

"It evolved from Roman and Greek ideas," Phoebe said, affirming the Pharaohs opinion.

Your cultures seems to follow the popular voting structure as does Rome," Cleopatra speculated. "The Greeks like to draw lots and hope for divine political involvement."

"Our culture follows the popular vote on almost everything," Phoebe agreed.

"She has told me that recently, they have given their women the right to vote." Cleopatra informed Calpurnia.

"Oh, wouldn't that be wonderful," Calpurnia wishfully replied. "But such an event would never happen in Rome. The men here are too caught up in their power struggles. I just wish they would give us the right to raise our children. Claudia gave birth to a perfect baby girl last week, and that horrible man she is married to wouldn't accept her. She had to expose her beautiful daughter."

"How awful!" Phoebe exclaimed. She had read about unwanted children being exposed, but never imagined that the mother had no right in the decision.

"Things can change," Cleopatra assured Calpurnia. "With a Dictator like Julius Caesar, much can be accomplished for the people of Rome, including its women."

"He thinks only of honor and revenge these days," Calpurnia replied bitterly. Phoebe was surprised that she would speak of her displeasure concerning Julius Caesar so openly. She didn't translate this unhappiness to Marcus. *It's not really his business.*

"The massacre of Crassus and his legions is weighing on him," Cleopatra agreed. "But Julius greatly loves Rome and her people. With both of us to give him wisdom, he will have a glorious reign."

"If he survives the day," Calpurnia voiced the underlying tension at last.

"Great Isis watches over him," the Queen assures her.

"And so do all the Gods, my dear Queen of the Nile," the voice of Cornelius Balbus answered from behind Phoebe. She turned to see who had arrived and stood up in shock at the sight of her friends.

Jaxom, Chris and Balbus stood in the doorway covered in the blood of battle. Chris looked the worst, with his entire tunic stained red. But they all were whole and Phoebe gave a prayer of thanks that no one appeared injured.

"What happened?" Phoebe quickly asked.

"Julius Caesar is victorious once again," Cornelius Balbus told them. Cleopatra and Calpurnia embraced with relief. Phoebe resisted the urge to run to embrace Jaxom and Chris. She had been trying to ignore the ache of worry in her gut over their safety.

"Almost a hundred Senators are dead," Jaxom informed them.

"And Jaxom saved my life!" Chris added.

"We will explain all," Cornelius Balbus told them. "First let us change."

"Of course," Calpurnia agreed, gesturing down the hall. The old Senator led the two out of the room to clean up, and Phoebe and the others retook their seats. Phoebe was anxious to hear their story, wondering what Chris meant about Jaxom saving his life. She would find out soon enough.

"What wonderful news," Calpurnia smiled. "I shall have a feast prepared for my husband's arrival. We have much to celebrate!" She stood and hurried out through a different doorway.

"Your arrival has turned fate to our favor," Cleopatra exclaimed, "and I am so grateful."

"You're welcome, your Majesty," Phoebe replied, with a slight bow of respect towards her new royal friend.

"What do you think Chris meant, and where did Calpurnia go?" Marcus asked. With the excitement she had again forgotten to translate for Marcus. *This translating is really aggravating.*

"It looks like they were in the middle of the trouble," Phoebe answered. "I'm just glad their safe. We will find out in a few minutes. Oh, and Calpurnia is getting a feast ready for us to celebrate."

"Chris's tunic was torn in the back," Marcus pondered aloud. "It looked like it was soaked in his blood."

"If he had lost that much blood, he wouldn't be walking," Phoebe replied. "Just wait a few minutes, Marcus."

Phoebe turned back to the Queen to translate the conversation.

"I did not understand your friend when he spoke," Cleopatra responded. "He is well now. What is next for you and your friends?"

"I hadn't thought about it," Phoebe answered the Queen. "I guess we go home. Though I would like to spend more time in Rome before we go."

"You are welcome to stay, my dear," the Pharaoh declared kindly. Phoebe thought about exploring this ancient region with great excitement. She could see the great wonders of the world that no longer existed in her time.

"I would really love to see the Library in Alexandria," Phoebe told Cleopatra. "It was destroyed in my timeline, after Julius Caesar's assassination." The Queen smiled widely anticipating the trip.

"Then you shall journey with me to see it," the Pharaoh announced. "It is the most wonderful of places and we will keep it safe. For generations we have been gathering all the written knowledge we can find and new works are continuing to be produced." Marcus bumped her shoulder and Phoebe turned to translate for him.

"Are you sure you want to travel that far?" Marcus said after she had explained the Queens offer. He looked worried over the idea, but just then

Jaxom and Chris returned, still accompanied by Cornelius Balbus. They were both clean and were wearing simple robes, Jaxom again wearing a blue matching her dress, she noticed. The boys settled onto a sofa near to Phoebe, and Cornelius Balbus took Calpurnia's spot next to Cleopatra.

"Where are Benjamin and Kristy?" Jaxom asked.

"They left and good riddance," Marcus answered. He apparently didn't like his two missing classmates much.

"They decided to go find the Synagogue," Phoebe added. Jaxom and Chris looked at each other and just shrugged. No one seemed to care much about what happened to Benjamin and Kristy. Phoebe was feeling nervous still about their safety, especially Kristy's, but decided to let the subject drop for now.

Calpurnia rejoined the group sitting on the remaining divan. Cornelius Balbus asked Jaxom to tell what happened so no one would need to translate. All eyes locked onto Jaxom as he began.

"After we left the country house, we rode straight here," Jaxom began. "Julius Caesar met with his Centurions and then Balbus escorted us to the Senate meeting. When Julius Caesar arrived at the meeting, the Senators clustered around him just like the history book's description. But when Cimber began the assassination, the Dictator ordered his legionaries to attack. The soldiers stormed the meeting and wiped out anyone who stood opposed to Julius Caesar, but then the gladiators from next door joined the battle," Jaxom continued. He looked nervously at Marcus. "Chris got himself stabbed during the attack, but I healed him with the magic ring." Marcus looked stunned. Phoebe wondered how he would take the news. Then it hit her. *That was Jaxom's third wish!*

"That ring is what brought us here?" Marcus questioned as he s stood up. Jaxom nodded. "And you knew." Jaxom nodded again and Marcus turned to Phoebe. "What about you, Phoebe? Did you know?" Marcus asked her.

"Cleopatra and Balbus figured it out for us," Phoebe answered hoping Marcus would not be too angry. Marcus glared between the two not saying anything. He looked pretty upset.

"If Jaxom hadn't been there," Chris broke the silence and stood up next to Marcus, "I would be dead right now." Marcus looked at his best friend who opened his robe to reveal a horrible scar on his chest. "You should see my back where the sword went in. Jaxom says it looks much worse."

The anger drained from Marcus's face and he grabbed Chris in a firm embrace. "I am so glad you're ok," Marcus told his friend. "Hope you learned your lesson about running off to stop assassins."

"It was quite chaotic. I'll file that one with my recent Chemistry lessons." Chris said grinning. Marcus laughed and hugged his friend again. Phoebe was glad the confrontation was over but didn't think that was truly the end of things. *Jaxom used his third wish to heal Chris. Will we ever make it home?*

Chapter 16:

"Bring out yer dead"

Monty Python

Leaving the Roman Synagogue, Kristy felt even more depressed than before. Now even Benjamin was getting excited about being in ancient Rome. To her, everyone speaking Hebrew was no better than everyone speaking Latin. She couldn't understand anyone or anything that was going on. *I'm not even sure that any of this is real.*

As she and Benjamin walked through the crowded streets towards the forum, Kristy wondered if her mother's hallucinations were like this. Since she was small, Kristy had always worried that she would inherit her mother's mental illness. When she arrived at Julius Caesar's country villa, she thought it must be a delusion. *Yet everything seems so real and even my friends are seeing it all.*

It must be real, she decided. *Some magic had brought us to Rome just like Phoebe said.* She wasn't any happier about being stranded in a strange foreign city, then when she thought she was going crazy. *There has to be some way to return home. Mother can't cope without me*, she thought. They turned the corner and suddenly encountered a decapitated head, its vacant eyes staring right at her.

Kristy screamed. Bloody heads of recently deceased men were mounted on poles lining the road. She took off running, pushing through the crowd to get away from the awful vision. *I must be going crazy.* As she ran into the forum an even worse scene confronted her. A gruesome pile of dead bodies stood in front of her. A Roman soldier dragged a body from the pile. With his sword, he quickly decapitated the corpse. The world began to spin and then Kristy fainted.

When she came to, Benjamin was by her side gently shaking her. "Kristy, wake up. We need to get off the street," he was saying. "You're making a scene." She looked around and saw a few people watching them, but keeping their distance. Most of the people were just going about their business, ignoring them as well as the horrible spectacle still occurring near them.

"I'm causing a scene!" Kristy roared at him. "Look at that pile, Benjamin. That is the problem, not me." She couldn't believe how calm he was, how calm everyone was when someone had just murdered all those men and were using their heads as roadside decorations. *This can't be real! If it was real, everyone would be freaked out!*

They were suddenly joined by the soldier that had been in charge at Julius Caesar's country place. Mark Anthony tried to speak to Benjamin but the two could not understand each other. So instead the frustrated Roman gestured for them to follow him. Benjamin helped Kristy to her feet and they followed him away from the gory forum towards Julius Caesar's mansion. *Why is this happening!?*

Kristy felt numb except for a spot on her head which throbbed with pain. She must have hit it when she fainted. She followed the soldier, holding tight to Benjamin's hand. His hand felt genuine, warm and slightly callused. She could see and hear the busy city around her, and smell the animal waste and incense from the temples mingling in the air. *But it must not be real. When did I start hallucinating and why would my mind create a trip to ancient Rome? Perhaps I'm already institutionalized, strapped to a bed like they did to mom for a while.*

As they entered Julius Caesar's mansion, Kristy could hear laughing and wondered how anything could be funny right now. She recognized Jaxom's voice as they followed the soldier deeper into the ancient home. Mark Anthony led them to a huge dining hall where all her classmates sat on couches lining the room. Everyone was enjoying themselves, chatting with the Queen and Julius Caesar himself. A large table lining one wall was filled with a delicious smelling feast which reminded Kristy she had not eaten since breakfast. No one seemed to notice their arrival.

"I couldn't believe it when he ran right towards the conspirators," Jaxom was saying to the roomful of people.

"I'm just glad you healed him with that magic ring," Marcus responded happily.

"What magic ring?" Benjamin bellowed, and the room fell silent. Everyone looked towards them in surprise. "That ring you found brought us here," Benjamin continued questioning Jaxom without waiting for an answer. "So much for being honest with everyone, Jaxom. You knew all along didn't you?"

"I didn't know at first," Jaxom stood and began explaining himself as `Benjamin strode into the room until he stood directly in front of Jaxom. Kristy was hauled along with him since they were still holding hands. Benjamin's grip was so tight that her hand was beginning to ache. *Can you feel pain in a delusion?*

"Well, now we all know," Benjamin interrupted Jaxom. "So why aren't we heading home?"

"The danger is passed. We stopped the assassination," Chris said, coming to his friend's defense.

"And the ring's three wishes are used up," Phoebe chimed in. Kristy looked at her friend, surprised that Phoebe would support Jaxom in anything. Phoebe smiled at her as if to say everything would be alright. Kristy wished she could believe that it would.

Benjamin looked around at the group with growing anger in his eyes. Kristy was worried that he might actually attack Jaxom. Yet more than anything, she just wanted to go home. No one in the room said anything for a few minutes. The ancient Romans and Queen stayed in their seats, watching to see how this conflict would play itself out.

"Give it to me," Benjamin growled at Jaxom, holding out his hand.

"No, it's not yours and it won't work," Jaxom answered in a calm tone. "Like Phoebe said, the ring only had three wishes and they have all been used."

"Maybe it will work for us," Kristy said, hoping that it would be true. *I have to get out of this hallucination and get back to mom.* Benjamin grabbed Jaxom's arm and Jaxom struggled to pull away.

"We're going to wish ourselves home!" Benjamin hollered just as Jaxom pulled his arm away. Suddenly Kristy felt the ground shake again and squeezed her eyes tightly closed. *Oh, please let us be going home!* The room began to spin and Kristy braced herself against Benjamin as wind roared around them. Then suddenly everything was silent and still.

So many mysteries to unravel, thought Marcus Cicero as he watched Cornelius Balbus lead away his two newest protégées. Julius's engineering friend had not dropped many clues as to the significance of these foreigners, but anyone under the protection of the Dictator was important. He had moved closer to overhear Cornelius speak to the boys before leading them out of the Forum. These new players were staying with the Julius Caesar and he would be meeting with them later. *And Cornelius is right about their native tongue. I've never heard it before.*

The Dictator was going on about the victims and then more about the glory of Rome. Cicero had heard it before. Julius Caesar had always possessed the power of rhetoric. The Roman people had forgiven this man a great many crimes, and will do so once more. *Julius Caesar holds the threat of another civil war at bay. The people will believe in him if only to keep the peace.*

This tragedy in the Senate was disastrous. Some of the most influential and traditional men in Rome had just been killed and they had already lost so many patricians during the civil war. *Such noble families destroyed!* The dynamics of the Senate had just change dramatically and Cicero knew it could get worse when Julius Caesar began finding replacements for the lost Roman men.

As the Dictator finished his speech, Cicero watched the crowd disperse and the centurions began their gruesome task. Most of the remaining Senators were hurrying across the forum towards home to remove their bloodstained tunics. Cicero glanced at his own, finding it stained dark red across the side. Glancing around the Portico, he noticed Aulus Hirtius and Vibius Pansa deep in conversation. *Perhaps they know something about this attack or these strangers staying with the Dictator.* He strolled their direction hoping to pick up a bit of their conversation before he was noticed.

"I'm sure he had a dagger," Vibius was telling Aulus. "When he saw the centurions he threw himself to the floor and slide the knife away."

"Hello Cicero," Aulus loudly called out, quieting his friend. "I am glad we will still have your wisdom to guide us in Senate meetings. We have lost so many."

"Between the civil war and now this, we have lost too many," Cicero replied hearing bitterness in his own voice.

"Julius Caesar did what he had to do in stopping this attack," Vibius retorted. He was a faithful follower of the Dictator. Actually they both were, but Vibius was a little more zealous about his loyalties. Yet they were also students of Cicero's, taking classes in rhetoric from him throughout the past year.

"I mean no disrespect to Julius Caesar," Cicero responded calmly. "Only that it grieves me to lose so many colleagues. I fear that I am passing through my prime years too quickly."

"You will be greatly needed for many more years," Aulus assured him as Cicero knew he would. "The intensity and vision you bring into the Senate has always inspired me." Cicero gave Aulus a smile and a nod of thanks. Cicero was pleased with the praise though he wished to direct the conversation towards the events of today.

"Did you have any foreknowledge of the attack today?" Cicero questioned the two young Senators. Vibius shook his head in negation than looked to Aulus whose eyes glimmered with secret knowledge.

"Mark Anthony spoke to me just before it occurred," Aulus told them. "I spied his sword hidden beneath his toga and he said Julius Caesar had gotten word that something was to occur at today's meeting. He warned me to stay out of the way."

"Aulus watched the entire incident from behind the farthest row of seating," Vibius told him.

"And that is where you saw Brutus with the knife," Cicero responded. Aulus and Vibius looked surprised and stepped in closer to Cicero. *Just as I suspected.*

"Did you also see him," Aulus whispered. "We should go to the Dictator with this news."

"No, that cannot be done," Cicero told them.

"We must inform Julius Caesar," Vibius uttered.

"There are factors you two are not aware of that would cause great conflict with your plan," Cicero sighed. "Marcus Brutus is Julius Caesar's son." The two young Senators reacted in shock.

"So that is why Julius Caesar let him leave without being searched," Aulus replied and Cicero nodded in affirmation.

"Did you see the two young men attend the meeting with Balbus," Cicero asked, changing the subject.

"Yes, did you see the fool run towards the fight unarmed," Aulus smirked.

"I then saw him walk away after being stabbed," Vibius reported. "How is that possible?" The two Senators looked to Cicero for answers. Cicero remembered the blood soaked tunic of Balbus's protégée, though the young man did not appear injured.

"That is something I did not see," Cicero replied. *Vibius must be mistaken. It was just not possible.*

"The Dictator placed them under his protection after you were released," Aulus informed him.

"Yes, I expected he would" Cicero answered as if he knew more than he really did about the strangers. "They are friends of Julius Caesar's and staying at his estate."

"Do you remember that today was the day the oracle said Julius Caesar should beware of?" Vibius whispered.

"Some kind of magic is at work today," Aulus murmured. Cicero scoffed at the thought of magic. These young Senators were always being deceived by the Etruscan swindlers. *There is always a logical explanation.*

"I must head home," Cicero decided aloud. "I would like to remove this ruined toga. I will give thought to what you have seen and we will speak again tomorrow."

"Good day," the young Senators called to him as he headed down the steps of the public portico. He now had another mystery to solve. Perhaps Vibius was wrong, though he was usually a man of great intelligence and integrity. The mystery surrounding these newcomers was intriguing. How had they gotten so close to Julius Caesar that he would welcome them to stay in his home. *I need to know more. Perhaps I should take a walk by Julius Caesar's home later. Besides, I've not seem his completed pediment yet.*

Chapter 18

*"Efforts and courage are not enough
without purpose and direction"*
John F. Kennedy

Jaxom was finally feeling like everything was going his way. Julius Caesar had finally arrived home and they were heading to a feast to celebrate the day. They had stopped the assassination and Chris was whole. Marcus wasn't too angry about them keeping the ring secret and as they headed to dine with their hosts, Phoebe had given him a quick hug and told him she was glad he was alright. Of course, she had also hugged Chris, but he couldn't help but think that she lingered by his side out of more than just relief. He hoped so, anyways.

"I was talking with Cleopatra about taking a trip to Egypt," Phoebe stated as they entered into the dining hall. "Wouldn't it be cool to see the libraries in Alexandria?" The elegant marble room was filling with the delicious aromas of their victory feast being brought in by a troop of servants.

"The lighthouse should still be there also," Chris commented.

"We could travel the Nile and see the Great Pyramids," Jaxom responded, excited by the prospect. He and his friends wandered towards a long table filled with a huge array of appealing cuisine. There was bowls heaped with fruit and trays piled high with bread. In the center of the table was a huge roast as well as seafood of various sorts. There was some dishes there that Jaxom didn't recognize. *But everything looks and smells delicious!*

"Smells great," Phoebe commented to him, as they both accepted slices of roast on finely crafted silver plates from one of the servants. Jaxom helped himself to a pile of cherries, some sort of bean mix and a salad with cucumbers and olives. Phoebe was already sitting next to Cleopatra and Julius Caesar, asking the Queen about the fish varieties, so he settled himself on a sofa nearby.

Everyone enjoyed their meal for a while without much talk. Servants circulated through the room, offering tea and wine and helping to refill plates. Jaxom tried some roasted peacock offered to him but was disappointed that it just tasted like chicken. He began to get used to the watery wine finding it similar to the flavored waters sold back home. As everyone began to fill up, Calpurnia dismissed the servants and conversations began around the room.

"I am grateful for the help you provided today," Julius Caesar told them. "If you choose to stay in Rome, I offer you a choice from one of the many estates just confiscated."

"Thank you, that would be of great use to us," Jaxom told the Dictator and then translated the offer for Chris and Marcus. Everyone was excited about the prospect of acquiring their own place in Rome. Even Phoebe seemed delighted, giving him a radiate smile than going back to her private conversation with Cleopatra.

"I have my own reasons to keep you comfortable in Rome," Julius Caesar continued. "I would like your assistance in translating the text found within your school building. The maps will give my legions a great strategic advantage in their future engagements. "

"As I said before, I will translate anything you need, sir. We are at you service in anything you require." Jaxom assured the Dictator. *Working for Julius Caesar in any function would be a privilege. I can't believe I'm becoming friends with this man. I bet the others all agree now that that we should stay in the past for a while.*

"Jaxom," Marcus called to him. "Ask Caesar what they will do with the rest of the property that was just confiscated." He turned to the Dictator and repeated his friend's question.

"We will be selling most of it, though a few places will be given to the families of the victims in the Senate attack," Julius Caesar replied. "Why does Marcus ask?" Jaxom again translated for his friends. He was getting really tired of repeating everything.

"Real-estate can be more valuable than cash at times," Marcus began. "I was thinking that Rome might be able to lease some of the properties and bring in a continuous cash flow instead of a one-time chunk of funds. There's areas in this city that could use some major renovation as well and that would increase Rome's real estate value overall." Jaxom translated again, adding that Marcus's mother was a real-estate agent. Julius Caesar looked thoughtful for a moment about the matter.

"We should address this proposal more," the leader of Rome informed them. "The idea bears more thought."

"I have an idea, too," Chris added with a smile. "I want to start a Roman bicycle business." Jaxom looked at Chris in surprise for a moment. Then Marcus fell back in laughter. Everyone else looked over wondering what the merriment was about, so again Jaxom repeated what was said. The ancient adults looked about in confusion as Phoebe also began to laugh and then Jaxom had to join in.

"What gave you that idea?" Phoebe asked still giggling.

"My sore ass and legs," Chris answered trying to look serious. "That ride into Rome was the second most painful thing I've ever dealt with. You healed that too, Jaxom. Thanks." Marcus was in such hysterics now that Jaxom thought he was going to fall off the sofa. Jaxom translated, again, for the confused adults who began to see the humor in the suggestion.

"What is this bicycle he speaks of," Calpurnia questioned, clearly not getting the joke.

"A much less painful way to travel," Marcus sputtered through his glee.

"We should have had him carried to the Senate house," Balbus joked.

"I figured you were sore, but I didn't know it was that bad," Jaxom told his friend.

"He wasn't gonna let a sore ass, keep him from saving the day," Marcus commented, finally getting control of himself. Jaxom translated everything for his friends than looked at Marcus.

"I couldn't believe it when he ran right towards the conspirators," Jaxom told Chris's best friend.

"I'm just glad you healed him with that magic ring," Marcus responded happily.

"What magic ring?" Benjamin suddenly bellowed from the doorway. The room fell silent as everyone looked towards him. He was standing there holding tight to Kristy's hand, with a look of fury on his face. Mark Anthony stood beside them. "That ring you found brought us here," Benjamin continued without waiting for an answer as he advanced into the room towards Jaxom. "So much for being honest with everyone, Jaxom. You knew all along didn't you?"

"I didn't know at first," Jaxom said, standing up and hoping to explain himself to Benjamin. He had completely forgotten the existence of his other two classmates. Benjamin and Kristy had crossed the room and now stood right in front on him.

"Well, now we all know," Benjamin interrupted Jaxom. "So why aren't we heading home?"

"The danger is passed. We stopped the assassination," Chris said, coming to Jaxom's defense.

"And the ring's three wishes are used up," Phoebe chimed in. Jaxom was glad to hear everyone supporting him. The guilt he had felt for keeping the ring secret began to rise within him again. Though, Benjamin's angry response to everything today was the main reason for his underhanded behavior. Seeing the red in Benjamin's eyes, he knew better to mention this fact. Jaxom stood there for a minute not knowing what to say. No one else in the room spoke again either.

"Give it to me," Benjamin growled at Jaxom, holding out his hand.

"No, it's not yours and it won't work," Jaxom answered trying to stay calm. "Like Phoebe said, the ring only had three wishes and they have all been used."

"Maybe it will work for us," Kristy said as Benjamin grabbed Jaxom's arm. He twisted his arm away from Benjamin as his angry classmate shouted again.

"We're going to wish ourselves home!" Benjamin yelled, and suddenly he and Kristy disappeared. Everyone not standing, jumped to their feet in surprise. *The ring must have worked. They had wished themselves home!*

"Balbus," Phoebe quickly asked in amazement, "didn't you say the ring only had three wishes?"

"That is how it reads," the elderly Roman answered her. "I now believe I have inadvertently mislead you."

"Anyone can make three wishes," Marcus made the obvious conclusion. Phoebe smiled again at Jaxom with a devilish grin and stepped around the low table to Jaxom's side. He wondered what she was up to as she took hold of his hand. *I can't believe that she would want to go home now.*

"I wish we could all understand each other," Phoebe said. *She sure is clued-in. I hadn't even thought about that wish,* Jaxom thought with a laugh.

"Did it work?" Chris asked.

"Yes it did, my young friend," Julius Caesar announced, thumping him on the shoulder. Everyone in the room was grinning.

"Finally, Jaxom chuckled, "the constant translating was driving me crazy."

"And now we have yet another reason to celebrate," announced Cleopatra, passing around another flask of wine.

"And speaking of celebrations," Cornelius Balbus remarked, addressing the Dictator, "have you made any plans to celebrate your success today?" All eyes turned towards Julius Caesar. Jaxom realized where this was going. The excitement he had felt a moment before sunk into his belly and began to twist into apprehension.

"Games are in order for such an event," Mark Anthony added. "Rome is safe once again."

"Yes," Julius Caesar answered. "Silver adorned gladiators are popular, but we should leave out the elephants." The Dictator laughed at his own comment. Cornelius Balbus and Mark Anthony chuckled at this private joke. Jaxom and his friends looked confused so Balbus explained the Dictator's comment for them.

"At Pompey's last public games, he used twenty elephants. It was in celebration of the completion of his new Senate house and temple but instead of being thrilled by their deaths the entire audience broke down in tears."

"It was the strangest thing," Mark Anthony declared. "Everyone in Rome seemed mad at him over the deaths of those beasts. He never understood why."

"Do you understand why?" Phoebe demanded of the Roman men. Jaxom recognized those awesome fiery eyes that had been directed at him so many times in the past. He felt his usual thrill that he got from her righteous anger. "Those beasts as you call them are amazing creatures and in our time they are in danger of going extinct. Did you know that elephants love their family as much as we do? They mourn for their dead, even returning a year after to stand vigil over their lost loves place of death." The Roman men seemed shocked by her outburst, though Calpurnia and Cleopatra had small understanding smiles on their faces.

"Why sacrifice these animals at all?" Jaxom jumped in, wanting to support Phoebe. He couldn't believe that she had just scolded Julius Caesar and his friends like that.

"The people need thrills in their lives," Mark Anthony answered looking unsettled.

"The masses have such dreary lives," Julius Caesar tried to patiently explain, "The games give them excitement to look forward to."

"There are other ways to bring excitement to the people." Phoebe said.

"And how does your culture do this?" Calpurnia jumped into the conversation.

"We have football!" Chris announced.

Chapter 19

"There is nothing permanent except change"
Heraclitus

The room shook and went dark for a moment. Then they were back in the schoolhouse, finally home. Benjamin looked around quickly, first noticing that only Kristy had come with him. She stood with her eyes tightly closed, trembling next to him. He pulled his aching hand from her tightly clinched fist. *I am so tired of holding it.* Then he realized, with a sinking feeling, this was not their classroom.

The room was the same size with a similar layout and his backpack still stood next to his desk which was now made of wood instead of plastic and metal. There were other differences throughout the room. The walls were not made of sheetrock but gleamed like marble. The door was missing and had been replaced by columns such as those he had seen in ancient Rome. *What do the Romans have against doors?* Then the world map on the wall caught his attention.

Benjamin slowly crossed over to the wall upon which the map was hung. The contours of the continents were of course the same. North and South America still held the same names, but all the countries were missing and the entire landmass was label the Western Roman Empire. The Eastern continents were labeled incorrectly as well. Instead of the European nations he knew, he beheld the country of the Roman Empire stretching all the way east to the great wall of Yuan China and north to the Viking Empire. The entire of Africa was now the country of Egypt and Australia was named the Southeastern Roman Domain.

"I guess Phoebe was wrong," Kristy meekly commented from behind him. He turned to look at his new girlfriend. Kristy's face was red from crying and her eyes were large and glazed as if she was in shock. Benjamin wondered what else would be different in this changed reality. *Whatever we encountered here, I don't think Kristy can handle it.*

"Hey what are you kids doing in here?" Mrs. Branson's voice yelled at them from the hallway. As their teacher entered the room, Benjamin was surprised to see her looking forty pounds thinner and dressed in a revealing low-cut gown, much different than her usual slacks and conservative tops.

"Sorry ma'am, we were just leaving," Benjamin stammered as he grabbed his bag and Kristy's hand again and dragged her from the room. *How creepy*, he thought, *to see that much of the old lady.*

"Benjamin, remember to study for your test over the Roman treaty with Eric the Red," his slimmed down teacher called out to them as they hurried down the hallway. Apparently, he still attended school here, but Mrs. Branson hadn't said anything to Kristy. They departed the building through another archway supported by marble columns and then stopped short to view the unusual changes all around their modern world.

The rest of the school was present again but looked as if it also had been through a strange time warp. Everything was built out of marble and stone instead of the concrete block and there were columns everywhere. All the doors were missing and statues and fountains had been added to the schoolyard. There was also a lot more trees and other plants all over the grounds.

"Wouldn't there be a lot more theft without any doors?" Kristy asked.

"Yea, probably," Benjamin agreed wishing she would think about something more relevant. "Let's head for my house. It's only a few blocks away, if it's still there at all." Benjamin headed down Roosevelt High Drive towards Main Street praying that his family was still around. The roads seemed to be laid out as they should be, but the asphalt had been replaced with solid stone. As a horse and cart rounded the corner, Benjamin realized something else that was missing. There was not a car in sight. *Did the industrial revolution not take place in this timeline?*

He led Kristy to the corner of Main Street and turned left towards what should have been the grocery store and a couple fast food joints where school kids hung out after school. Instead a huge open air market spread across the street, bustled with customers weaving about booths and wagons filled with all varieties of products.

As they moved through the market, Kristy seemed to revive. First stopping to admire a row of long silky skirts, Kristy then pulled Benjamin towards a smelly array of blooming plants. The sellers hadn't even cut the stems, but had left a dirty ball of roots wrapped in flimsy cloth.

"This is an improvement," Kristy commented as she admired a blue and white blossom. "Better than the ugly grocery store and unhealthy fast food." Benjamin looked around at the crowded street and disagreed. *It a lot filthier and smellier, kind of like Rome.*

"We should keep going," Benjamin told her. "I need to know if my family is still here."

"I need to find my mom," Kristy suddenly gasped. "She can't function without me and I can't imagine what all these changes are doing to her!" Kristy turned to head out of the market the way they had come, but Benjamin pulled her back close to him.

"I'm only a block from home," Benjamin informed her. "After we check on my family, we'll find your mom." Without waiting for her to answer, he dragged her to the junction of Main and Tenth Street and turned the corner, leaving the noise and aromas of the market lingering behind them.

As they advance towards the only home Benjamin had ever known, the area became more familiar. Several kids rode their bikes past them, racing down the hill. Tenth Street ran up the same hill and similar middleclass houses dotted each side of the stone road connected by driveways. Yet these driveways led not to garages, but to horse stables. Plastic siding was replaced with a colorful variety of stone and wood surfaces. The yards here were also decorated with many more plants than before including a small orchard of pears, heavy with ripe fruit in his neighbor's yard.

His family's home looked very different. It was now built out of dark stone and had a huge open porch attached to the front. The house was bigger than it used to be and their smooth grass yard was cluttered with raised garden beds. Benjamin knew it was the right place though, because his sister, Naomi sat on the porch swing, chatting with her best friend. Benjamin turned up the driveway towards the unfamiliar residence dragging Kristy along with him.

"Who's that, Benny?" Naomi called out. "Does daddy know you're bringing a girl over?"

"Stay out of my business," Benjamin grumbled at her as he and Kristy ascended the steps. *At least we have a door*, Benjamin thought as he entered his unknown home. There was a large formal entryway leading either into a spacious front room or down a long wide hallway. Benjamin could hear the sounds of a sportscaster on the television coming from down the hallway so he went that direction. *That must be coming from dad's study. At least we still have electricity.*

Following the sound down the hallway, they passed several closed doors and an archway that led into a dining area. The next door was open from which the televisions dialogue could be heard announcing the start of the second quarter. The voices of his dad and Aunt Faith could also be heard discussing his cousin Sam.

"Sam's blocking was weak," dad was saying. "He's not putting enough power behind his shield." He could see his dad through the doorway, sitting on a couch with a soda watching a ballgame. *He looks exactly as he should,* Benjamin thought with relief.

"You know how useless the receiver shields are, his guards should be punching him a hole to get downfield," Aunt Faith argued. Then she noticed Benjamin's arrival. "Why are you lurking, Benjamin. Come on in."

"Your cousin's team is playing against the Vikings," his dad called out without looking up. "Check out the crazy helmets on those foreigners." Benjamin walked a little farther into the room to where he could see a huge flat screen TV on the wall. *Cousin Sam was supposed to be up north studying to be a Vet. Now he's playing football.* But as Benjamin looked at the game, he saw this was not the ballgame that he had grown up on.

Shiny metal armor encased the players on each team as they took their positions on the field. The Viking helmets were crazy, with large horns sticking out, but the Carolina Wildcats were even weirder. Their helmets were actually shaped like cats, complete with pointed ears and creepy glowing cat's eyes. A kicker and receiver stared from opposite ends of the field holding small shields while the other players, also holding weapons and shields, lined up ten yards apart.

"They shouldn't even let the foreign teams into the league championships," Aunt Faith complained. Benjamin watched as the ball was kicked and the two lines smashed into each other. Behind him, Kristy gasped with shock as a Viking swung his war axe, crushing a Wildcats between the turf and a small shield.

"Who is this?" Dad asked looking over at Benjamin and Kristy for the first time.

"This is Kristy," Benjamin told his dad. "We met in history class. We're gonna work on a project about Julius Caesar together."

"The first of our Caesars, what a wonderful assignment," his dad declared. "And which district are you from, young lady?" *What districts is he talking about, and since when did dad ever care about Roman history,* Benjamin wondered?

"What do you mean sir," Kristy asked, looking as confused by the question as Benjamin was. His dad looked at him and then back at Kristy again.

"Where do you live?" his dad asked talking slower to Kristy. He was obviously getting annoyed. He was a man that never had any patience with anyone, *especially when a ballgame is on.*

"Oh, I live over on Holly Street," Kristy answered, then she gave his dad a lovely smile. But the smile seemed to have the opposite effect then she had expected. His dad jumped off the couch so suddenly that Kristy jumped behind him in fear.

"Oh Benjamin, how could you?" his aunt gasped in disbelief. Something had just went very wrong and Benjamin had no idea what it was.

"Benjamin," his dad was suddenly yelling, "why would you bring her here? I didn't even know they would let one of them into your school. You will not associate with her again." His dad grabbed Kristy by the arm and dragged her out of the room. Kristy began to cry again but let herself be pulled down the hallway and out to the front foyer.

"Antonio," his dad called out to an armed guard who was rushing in to see what the commotion was about. "Take this girl home to her Serpents Lair."

Chapter 20

"Life is not measured by the number of breaths we take,

but by the moments that take our breath away"

Maya Angelou

Queen Cleopatra found this new young friend quite intriguing. Phoebe was witty and knowledgeable and had enough spunk to stand up to the top dogs of Rome. During their meal, Cleopatra had switched over to her native Egyptian tongue. Phoebe had not seemed to notice the change. *Great Isis has granted her an amazing gift. This is a young woman I wish to know more about,"* she decided.

The success of today's battle and this fine dinner had relaxed the nervous tension that she had carried around for so long. The conflict between Jaxom and his vulgar colleague was unexpected but the offensive parties had departed quickly and not spoiled the mood too much. Then Phoebe had made her wish and proceeded to lecture Julius. *I bet he wasn't expecting that!* Cleopatra smiled at the memory. *And he put up with her, even more amazing!* She looked over at her love and smiled.

The men were heading back towards the food busy discussing some competition from the future, leaving her and Phoebe to continue their conversation. Phoebe had been explaining to her how to use moveable letters to print the books that arrived with the schoolhouse. Then the conflict with the other students occurred and then the magic and ensuing argument. She was about to ask about their manner of printing the text when Calpurnia pre-empted her to speak on another topic.

"I guess the men will hold their competitions in any era," Calpurnia began. "What do the women of your world do for entertainment? Our lives here are do not provide for much excitement."

"Many women in my culture participate in competitions as well as the men," Phoebe responded. "We have so many paths to joy in my time. We dance, sing, paint and write. Some hike or garden or climb mountains. In the city about an hour away from my home, I've been to great science museum, a zoo and an awesome water park."

"That sounds wonderful," Calpurnia exclaimed. "What is a water park?"

"They have waterslides and swimming pools. It's a place just to have fun," Phoebe answered her. *What an interesting world she comes from,* Cleopatra thought. *The people seem to have such freedom with their time. How is that possible without slaves to do much of the work?*

"And how do your people support and feed themselves?" the Pharaoh asked.

"They own a business or work for someone else." Phoebe informed them. "There are still some small farms that support themselves but most of the food is produces by massive corporations that hire lots of employees to do the work."

"We have that here too," Calpurnia told Phoebe, "but most of the work is done by the slaves."

"There is no slavery in my time," Phoebe told Calpurnia. "No one is allowed to own another person, at least in my country, and a lot of others nations too." Caesar's wife seemed surprised by this concept.

"I also find this strange," Cleopatra stated. "Am I correct in presuming, these are the same laws that gave women their freedom."

"Actually women's rights came shortly after the antislavery movement but the two changes tied in together," Phoebe stated. "It is the beginning towards a truly free society."

The women looked over at the men who were returning to their seats. Chris, plate piled high again, was giving Balbus detailed instructions on how to build bicycles. Marcus and Jaxom were eagerly explaining sporting rules to the other Roman men. *Julius looks intrigued*, Cleopatra thought. *He seems to be taking a liking to these young travelers.*

"I am planning to give Phoebe a tour of our home," Calpurnia announced. Cleopatra smiled knowing that Calpurnia hoped to continue their conversation without the presence of the men.

"Then we shall retire to my chambers," Julius Caesar answered before he took a seat. "I was wishing for a scroll to record these complex rules anyways."

"And I can draw out my bicycle for you, if you have extra paper." Chris stated excitedly.

"We shall find you some," Cornelius Balbus responded.

"If I may join you, Calpurnia. I'd like to see the house too," Jaxom surprisingly stated, "if ya'll don't mind?" Jaxom quickly looked at his friends to get their consent. Chris just shrugged and Marcus didn't seem to care.

"I can explain the rules simply enough," Marcus responded.

Calpurnia looked a little disappointed over the intrusion and the Pharaoh wondered why Jaxom would want to see the house instead of speaking with the leaders of Rome. As Jaxom gave a nervous glance towards Phoebe, Cleopatra realized why he wanted to come along. *This young man has an interest Phoebe, and she doesn't even realize. Perhaps he needs a little help in his wooing.*

"We would love the escort," Cleopatra stated giving Jaxom a friendly smile. His cheeks flushed slightly and he quickly looked away. *He is so nervous around women. No wonder Phoebe hasn't any idea of his feelings.*

"We will see you later than, Jaxom. Someone will show you to my rooms when you are finished," Julius Caesar said as he turned towards his wife and his love. The Dictator gave Calpurnia a quick nod and then pulled Cleopatra into a tight embrace. *He will be by later to see me*, the Queen thought as she melted into him for just a moment. Then Julius Caesar, followed by the other men, departed through the door at the end of the long room.

"First let me show you the kitchen area," Calpurnia began, commencing the tour that she had promised to Phoebe and Jaxom. "It has an amazing amount of prep space as well as running water at one of the wash basins."

"How do you have running water inside?" Jaxom asked startling Calpurnia with his question. Cleopatra wondered if Calpurnia had started the tour in this area thinking that Jaxom would get bored quickly and leave them to their women's time*. She hasn't noticed his infatuation for Phoebe yet,* Cleopatra thought, smiling to herself.

"It flows from the cistern just outside," Calpurnia explained, pointing out the large stone water tank that could be seen through the open windows.

"This bread oven is incredible," Phoebe announced, admiring the stone structure. The oven had been cut from huge slabs of granite and was decorated with beautiful red tiles. Cleopatra knew how much Calpurnia loved her kitchen, and watched as her friend glowed with pride at the attention given to the space.

"It looks like you could bake a dozen loafs of bread," Jaxom commented moving closer to Phoebe.

"Oh, even more," Calpurnia declared excitedly. "Before festivals we will sometimes fit over twenty."

Calpurnia's talents in this kitchen are well known around Rome," Cleopatra praised her friend. "She is a fantastic chef. I bet most of our feast came from her recipe box."

"Actually, everything did," Calpurnia declared with a chuckle. "And I had to begin the preparations this morning before Julius had even left." Turning to Phoebe she asked, "so what talents are you pursuing, Phoebe?" Cleopatra watched as her new young friend was caught off guard. Phoebe looked flustered for a moment glancing awkwardly at Jaxom, then regained her center as she found an answer.

"For the past several years I've been studying the ways of the woodlands with my grandfather," Phoebe disclosed to their small group. "He has taught me so much about how the ecology flows in our mountains and how to identify plants and animal tracks. I've been reading everything the school library has also."

"That is wonderful!" Calpurnia proclaimed. "You should visit the temple of Artemis while you are still here. The women there have dedicated themselves to the same path."

"And you Jaxom," Cleopatra asked, pulling this nervous young man into the conversation, "what talents are you learning at home in your North America?"

"Well, since I live above my Uncles mechanic shop, I get to work on cars all the time. Those are vehicles we have in the future," Jaxom explained. "But in my free time, I've been practicing carving." Jaxom was looking at Phoebe the whole time as he spoke, and Phoebe smiled back seeming glad to know more about him. Cleopatra saw the realization dawn in Calpurnia's eyes. She smiled at the Roman aristocrat to show that she saw it too.

"Let's head out to the gardens next," Calpurnia suggested, obviously ready to add her own influence to the situation. Calpurnia proceeded out a side door and Phoebe and Jaxom followed together.

Cleopatra trailed behind the two, remembering when she fell in love with her Julius. *I had just turned twenty one and my treacherous brother was raising an army against me in Alexandria. Then Julius Caesar sailed into my world three days after my brother murdered Pompey the Great. Julius Caesar immediately took up residence in the palace with his guard of four thousand men and began ordering my brother around. Sneaking past my brothers' army, I meet this Roman hero wrapped within a carpet. To my great joy, I found in him*

compassion; comfort that I had not ever known.

Cleopatra followed slowly, savoring the memory of her time with Julius in Alexandria. *My furious brother was furious besieged us in the palace together. Wrapped in his arms and secure in his strength and intelligence, I watched as my new love contrived to trick my brother into a reluctant truce until his reinforcements arrived. When my brother fled and drowned in the Nile, I found my throne safe and myself completely in love with my Roman warrior.*

They had sailed the Nile together before he left to end Rome's civil war. *I must return to my own duties soon,* Cleopatra thought with a brief twinge of regret. But the Queen loved Egypt and knew she would soon sail south on the Mediterranean again.

The night air was cool and the full moon shone brightly overhead. Calpurnia was showing the teens the gardens. Jaxom stood close to Phoebe as she delighted in each variety of herbs. He obediently smelled each blossom that she pointed out and listened with interest to the women's plant talk.

"This Rosemary is huge," Phoebe declared, "and it smells amazing." Jaxom leaned in close to breath in the scent of the herb. Cleopatra watched as the young foreign couple wandered together enjoying the beautiful space. "Is this Anise?" she asked, admiring a low growing feathery herb.

"Yes," Calpurnia agreed. "I use that in Caesar's teas to help control his epilepsy." Phoebe seemed delighted by Jaxom's attention and the Queen decided it was time to leave the two alone for the evening.

"Calpurnia, I have need of your assistance on a private matter if you have time this evening," Cleopatra called out to the Roman aristocrat.

"Of course, Queen Cleopatra," Calpurnia answered her than turned to the two. "Shall we complete our tour tomorrow? You are welcome to remain in the gardens and continue enjoying the lovely evening."

"That would be nice," Phoebe replied as she smiled at Jaxom.

"Phoebe, your rooms are just through the entrance at the far end of the garden, third door on the right," Calpurnia explained. "Jaxom, the men's private chambers are passed the dining hall. Someone will be around to show you where you're other friends are resting. Blessed dreams to you both."

"Good night, Calpurnia,' Jaxom replied. "Thanks for such a lovely dinner."

"Rest well," Phoebe also answered, then turned to Cleopatra. "Thank you for everything, your Majesty." The Pharaoh gave her new young friend a quick embrace and turned to follow Calpurnia inside.

Chapter 21

"It is difficult not to cause him pain and
yet to escape from him for good"
Andrew Lloyd Webber

The evening was perfect. The full moon illuminated the lovely herb garden and Phoebe felt relaxed and happy hanging out with Jaxom, Cleopatra and Calpurnia. She didn't even mind that the ancient ladies were leaving her alone here with Jaxom. *I wonder if the wine is going to my head. Even watered down, it's gonna affect me.*

Phoebe looked at Jaxom as he waved goodnight to the foreign women. He was being so sweet this evening, acting like a friend instead of the tease that he usually was. *Remember who this is*, she thought as Jaxom beamed a carefree grin her direction then turned back towards the garden.

"What is this herb, Phoebe," Jaxom asked pointing to a small branching shrub with tiny closed blossoms covering the stems. *At least he's using my name now.*

"That looks like a variety of thyme," Phoebe answered him, wondering if he really cared about the plants. "My mom has thyme in her garden, though it doesn't grow so tall."

"I thought I recognized it," he called back. Looking across the garden, Jaxom smile widened. "I know this one, chives," Jaxom said as he plucked a long green stem and began to chew on it. "I used to eat these all the time when I was young."

"Did your mom have a garden?" Phoebe asked realizing that she still knew nothing about his family. This was the first time Jaxom had said anything to her about his childhood.

"Yes, she did," Jaxom whispered and then he got very quiet. The grin had disappeared from his face and was replace by a look Phoebe had seen before. An absent look, as if Jaxom was a million miles away, in a place he did not want to visit. *He's in pain*, Phoebe realized for the first time. *Something happened to him.* He just stood there, slowly chewing his chive and staring into the past.

"Did something happened to your family?" Phoebe asked not knowing what answer to expect. *He can change so quickly, maybe I shouldn't pry.* Jaxom didn't say anything for a few minutes. He just froze. He stopped chewing on the leaf and stared at the sky. Then Phoebe noticed that he was crying. She watched as a tear roll down his cheek and she had no idea what to do.

"Why is it always you who asks these questions?" Jaxom finally answered as he sank to the ground. Phoebe remembered the similar question she had asked on the day he had arrived. *Wow, I really am nosy.*

"I'm sorry, Jaxom. I shouldn't pry," Phoebe apologized. She sat down next to him on the garden path. *We were having such a great time and now I've spoiled it.* He didn't say anything for a few more minutes and Phoebe tried to think of something to change the subject to.

"I had a little sister named Jessica," Jaxom suddenly opened up. "My dad ran off with some other woman when mom was pregnant with her, so I got to help mom through all the baby things. It was great but I was so glad when Jessie was potty trained and I was so proud of her too. She had just turned four years old and she had got this book set all about animals for her birthday. She was crazy about it. I sat in the library reading those little books to her every night all week." Jaxom stopped talking and stared into the starry night. Phoebe felt her heart tighten in her chest. *I'm not sure if I want to hear the rest of this memory.*

"You really loved her," Phoebe softly answered breaking the silence. Jaxom looked at her and smiled through his tears. It wasn't his normal cocky smile but one of true emotion. She reached out and squeezed his hand. He held it tight as he answered.

"I loved her with all of my heart and my mom too," Jaxom told her. His smiled disappeared as he continued his story.

"There was these oil lamps in the library," Jaxom continued. "Mom had taken Jessica upstairs to bed and I was playing with this wand things she had also gotten as a gift. I threw it wrong and when I jumped to catch it, I hit one of the lamps. It broke and the oil splashed all over everything. The fire spread so fast! I didn't know what to do. I tried to save Jessie's books. I started piling them back into their box but then several caught fire and I realized the whole room was burning. I ran out of the house with the stupid box of books and left my sister and mom behind. I wanted to go back in, but the neighbors wouldn't let me. Mom and Jessica both died in the fire that I started."

"And then you moved in with your Uncle," Phoebe gasped, realizing how painful her questions to Jaxom had been. "I was so stupid, Jaxom. I really am sorry." The sat together still hand in hand quietly thinking about the past. Phoebe wished she could help him with his grief but she had never dealt with such tragedy before.

"Actually I stayed with my cousins for about a month," Jaxom told her as he wiped his eyes with his free hand. "But then I tore up my aunt's kitchen and she said she couldn't handle watching me all the time."

"You tore up her kitchen?" Phoebe repeated.

"Oh, yea," Jaxom chuckled slightly. "I broke a bunch of her dishes and really thrashed the place. I was just so angry at myself." Phoebe heart melted as she looked into Jaxom's chocolate brown eyes. She had never seen him look so honest and vulnerable.

"Did it make you feel any better?" Phoebe asked. Jaxom laughed softly again. His tears had stopped but sadness still filled his eyes.

"Yea, it felt great to release all that anger," Jaxom answered. "But it still comes back. I lost everything that evening because of my stupidity and cowardice."

"Jaxom, it was an accident and you were young," Phoebe told him. She knew it wouldn't help him much to hear this. *Not after he's carried around so much guilt for all these years.*

"When I found out about the ring's magic, I had hoped I could bring them back," Jaxom shared with her.

"Maybe when we get home, we still can," Phoebe told him. "If anyone can make three wishes, we still have a lot of wishes to go around." Jaxom's eyes brightened at the thought.

"Would you really help me and wish them alive again?" Jaxom questioned her. She could feel his guilt release its hold on him a little and she hoped it was possible to fix things for him. Her grandpa used to tell her, since you can't change the past, you should instead try to learn from it. *But here we are in ancient Rome and even stopped Julius Caesar's assassination. Would it be right to also change his past?*

"I will try for you Jaxom," Phoebe agreed. "I don't know if it's possible, but I didn't think this trip would be possible." Jaxom smiled again and sighed.

"I know, it's an unlikely miracle. This trip had been pretty amazing though, hasn't it?" Jaxom replied changing the subject.

"You actually helped to save Julius Caesar's life," Phoebe exclaimed. "I didn't think that our presence here could make such a difference."

"I knew we could save him," Jaxom boasted, his usual confidence beginning to return. "Why else would we be here?" Jaxom still held her hand and Phoebe wondered if he was still needing emotional support or if his intentions were more physical. She couldn't let go though. *Why don't I want to escape from him*, she wondered? *Would I really want to begin a relationship with Jaxom after all our years of problems?*

"I think Isis wanted you to save him so he could keep Cleopatra safe," Phoebe answered after a few minutes. "She is deeply devoted to her Goddess and her culture is in danger of being destroyed."

"What really surprises me is that these ancient deities are actually real," Jaxom told her. "I guess you already knew that being pagan and all."

"I am surer now than I ever was before," Phoebe admitted. "Just because I'm pagan doesn't mean I see magic like this every day."

"How many times have you seen magic like this?" Jaxom questioned her. *Is he truly interested in knowing?*

"I've never seen anything like this," she told him. "I think my high Priestess can control the weather though. It was pouring rain once when mom and I headed to an Ostara ritual and by the time we arrived there was a beautiful blue sky for our circle. When it was over the rain started up again. She always has perfect weather around her." Jaxom smiled at her and then looked up at the lovely night sky.

"Then I guess you didn't magic up this wonderful evening with that magnificent full moon," Jaxom chuckled.

"No, the moon is supposed to be full. This is the Ides of March, remember?" Phoebe answered back. "Their months began on the New moon and the Ides was the Full moon at the month's center."

"Is that what the Ides means?" Jaxom questioned. "I never knew that." Phoebe felt so peaceful sitting here with Jaxom that she wondered how she had ever despised him. There was just so much misunderstanding between the two of them that she had never gotten to actually know him. *It is amazing how things can change in just a day,* she thought as she smiled at Jaxom.

"Lots of weird things happen on the full moon," Jaxom commented.

"More women birth their babies on the full moon than any other time," Phoebe told him.

"Really, I wonder if anyone around us is giving birth," Jaxom questioned?

"I hope not. Rome is not the safest place for women to create children," Phoebe commented. When Jaxom questioned why, she explained what she heard earlier about Clodia Metelli's daughter.

"That's horrible!" Jaxom declared. "I can't imagine how anyone could abandon a tiny infant. Maybe we can talk to Julius Caesar about stopping the practice."

"Maybe you can, the Dictator doesn't even speak to me," Phoebe said, hearing a little bitterness slip into her voice. Jaxom turned to her with a look of concern.

"He'll talk with you, I'm sure," Jaxom assured her squeezing her hand. "He's just been busy. He had to stop his own assassination."

"It's not just child exposure that is the problem," Phoebe declared. "Roman women have no rights at all. Their fathers choose who they marry and their husbands control them after that. The women here are basically slaves."

"Calpurnia seems pretty happy. Look at this mansion she lives in and all the gems she was wearing," Jaxom argued back. "She has everything that she wants." *Why can't he see the obvious!?*

"No, Jaxom," Phoebe countered. "She has no rights. Julius Caesar could divorce her and she would lose it all. She's a puppet like every other Roman woman. I just wish Caesar would give the women their freedom!" Jaxom pulled his hand quickly away and as Phoebe saw the shocked look in his eyes she realized her mistake. She had just made her second wish!

"Jaxom, I didn't mean to!" Phoebe cried. She could see a look of betrayal in his eyes and knew that he didn't believe her. *I've caused him pain again!*

"Well you have your wish now," Jaxom commented angrily as he stood up. "I hope it was worth it, wanna be witch." Then he turned and headed back towards the kitchen.

"Jaxom, wait," she called out but he did not even look back before he disappeared into the mansion. *How could I betray his trust like that?* Phoebe leaned against her knees and began to weep.

Chapter 22

"Sometimes underneath the load is where I show my best"

John Bell

Chris finished his sketches and held them up for Balbus to inspect. His bicycle business was a great idea, even if everyone else thought it was funny. They needed income if they were going to stay in ancient Rome for long. Selling bicycles would provide that, as well as a great form of transportation for the Romans. *It's a win, win situation for everyone*, he thought.

They stood around Julius Caesar's long wooden table in his private study. Textbooks from their schoolhouse were piled on one end, brought over from the country house by the Dictators servants. Julius Caesar was on the other side of the table watching Marcus sketch out football plays.

"This is an ingenious design," Cornelius Balbus announced after looking over the scroll for a few minutes. "And these gears provide different levels of force. I know a smith that I think would be interested in this challenge."

"Yea, the amount of gears can decrease but then we lose our top speed," Chris commented back. He glanced across the room to where Marcus was eagerly explaining football rules to Julius Caesar. These Roman men were very receptive to their ideas and Chris was having a great time in ancient Rome.

They treat us like intelligent men instead of wayward teens. Of course I did almost die helping to save Caesar, Chris thought shuddering at the memory.

"Hello young Jaxom," the Dictator called out, and Chris turned towards the door to see his friend arrive from his tour with the women. *Why would he want to look at a house when he could talk with Julius Caesar and Mark Anthony?* Then Chris noticed that standing next to Jaxom in the doorway was the lovely servant Miriam, carrying a heavy looking sack.

"I met Miriam in the front room," Jaxom told Julius Caesar as he entered the study. "She has news for you, sir and says it has to do with all of us." Jaxom seemed agitated about something and Chris wondered what could be wrong. Miriam remained silently waiting in the hallway. Chris was delighted to see her again hoping he would find time to talk with her soon. *Because of Phoebe's wish, I can now understand her.*

"Let us listen then," the Dictator said as he stood from the couch. They followed Julius Caesar into the hallway and headed towards the front room.

"Where's Phoebe?" Marcus asked Jaxom.

"I don't know," Jaxom snapped. When seeing Marcus startle, he added, "She's probably heading to bed." *I bet they were arguing again,* Chris thought.

"We can tell her anything important tomorrow," Chris commented. Then he noticed how Miriam was struggling under the weight of the bag she carried. "Would you like help with that?" he offered.

"No, I am fine," she shyly responded. She seemed to have a hard time handling the load so Chris pulled the sack away from her despite her protest. *It isn't right not to help a lovely lady in need.* He almost wished he hadn't been such a gentleman. The sack was really heavy and bulky too.

"As they settled into the seating area of the front room, Chris dropped the bag and sank into one of the soft cushions. As everyone settled around him, he noticed that Miriam was not sitting down with the rest of them.

"Miriam, there's room here for you," Chris called to the lovely servant. Miriam gave him a look of surprise, then a nervous glance towards Julius Caesar. When the Dictator gave her a simple nod, she carefully settled herself down next to Chris. He gave her his friendliest grin and was rewarded with a shy smile. Her long blond hair was tousled, her face beautifully flushed and her simple dress was dusty. Chris guessed that she had just rode one of those painful beasts into Rome. *She is still lovely*, he thought.

"What news have you brought me?" Julius Caesar questioned.

"The building in the garden, sir," Miriam explained, "the one that these travelers arrived in, has disappeared." Everyone in the room was surprised by this announcement. "All that was left was several travel bags, so I brought those with me," Miriam pointed at the sack that Chris had just carried for her. Chris quickly untied the sack and pulled out his backpack.

"Yours are in here too," Chris told his friends as he passed the bag to Marcus. He was glad to have his stuff even though he didn't really need it. Chris wondered if the schoolhouse really mattered. *This doesn't really change any of my plans*, he thought.

"When did this happen?" the Dictator asked.

"A few hours ago, sir. A little before the sunset," Miriam answered.

"Why would that happen?" Jaxom wondered aloud.

"That would be about the time that Benjamin made his wish," Marcus commented.

"Perhaps your structure was pulled away with your classmates," Balbus surmised. That made good enough sense to Chris. He was past the concern of the schoolhouse and instead wondering about this young lady. He glanced at Miriam sitting next to him. *I wonder why she lives with Caesar and if she's single*? She was shyly glancing around at the group and seemed to be happy to be included. *That sandy blond hair didn't come from Rome.*

"At least the maps and texts remained," Mark Anthony commented.

"Thank you for bringing us this news, Miriam," Chris kindly thanked the servant. She startled for a moment then turned and looked him in the eye. Her eyes were as blue as the sky, unlike the dark eyes of the Romans. *Another difference we have in common.*

"You are most welcome, sir," Miriam answered. "The soldiers had all left, and the Queen had ordered her eunuchs to remain at the villa with Caesarian. I thought it was important enough news to be delivered quickly." Miriam blushed a bit as she spoke to him which Chris thought was incredible charming.

"It was a wise choice," Julius Caesar praised her. Then looking at Chris he added, "Miriam has been my slave for years. She is a great help to me and Calpurnia." Julius Caesar had a gleam in his eye as he looked at Chris as if he was amused by his attention to the servant. *Not servant, he said slave!* He looked at the beautiful slave girl next to him. *No, to me she is a princess.*

"Please call me Chris," he told Miriam and offered her his hand to shake. Miriam raised her hand and as Chris started to shake it he changed his mind and brought it to his lips for a gentle kiss. "These are my friends, Marcus and Jaxom," Chris added feeling a little embarrassed by his spontaneous action.

"Yea, thanks for bringing us the news," Marcus remarked.

"And our things," Jaxom stated.

"It is nice to meet you all," Miriam smiled at each of them.

"I believe I will have Miriam show you the estates tomorrow," Julius Caesar commented. "There are several nice places for you to choose from and she knows the city well." Miriam brightened at this and Chris was glad she was happy with the idea. *She wants to go.* "Cornelius would you like to join them?" Julius Caesar asked his friend.

"I would be glad to," Cornelius Balbus answered.

"So your new protégées will be staying with us," came a comment from the entryway. Everyone looked towards the unexpected voice. An older Roman that Chris remembered seeing in the Senate stood under the archway. He had not been able to understand the conversation when Cornelius had spoken to him earlier, but Chris had felt this man's shrewd, calculating eyes judging them, then and now.

"Marcus Cicero, it is an unexpected pleasure," Julius Caesar called out to the newcomer. Chris remembered reading about this Roman. *He is one of the great orators of the time.* "Please join us," the Dictator continued. The skinny old Senator crossed the room and settled himself onto the last remaining sofa.

"I was out for my evening stroll and decided to walk by and see your completed pediment," Marcus Cicero explained. "It is quite grand. Since I heard voices, I decided to stop in for a short visit."

"Yes, the pediment was completed quickly," Julius Caesar continued the small talk. "The workmen did an excellent job, though and am glad to have them gone." *Why would Caesar invite this man to join us? We shouldn't talk openly in front of too many people.*

"I wish to commend you on your success today, Julius," Marcus Cicero told the Dictator. "I met your young friends, Jaxom and Chris after the attack." The Roman nodded to each of them. "I have not met this other young man," the senator looked at Marcus, again looking like he was evaluating what he saw. *He has eyes like a dirty lawyer.*

"My name is also Marcus," Chris's best friend introduced himself, "Marcus Brooks."

"Wonderful!" Marcus Cicero cheered. "I am always glad to meet a fellow namesake. It is a name which shows ties to Rome. You must not have had to traveled far to visit our noble city?" Chris hoped that Marcus would be careful in answering Cicero. *My instincts don't like this man.*

"We have traveled quite far," Marcus replied to Cicero's query. "Though I do have ancestors who came from this part of the world."

"Your father does you honor in giving such a name," Cicero praised. "I heard you will be going estate shopping in the morning. Perhaps you would like to view several spaces that I am looking to sell."

"Actually, the Dictator has granted them an estate at his own expense," Mark Anthony informed the Senator. He was frowning at Cicero obvious not liking the old man at all. *Makes me trust Mark Anthony a bit more.*

"Miriam and I can handle the tour tomorrow, but your offer is appreciated," Cornelius spoke kindly to the Senator. *Cornelius Balbus is always the perfect aristocrat*, Chris thought. *He's my favorite Roman so far.* Chris was sure Miriam wasn't from Rome, so she didn't count as a Roman. *She's my favorite ancient by far.*

"Tomorrow will be full of activity," announced Julius Caesar. "I believe we shall retire for the evening. Thank you for the visit, Cicero. I shall see you in the morning in Senate." After dismissing the Senator so abruptly, Julius Caesar rose and led their group from the room. Chris looked back at the old Senator. Marcus Cicero was leaving with a look of disappointed across his face. *He didn't find out much from that short dialogue. He's looking to take advantage of anything he can*, Chris's intuition knew.

Then he noticed Miriam departing towards the women's quarters carrying her sack slung across her back. She was having no trouble with its weight now that it only contained Phoebe's shoulder bag. As she headed away from him, Chris realized that he had missed his opportunity to say goodnight to the lovely slave. *A true damsel in distress.*

Chapter 23

"What fools these mortals be"
William Shakespeare

Julius Caesar finally strolled his way towards the sleeping compartments which he shared with Calpurnia. This had been a significant day and he felt weariness deep within his muscles. After settling his visitors into the guest quarters, he had met with Cornelius and Anthony to formulate his campaign schedule for the attack on Parthia. Mark Anthony was as usual quite inebriated by this time of night, so he sent his intoxicated general home. After saying good night to Cornelius, Julius Caesar had attempted to visit Cleopatra in her quarters but was told by a eunuch that the Pharaoh was not receiving visitors this evening. *That is strange.*

He entered the dimly lit room and saw that Calpurnia was already sleeping. Julius Caesar quietly crossed the room to the private bathing chamber. He was glad he had granted his wife's request to install one of Orata's Hanging Baths. *The soak will do my muscles much good.*

The bathing room was dominated by the large tub. Earlier he had ordered a slave to stoke the fire for his bath and as he turned on the water, the welcome spray of a warm waterfall washed down his body. He remained standing for a time, waiting for the tub to fill as he washed his thinning hair. Then Julius laid down in the warm soapy water and allowed his muscles to soak.

As Julius relaxed he began to daydream. He found himself drifting down a pleasant stream, floating past banks lush with greenery. The current pulled him along at a moderate rate and seemed to be increasing, though not uncomfortably so. The leader of Rome leaned back to enjoyed the buoyancy of the water for a moment, staring into a perfect blue sky. Then his foot knocked against something sharp in the water. As he sat up his leg struck another obstacle and Julius Caesar found himself in the middle of a deeper swifter flowing river. He dismayed as he saw that he was being pulled into a series of rocky rapids. *Where am I?*

As his leg struck another jagged stone, Julius surveyed the river in front of him. About a hundred pes ahead, there was a large outcropping of flat boulders penetrating far into the river. *If I can get to those rocks, I can pull myself out. Then I can figure out this strange vision.* He began swimming towards the outcrop, trying to avoid the protruding river rocks as best he could. The current was now fiercely shoving against his strokes and his leg throbbed where it had hit the last sharp stone. A mist of cold droplets swirled about his face as he struggled to keep himself from being pulled under.

Julius soon realized he was not going to make it to the outcropping. The current pushed him passed his unrealized exit and through several drops. He was flung through roaring rapid having completely lost control of his direction. He smashed his ribcage against a rocky ledge and struggled to catch precious gulps of air as the waters tried to submerge him. Julius saw the edge of the fall just before he reached it, a sheer drop of unknown depth. *Oh Great Goddess Venus, help me!*

Then there was sudden silence and a hard flat surface stopped his fall. Every point on his body screamed in pain. Julius slowly looked up from where he was laying and found himself on a stone ledge behind the waterfall. The water was frozen like an iridescent ice curtain and before it stood his ancestral Goddess Venus. In one hand she held the branch of an apple tree. On her shoulder of her flowing robes rested her sparrow and at her side crouched her lynx. He felt in awe at the power he sensed radiating from his Goddess.

"I am pleased you still remember me in your time of need," the Goddess addressed him. She was the same stunning image as the statues placed around his childhood home. "I am troubled, Julius, that I do not hear much from you in your myriad times of triumph. I have granted you many successes through your Love of Rome, my son."

"You are a gracious Mistress," Julius declared to his ancestress, the great Goddess of Love. As the Julius pulled himself onto his knees pain ripped through his body. He fought to hold back the nausea he felt.

"Have you not learned perseverance? Rise Son of Rome!" Venus commanded him. The lynx flattened its tufted ears and snarled at him. Julius Caesar pushed against his pain and forced himself to rise before his Goddess. Venus smiled at him and said, "While pain will teach perseverance, compassion creates the way for love." The Goddess reached up and plucked a leaf from the apple branch. Julius felt a wave of healing pour over him beginning with his pounding head. He felt the soothing power flow down his body healing his broken ribs and mending each bruise and laceration.

In a few moments Julius again felt healthy and whole. He quickly knelt on one knee before his deity and pledged his loyalty to her. "Thank you, your graciousness. I am honored to be your son, and shall do whatever you require of me." Julius waited to find out why Venus had chosen to visit him. The Goddess stroked the grayish tan pelt of the feline as she regarding him with her stunning eyes. *I have also learned patience*, he thought as he waited.

"Let us sit and talk for a spell," the Goddess decided aloud and as she plucked another apple leaf, several large soft cushions appeared beside the Dictator. "I have frozen time so that we may speak without interruption." The Goddess of Love settled herself onto one of the cushions so Julius sank into the other. The lynx curled up on the stone floor between them, as if settling down for a nap.

"This waterfall is lovely," Venus commented. Julius considered the frozen shimmering veil of water in front of them. *That waterfall almost killed me.* Julius wondered why was it necessary for him to experience the near death before the Goddess revealed herself to him. *She will tell me if see chooses to. One should not question the motives of the Divine.*

"Lovely but deadly," he replied.

"Yet while floating in the stream you did not consider where you were headed," the Goddess pointed out. No, he had not concerned himself with what was downstream. *I was just enjoying the moment,* he thought.

"Living in the moment can bring great joy," Venus told him, hearing his thoughts. "However the lessons of the past and the plans for the future should not be ignored. Time flows just like this river, ever changing, yet always a seamless whole. In your lifetime you have seen Rome's power grow from a gentle stream into a great rushing river. A powerful future awaits her. Rome's place in this time flow is of great significance to the future of Earth. This is why I chose to save you in this reality."

"This reality?" Julius repeated, not sure what she meant. He understood the river analogy, though she didn't have to half drown him to make that point. *It is good to know Rome's future will be great, but how can there be more than one reality?*

"There are many levels to existence," the Goddess explained to him. "In other realities, the assassination was successful and the time flow will need many more generations to recover its balance. With these changes, I hope to find balance much sooner and spare my children much grief."

"I do not understand," Julius questioned, forgetting that he should not require answers from a Goddess. "How can I be dead as well as alive and why did you lead Cleopatra to believe Mother Isis saved me?" Venus gave him a radiant smile.

"My son, I have stopped time around us, but not for you," the Goddess answered. "To explain all I know would use up the remainder of your life. Know that I would not deceive Pharaoh Cleopatra." The Goddess of Love rose from the cushion and in a shimmering transformation became Mother Isis. Robed in regal Egyptian clothing, Isis resembled his beloved Cleopatra. The lynx transformed into a giant snake which began coiling itself around his cushion. The lovely sparrow launched itself into the air and became circling falcon.

"I am Mother Isis as well as Venus, and your beloved Cleopatra has always shown proper reverence. You would do well to listen to her counsel," Isis told him. "Understand that all Goddesses are one. Each Goddess is a facet upon the jewel that is the one Great Creatress. You choose to question the Mother of All?" Isis transformed again into Venus and returned to her seat.

"Forgive me for questioning, your Holiness," Julius apologized as the reformed lynx appeared glaring at him from top of his cushion. The agile creature leapt gracefully onto Venus's lap and the Goddess casually rubbed the creatures' tufted ear.

"The city of Rome has faced many troubled years of late," Venus shifted the subject as her sparrow gently settled upon her shoulder. "You do not see the rapids she is flowing through." Not knowing how to respond Julius chose to remain quiet. The Goddess waited for a moment but when he did not respond she continued. "Your society has forgotten to grant me the honors which I am due."

"Great mistress, we have not forgotten you," Julius assured his Goddess. "Rome has always honored you with the ancient rituals and traditions passed down from our ancestors."

"Did you honor me in your dealings with Pompeia?" Venus questioned him. Julius felt a wave of guilt as his memories flowed to the scandal surrounding his divorce eighteen years ago. Pompeia was hosting the festival of the Great Goddess at their home with the help of his mother, Aurelia. He and every other male in his household had withdrawn for the evening for it was strictly forbidden for men to witness the sacred rituals. Even the male statues were veiled for the occasion. Except on this evening, Clodius was caught dressed in women's clothes at the festival. Rich and well connected, Clodius was not someone Julius needed to alienate. So instead of confronting the man, he had divorced Pompeia and quickly left for his governorship in Spain.

"I did not support her as I should," Julius admitted.

"The day to day actions of my children are just as important to me as the festivals and rituals," Venus told him. Julius remembered the hurt look in Calpurnia's eyes when he had first brought home Cleopatra. He had never really considered the feelings of his current wife either.

"Calpurnia is also a devote follower and worthy of your ear," Venus told him. *She is right and in the future I will treat both with a greater respect.*

"How does your massacre's in the great coliseum honor the Goddess of Love?" Venus interrupted his thoughts. Julius felt a wave of her radiating power wash over him. Images of the countless coliseum games performed for the glory of Rome flowed through his mind. With her divine love pouring through him, Julius saw the memories in a new light. He saw brave men mauled by frightened animals who were in turn slaughtered. He watched as gladiators fought to the death, bearing their necks courageously to entertain aristocratic elitists. Instead of glory, he felt sickened by the sacrifice of so many brave lives.

"How did your conquest of Gaul honor me?" Venus continued to question. Now flashes of his time in Gaul played through Julius's thoughts. Entire tribes massacred or sold into slavery because of the disrespect to Rome shown by their leaders. He had not realized that his actions would be such an affront to his divine heritage. Julius found himself weeping for the loss of the brave Roman's he had seen die in battle, for unknown warriors dead for choosing to defend their homes, and for the innocent lives of women and children who had no choice as to when or where the massacres would take place.

"You have many lessons to learn from your past, my son," the Goddess said after a few moments. "The Empire of Rome is destined to grow and war is an inevitable part of that future. Rome will need to defend what she had created. But I believe your society can come to understand the balance between freedom and duty, love and honor. I have seen you perform acts of great compassion."

Images of men he had pardoned and peaceful treaties he had formed throughout his career now played through his mind. With great relief, Julius remembered his time as Aedile when he had worked hard to improve the roads and other public spaces in Rome. *I spent much of my life striving to strengthen and expand my country even if sometimes my decisions also had selfish motivations behind them. I love the Roman Republic.*

"It is good to look to your own needs as long as you stay in balance with your duties to your land and its people," Venus told him. He thought over the current plans he had drawn up to add a theater to the center of Rome. This action would bring him prestige as well as providing entertainment to the public. The games Jaxom and Marcus described could entertain the people as well, without the huge bloodshed he had provided before. His plans against the Parthian would need to be revised. *Actually*, Julius realized, *I can't leave Rome now.*

"Yes," he told his Goddess, "I can learn from the past."

"You can use your understanding to choose a better future for your people," Venus reassured him.

"What do you command of me?" Julius asked the great Goddess of Love.

"Love is not something one commands," Venus advised him with a smile. "I hope for you to see me in every face you gaze upon," Venus expressed to him, "for there is a piece of the divine in each one of my children. I desire to see you mend your mistakes and honor those who love you. I wish you to plan a noble future for your people, and I want you to listen to the womyn of Rome. They hold a brilliance and beauty that Rome is ignoring."

"I will do all that you ask, great Goddess," Julius promised Venus bowing low to his ancestral Goddess.

"Then it is time for you to return," Venus stated, plucking another leaf. The air was suddenly filled with the roar of the waterfall again flowing down into the dark abyss. Julius looked towards the curtain of water, wondering if this was how Venus meant for him to depart.

"There is only one thing Love ever commands, my son," Venus declared. "I command you to Jump!"

And so he did, tumbling down within the swirling currents. He felt himself sucked into a great river at the bottom, the force of the falls pushing him under. He swam with the current away from the falls until his lungs felt they would burst. He pushed himself towards the surface and found him splashing in his bath.

"Calpurnia," Julius Caesar called out. His wife stumbled into the bathing room awoken by the disturbance.

"What is it Julius? Is something wrong?" she asked.

"We need to speak," he told her in great exhilaration. "I have much to tell you!"

Chapter 24

"How wonderful it is that nobody need wait a single moment before starting to improve the world"

Anne Frank

As Benjamin's father shoved her out the door, Kristy collapsed onto the hard stone pavement. She felt overwhelmed with confusion and grief. *Why did he scream at me like that? What did I do?* She remained curled up upon Benjamin's porch unable to control her tears. Everything was so mixed-up she felt like she was being pulled under by harsh waves.

"Miss, please come with me," the young guard kindly said, offering her his hand. He was the only one who remained on the porch with her. "I will take you home." The thought of home and her mother brought Kristy out of her turmoil a bit. *Mom will need me*, she thought as she forced herself to accept the strangers hand and rise.

"I am sorry Mr. Ezra was so harsh," he apologized for his employer as he escorted Kristy off the porch and away from Benjamin's house. "I am Antonio."

"My name is Kirsty," she answered back as she rubbed the tears from her cheeks so she could see who was offering help. Antonio was tall and tan with a bright smile that made her want to smile back. So glad to see a *friendly face, I don't even care if he's real. It least he's nice.*

"See, you feel better already," Antonio cheered as they headed down the hill back towards the street market. "You should not have come into the Jewish district. Their grudge has been building for so long, they are likely to file a protest against your actions."

"What did I do that was wrong?" Kristy questioned him as she let go of his hand. She didn't even know him. Antonio gave her a curious look before he answered her.

"They don't like independent women," he answered her. "Don't you know the history about the religious feud between your districts?"

"I'm not very good at history," Kristy answered. Who know what history existed in this delusion. *I'm not sure of anything right now*, she thought.

"That's right, you don't have to involve yourself in education in your district unless you want to," Antonio remembered. "I wish my childhood was that carefree. I grew up in the Bolivar district. My mother signed me up for every class I qualified for. She wanted me to have every advantage possible and all its' gotten me is a job as a security guard."

"Security is a nice profession," Kristy responded. "You help keep people safe." Antonio beamed her another beautiful smile and Kristy beginning to relax, glad to have this man as her escort. The sounds and smells of the street market up ahead tantalized her senses and lifted her mood a bit more.

The lively market bustled with activity. As they entered onto Main Street, strong odors of citrus, coffee and cooked meat mingled with lighter floral overtones. Looking across a cart filled with cheese and bread, Kristy realized she was hungry. As she smelled the bread, her guide, noticing her interest and bought a large cinnamon walnut bun and split it into halves for them to share. Then he bought a large bowl filled with tiny woodland strawberries and offered some of those to her as well.

"Thank you, Antonio. I haven't eaten in hours," Kristy gratefully said as she tried one of the red berries. It was sweet and delicious. She was curious about this man who was being so kind to her. "What is the Bolivar district?" she asked trying to strike up a conversation. Antonio looked at her and chuckled.

"You don't get out much," he commented with an amused twinkle in his eye.

"Well, my mom has been sick," Kristy replied beginning to feel offended by his amusement. It wasn't her fault she didn't know what he was talking about earlier.

"I'm sorry," Antonio apologized, perceiving her annoyance. "I would do anything for my mom. The Bolivar district is for citizens from South American. It's named after our first Subconsul, Simon Bolivar. About two hundred years ago, he was one of the men who led the fight over Roman citizenship for our people. That's also why our largest state is named Bolivia."

"I thought Brazil was the largest," Kristy commented forgetting for a moment how different things were.

"No, Bolivia's twice as large," Antonio answered her. *Everything is twisted around*, she thought. *I hope mom is alright.* The wonders of the street market paled as she thought of her mother. *How will I ever find her with the entire world changed so much!*

"I'd like to go home now," Kristy announced to Antonio.

"Sure," he responded and led her up Main Street away from the market. Her town looked similar but different and Kristy felt weary as she walked next to Antonio, sharing the rest of the strawberries. Past the school was sections of middleclass homes and shops. They were a little unusual, constructed out stone and wood instead of modern materials, but the neighborhoods had the same feel.

As they walked, Antonio continued to chat about his district and his family. Kristy half-listened to his dialogue, but concern for her mom crowded into her thoughts. *She has to be ok. Maybe in this changed reality, dad never left and our family is whole again. But what if something terrible has happened to her instead!*

They turned onto Hawthorn Street heading towards the river. Kristy was pulled out of her thoughts by the sound of music. As she stopped to look around, Kristy began to panic. Everything was completely unfamiliar. She should be only a couple blocks from home but her house was no longer there. Instead rows of brightly colored tents stood rustling in the breeze. Where do I look? *Mother, where are you?*

Right in front of her was a life-sized statue of an Egyptian Goddess. It looked much like the Egyptian Pharaoh she had left in Rome. The statues arms were raised in welcome, one gesturing towards a large sign which read "Greeting friends of the Serpent District. All respectful public is welcome." Stretched out on the statue's extended arm was a large black cat which lazily inspected them through half opened eyes.

Kristy forced her feet to move as she looked around the river valley where she used to live. The road flowed toward a large circular courtyard filled with musicians and dancers enjoying themselves. All the streets connected to the courtyard like the spokes of a wheel and throughout the space lay a mixture of tents and wagons. Near the courtyard in each section of land was a large tree surrounded by lovely gardens. There were people everywhere dressed in a vibrant variety of styles. It looked to Kristy like a traveling gypsy festival had replaced her home. But the most incredible part of the setting was the huge temple rising in the background.

The grandeur of the temple added a striking contrast to the simple possessions of the people below it. It rose above the festivities with spirals of gold ascending a huge marble and stone complex. Amongst the shining towers soared a massive statue of an exquisitely beautiful woman. She wore a sparkling crown of stars and a long bell skirt of glimmering emerald. Her chest was bare of clothes with prominent breasts for all to see. Kristy felt herself blush wondering what Antonio would think of the statue.

"It's much different from the rest of the town," Kristy commented to Antonio, trying to act as if everything was normal. She was starting to fathom why Benjamin's dad had a problem with this area of town. Kristy startled as another cat brushed against her leg. She unconsciously reached for Antonio's hand again, needing the comfort of a friend. Antonio happily took her hand, looked around and grinned.

"Yea, your Serpent district is unique, but always charming," he replied. "Don't worry, I've been here a few times with friends for different festivals. Always have a great time."

As they walked towards the courtyard, Kristy looked around in astonishment at the neighborhood she was supposed to live in. Near the river, a group of drummers pounded out a steady rhythm which resonated throughout the area, while scattered groups danced along the shore. A wide dock reached into the river filled with a mix of small water crafts while several of the boats were out on the water. *In my world, that river is too polluted for anyone to fish or swim in,* Kristy though as she watched someone dive of the edge of a yacht.

On the other side of the road, a colorful circle of wagons contained a group of ladies in lively conversation working on crafts together, several working on looms and others working with clay. All around her, the district bustled with joyful activity. The cats were everywhere too, sunning themselves in chose warm spots. She watched several children playing with the little felines.

When they reached the central courtyard, Kristy was unsure of what to do. She didn't want Antonio to know that she had never actually been here. She began following the edge of the stone courtyard trying to stay out of the dancers' way. Antonio, staying close to her side was looking around with interest. It was too loud to converse which was fine with Kristy. *How could I talk about any of this without showing my ignorance?*

When they came to the next intersection, the wooden street sign gave Kristy a feeling of renewed confidence. Oak Street was just before Holly in her original world. Perhaps she was close to finding her mother. Then she noticed the giant Oak growing in the center of the next garden. *It can't be a coincidence.* She hurried toward the next street. She saw the prickly Holly tree before the street sign and quickly pulled Antonio down her unfamiliar block.

A rainbow of tents lined one side of the street and tables full of fall produce were clustered on the other side. The street was filled with chattering people and Kristy wondered how she would find her mom in this crowd. Then she heard someone call out her name.

"Kristy, have you seen Phoebe? I can't find her anywhere."

Chapter 25

"Never go to excess but let moderation be your guide"
Marcus Tillius Cicero

Jaxom awoke from troubled dreams. Images of his sister, mother, and Phoebe flowed across his mind. As he thought of Phoebe he felt anger rise within him, brushing aside the sadness from his dreams. *How could she make a wish like that? After I opened my heart to her.*

He sat up and looked around the room. It looked almost like a regular hotel room from his world. Next to the soft bed was an empty dresser and bookshelf, and across the room was a small couch and table set. His backpack laid on the couch next to a bundle of clothes that Caesar had delivered before he went to sleep. Last night, Julius Caesar had given them each a room to use until their own arrangements could be made. *At least we're moving up in the world,* Jaxom thought. *And today we get to look for our own place in ancient Rome.*

Jaxom climbed out of bed, used the chamber pot in the corner and looked through the pile of clothes. *Why was I worried about matching Phoebe yesterday,* he thought? *I dress for me.* As he slipped on a grey tunic, black sleeveless overcoat and black leather sandals, Jaxom thought about the previous day. He just wanted to help save Julius Caesar and now he and his friend were welcome in the Dictator's inner circle. While escorting them to their rooms last night, Caesar had even guaranteed them each a line of credit whenever needed. *I wonder if he meant Phoebe too.*

A knock at the door pulled Jaxom out of his thoughts. "Hey, you up yet," questioned Chris's voice. "We got things to do, man."

"Yea, come on in," Jaxom hollered and Chris entered the room followed by Marcus. They had both also changed into fresh clothes, and Jaxon was glad to see that Marcus looked as excited about things as his best friend did.

"The sun is up, the sky is clear and I have a lady to see this morning," Chris announced. Marcus laughed at his friend's enthusiasm.

"I'd like to see some breakfast first," Marcus countered. "I'm sure you will find Miriam soon enough. Caesar told her to help us today. You ready Jaxom?"

"Yea, let's go," Jaxom answered, grabbing his backpack. Everything important to him was in there and he wouldn't leave it behind again. He followed his friends out into the hallway and towards the dining room.

"So what should we be looking for in our own place?" Chris asked Marcus.

"I've been thinking about that," Marcus answered. "Rome's got plumbing in parts of it."

"That's a must," Jaxom interjected. He had been surprised to find the bathrooms had running water and real drains. *Though, I don't really mind using the chamber pot.*

"We need four bedrooms and I'd like to have a large kitchen," Marcus continued. "We can't expect others to feed us all the time."

"I'm gonna need lots of space for my bike business," Chris mentioned. "I'm telling you, it will make us rich," he added when Marcus made a face at him.

"We'll see what we can find," Marcus answered as they entered into an empty dining hall. Several bowls of unknown fruit sat on the serving table, but there was no sign of anyone else.

"Where is everyone?" Jaxom asked, already knowing the other two didn't have an answer.

"Someone will show," Marcus said as he headed towards the fruit. "I wish they had left more food, though." They each grabbed something to eat and sat to wait for their hosts. Jaxom munched on the bittersweet fruit feeling as if something was wrong. They finished the simple breakfast and continued to wait.

Jaxom was beginning to feel impatient. *Why isn't someone here to meet us and where is Phoebe?* Marcus and Chris were again talking about finding their own place. Jaxom's mind wandered back to the evening before. *Maybe this has something to do with Phoebe's wish. I can't believe she used me like that.* He wondered if he should tell Chris and Marcus about it. *I don't want to give them reason to stress when everything seems to be going our way.*

"I'm gonna look around," Jaxom decided aloud as he stood up. He wandered towards the kitchen and found it deserted. He glanced out into the garden finding it empty. Seeing a door at the other end of the garden, he was reminded again of last night. Phoebe's room was that direction, third door on the left. *Why should I care*, he told himself and went back inside. Heading back into the dining room, he saw his friends rise to join in his search.

"We ought to stay together," Marcus commented with a look of concern. The three went into the main hall and followed it towards the front room but there was not a soul around. Unsure of where to look next, Jaxom stepped out under the new pediment to look around at the busy city. A sunny morning greeted him and for a few minutes he watched as the people of Rome rushed to begin their day. A group of elegantly dressed women hurried past heading towards the forum and then a cart filled with wine flasks rumbled by the other way.

"There's your slave girl, Chris," Marcus pointed down the street. Chris punched Marcus in the arm, then turned to watch Miriam coming their direction. She beamed them a smile when she saw them waiting and hurried through the crowd to meet them.

"I was coming to find you," Miriam said breathlessly. "I had to deliver messages for Julius Caesar this morning."

"We're happy to wait for you," Chris replied smiling like an idiot at the slave. Jaxom hoped Chris wasn't going to spend all day flirting with this girl. She's cute, but after what happened, Jaxom was tired of thinking about women.

"Where's Balbus?" Marcus asked.

"He said he would find us on the Palatine," Miriam answered gesturing up the hill. Jaxom looked up at the rows of Mansions covering the slope rising above them. "Julius Caesar sent him on errands as well."

"Is that where we're looking for a house?" he questioned. The servant girl nodded and Jaxom looked up again in amazement. "The places are huge!"

"Fortune can change quickly in this city," Miriam responded, "and yours seems to be on the rise."

"Aren't we waiting for Phoebe still?" Marcus asked.

"She went out earlier with the Pharaoh," Miriam responded. Jaxom felt relieved to not have to deal with her yet. *Eventually I'll have to talk with her.*

"Then let's go," Chris announced taking Miriam's arm and leading the way. Jaxom followed them, astonished at the neighborhoods they were heading towards.

The homes that Miriam showed them were amazing. The layouts were similar to the Dictator's mansion with huge open front rooms, spacious kitchens and full wings full of rooms in both the women's and men's quarters. Each place that they viewed was also completely furnished.

There was a massive amount of outdoor space as well. Extensive gardens already filled with food as well as stables and courtyards. They were just leaving the fourth home when Cornelius Balbus hailed them from up the street.

"How is your excursion so far?" the old Senator questioned them as he joined their group.

"Wonderful," Marcus exclaimed.

"These places are amazing," Jaxom declared. *I don't know how we'll decide.*

"I was worried that we wouldn't find a place big enough to start my bicycle business, but these places are huge," Chris commented.

"No one does business on the Palatine," Balbus informed Chris. "We'll find a business property for you as well."

"The next place available is just up the road," Miriam announced. Their group continued up the hill to the very top. These homes were the largest they had seen so far and the air was fresh and clean up here. *It would be like living on the top of the world*, Jaxom thought. *We've got to choose a place up here!*

"Balbus, a moment of your time," a voice called out, and as they turned, Jaxom saw the Senator, Cicero heading their direction. *Not this guy again.* The senator looked flustered and upset. "Why is the Senate house still guarded? The centurions won't allow me entrance and I must speak with the Dictator soon."

"I told you this morning, Cicero," Balbus answered. "Julius Caesar is in private meeting and is not to be disturbed. The Senate will meet tomorrow morning as usual." The skinny old Roman did not look satisfied with this answer.

"Why would he need to meet with a bunch of women?" Cicero grumbled. Then he noticed the party of teens. "Ah, have you chosen a place yet?" Jaxom was startled by Cicero's comment. *This diffidently has something to do with Phoebe's wish.*

"No sir," Marcus answered.

"You must be here to see Atticus's place," Cicero declared. "I will accompany you. Without waiting for an answer, Cicero began to lead them in the direction he had come from. "This is my estate," Cicero said gesturing to a lavish poplar shaded mansion. Jaxom caught Marcus's eye and could see the same annoyance he felt over this senator joining their group. Chris was so infatuated with Miriam, he didn't even seem to notice that Cicero had joined them.

The next place was a little bigger than the rest. Cicero went on about the fine furnishings and the prestige of living above the rest of Rome. Jaxom was no longer feeling impressed by all the splendor. As they stepped out of the house, he noticed the hill of slums just across from them. Was riches and prestige what he really wanted? He listened to Cicero going on about the neighborhood, the only neighborhood worth living in. *I change my mind. Living on the top of the world is not worth being neighbors with this man.*

"I really like the second place we looked at better," Jaxom stated. Cicero looked at him with a shocked expression.

"Which place would that be," he asked.

"That was Decimus Brutus's old place," Miriam informed them.

"That place is halfway down the Palatine," Cicero said looking upset.

"We can go back and look at it again," Marcus said. "It had a better view of the Forum and Pompey's huge theater." Looking at his friend, Jaxom realized that Marcus was enjoying Cicero's distress as much as he was. The old Senator was looking back and forth quite bothered by their conversation.

"We don't really want to walk all the way up this hill every day," Jaxom continued turning back down the hill with Marcus. Chris and Miriam followed leaving Balbus standing with the upset Senator.

"I'm sure Julius will meet with you soon," Balbus told Cicero, "and I will see you tomorrow in Senate meeting. Have a good day." Then then Engineer hurried to catch up to them. Jaxom didn't look back because he couldn't keep his laughter from rising.

"You should not make enemies of Cicero," Balbus said, catching up with their group.

"Oh come on, that guy's a jerk," Marcus said with a smile as wide as Jaxom's.

"He holds a lot of influence in Rome," Balbus commented. "But let's not worry about him now. We shall instead go and see your new home."

Jaxom was glad to have chosen a home. They looked through the place again and then Balbus pulled out a scroll for them to sign. After the paperwork was complete their Engineering friend announced that he would treat them to lunch.

Balbus led them down to the base of the Palatine where they lounged in a fantastic outdoor seafood restaurant. During the meal they discussed possible business sites for Chris's bicycle shop. Miriam suggested a place in Subura near where Julius Caesar grew up. Chris immediately agreed, so after completing their meal, they all headed across town. Jaxom was getting tired of watching Chris flirt with Miriam but went along anyways. *I'm just aggravated because of what Phoebe did. It's not really Chris's fault he found someone and I didn't. Of course his girl is a Roman slave,* Jaxom thought with some concern for his friend.

As they crossed the forum, Jaxom noticed Pompey's theater doors were guarded by a group of legionnaires. He wondered what was going on in that secret meeting. *I bet that's where Phoebe is right now.*

The business property turned out to be an old tavern. It had big open space in front that Chris thought would be great for display and plenty of room in the back. It even had wine and liquor in storage and a bunch of fancy glasses left from before the previous owner's unexpected death in the Senate had closed the business down.

"It's perfect," Chris announced and opened a flask to celebrate. Everyone agreed as they drank their wine straight. *This tastes a lot better,* Jaxom thought. Again Balbus produced paperwork and suddenly they owned a business property to go along with their new home.

They headed back towards Julius Caesar's mansion excited over the success of the day. Again they crossed the forum, but this time the guards were gone. *The meeting must be over. I guess I'll have to face Phoebe now*, Jaxom thought. But when they arrive at the Dictator's estate, no one was around.

"I'm sure they will join us for dinner soon," Balbus stated. They headed into the dining room and found a simple spread of food laid out. They each filled their plates and settled down to eat.

"What do you suppose Phoebe will think of our new place?" Marcus asked him and Chris. Jaxom didn't want to talk about her right now so he took a huge bite of bread. Luckily Chris spoke up and he didn't have to talk.

"She'll love it! She has an entire wing of rooms just to herself," Chris commented enthusiastically. "And don't you think Miriam suggested the perfect place for our bikes." Chris sent a goofy grin to the lovely slave lounging next to him. Miriam smiled back. She seemed to have lost the shyness from before and was obviously enjoying Chris's attention.

"Julius Caesar will be glad to see his old neighborhood improve," Miriam commented.

"Hey, maybe Caesar will let you come over and help set the place up," Chris remarked. "You know so much about Rome and he said you were great with numbers. We could use help with our finances."

"That's because I've spent most of my life in Rome," Miriam revealed to Chris. "I would love to help you but I must get Julius Caesars permission. I have other duties I must attend to."

"I will speak to him," Balbus offered, "and here is the lovelier of our hosts." Jaxom looked up to see Calpurnia entering the room alone.

"Julius is still a good looking man," Calpurnia joked. She smiled radiantly at them and went to prepare herself a plate. As she settled near to Balbus, Jaxom noticed she was still smiling and he realized that she knew what was going on.

"So what happened today in the meeting?" Jaxom asked, not being able to stand the suspense any longer. Calpurnia looked a little surprised by his forwardness but the smile never left her face.

"You will have to ask Julius when he returns," Calpurnia told him. "He is escorting Cleopatra to her ship right now."

"Where is Phoebe then?" Marcus questioned.

"She is with the Queen, traveling to Egypt."

Chapter 26

"Knowledge speaks, but wisdom listens"

Jimi Hendrix

Phoebe couldn't remember where she was when she first awoke. As she sat up and looked around, last night's troubles can crashing back upon her. Jaxom was furious at her for making that wish. *Will he ever forgive me?*

She was lying on a sofa in Cleopatra's sitting room. The kind Queen had found her last night, sobbing in the garden. Cleopatra brought her inside and the two had talked long into the night. Phoebe was so glad to find a friend like Cleopatra who was willing to listen to Phoebe's troubles without judging what she had done. *I think it might help Rome but it really was an accident!*

The Pharaoh was excited to hear Phoebe's wish last night and thought that today would bring great excitement. She could hear her royal friend stirring in the next room, so Phoebe got up and splashed her face with water from the wash basin in the corner, readying herself for the day. *I just wish there was a way to wash away this ache from my heart.*

Phoebe thumped on Cleopatra's bedroom door and the Queen called for her to enter. Entering the room, Phoebe found Cleopatra being dressed in regal fashion by two of her eunuchs.

"How do you feel this morning?" the Pharaoh asked.

"Tired, but better," Phoebe answered. "Thanks for coming back for me, your Majesty."

"You already thanked me, my dear," Cleopatra replied. A loud knock at the door in the sitting room interrupted their conversation. The Pharaoh ordered one of the eunuchs to answer but before he had the chance, Julius Caesar burst into the room. He strolled quickly to Cleopatra and swept her into a tight embrace.

"Last night I received an astonishing vision," the Dictator announced with great excitement. "I spoke with the Goddess Venus and Mother Isis also. Did you know that they are the same divinity?" He was staring deep into Cleopatra's eyes with such devotion that Phoebe felt like she didn't belong in the room. *I don't think he even noticed that I'm here.*

"Of course, Julius," Cleopatra sweetly laughed, caught up in his heightened emotions. "All the deities we worship are a part of the Divine Mother. Tell me what you learned in your vision." The Pharaoh led her love to a couch in the corner and they sat close together to talk.

"The Goddess Venus told me to seek your counsel," Julius Caesar revealed to Cleopatra. Phoebe felt torn between wanting to hear what he had to say and feeling like an intruder. She quietly slipped back to the sitting room to wait. She had been waiting for some time when another knock sounded through the rooms. A eunuch rushed into the sitting room and opened the door for Miriam who was carrying a generously filled tray of food as well as Phoebe's shoulder bag.

"The Queen asked that I deliver breakfast to her room this morning," Miriam told Phoebe as she set the tray on one of the tables. "And this is yours, left behind when your school building disappeared last night." Phoebe thanked the servant and asked about the schoolhouse. Miriam explained what she knew to Phoebe including the conversation last night with the men.

"Miriam," Julius Caesar called, surprising Phoebe. He and Cleopatra stood in the doorway hand in hand. "I have an additional task for you this morning. Come with me." The Dictator gave his Pharaoh a quick kiss and strolled out of the room followed by the servant. Cleopatra rushed over and sat near Phoebe, a look of elation across her beautiful face.

"Julius is calling a meeting this morning for all the patrician women of Rome," she announced to Phoebe. The Queen selected a soft pastry from the tray and indicated that Phoebe should eat. Phoebe grabbed a bundle of grapes, feeling too nervous to eat very much. *My wish is coming true*, Phoebe thought with mixed emotions.

"They are to meet in the Senate in two hours. Would you like to attend?" Cleopatra asked.

"Yes," Phoebe answered quickly, surprised that she would be included.

"I thought you would like to see what you have accomplished with your wishing," the Queen replied. "I already told Julius we would attend. Do not worry, I did not reveal your wish to him." Phoebe was glad of Cleopatra's discretion, unsure what the Dictator would think about being manipulated by her wish. *I hope this works out and that Jaxom forgives me.*

They spent an hour finishing their meal and dressing. Cleopatra had given her another amazing dress to wear, this one red with a split skirt and low neckline. Then the Queen skillfully applied paints to Phoebe's face as well as loaning her bracelets and a necklace to accent her outfit. Phoebe was not used to such finery and hoped she could get out of the house without seeing the others. *I don't want to talk to Jaxom yet anyways.*

They met Calpurnia in the main room of the women's quarters. She was also dressed in her finest, with jewels glittering as brightly as her smile. She began to chatter with excitement over the coming meeting.

"Isn't it amazing that Julius decided to meet with the women of Rome," she announced. "This is a momentous occasion. Did he tell you about his vision?"

"Yes," Cleopatra answered her friend with an equally beautiful smile. "We shall see a great change in him after such an experience."

To Phoebe's relief, they left the house without seeing anyone and were carried to the Campus in royal style. The eunuchs brought their carriage through the arena and private gardens to the base of the Senate house. As the Pharaoh and Calpurnia descended, all eyes turned their direction. A pair of centurions guarded each entrance and many well-dressed ladies were milling around the steps. They seemed unsure of what to do and looked to Julius Caesar's women for direction.

"Come, ladies," Calpurnia called, "our Dictator has summoned us."

"This will be an occasion you do not want to miss," the Pharaoh told them and then she and Calpurnia swept passed them and headed up, towards a Senate room that no women had ever been in before. Phoebe followed closely behind them, her stomach filled with butterflies, and the aristocratic ladies followed her, not knowing what to expect.

As they entered into the Senate, they found Julius Caesar deep in conversation with Lepidus and Mark Anthony. The Master of Horses looked radiant with excitement, in contrast to the Consuls solemn expression. When the Dictator saw them enter, he interrupted his discussion and hurried to greet them. Phoebe was surprised when he first greeted Calpurnia with a gentleman's kiss on the hand.

"You look lovely today, Calpurnia," Julius Caesar complemented his wife. "As do you Cleopatra," he turned to give his lover a similar kiss. He settled them in the front row, Phoebe sitting next to the Pharaoh and he returned to finish his dialogue with the men. The seating began to fill as more and more women arrived. Julius Caesar dismissed Lepidus, who strolled confidently from the room. Mark Anthony sat in his consul seat, holding pen and scroll and the Dictator of Rome stepped forward to greet the women.

"Welcome, noble women of Rome," Julius Caesar began. "Thank you for coming to my unusual summons. Our proud Republic has gone through many transformations in my lifetime. Through the efforts of our legions, our territory and citizenship had grown immensely. We have struggled through civil wars, slave revolts and pirate raids. Still the Roman Republic stands strong. As Dictator of this great nation, I plan to watch Rome grow in prosperity and prestige until we reach a golden age where Roman ideals and traditions are respected worldwide."

"Julius Caesar, drop the rhetoric," a holler came from the back of the room. Phoebe turned to see a tall dark-haired beauty standing in the back of the room glaring angrily at the Dictator. She was surrounded by several others who looked equally irate. "We know our history. What do you want of us?"

Anger flashed in Julius Caesar's eyes for a moment. Then he closed them to regain his composure. *He's not used to being questioned,* Phoebe reasoned. The Dictator turned and stepped back to the Consul seats, dropping into his gilded chair next to Mark Anthony. He looked across the room filled with women ending with Calpurnia and Cleopatra. They both were smiling at him in encouragement. Julius Caesar took a deep breath and addressed the group again.

"Last night I had a vision and spoke to my ancestral Goddess Venus," Julius Caesar revealed to the ladies listening. Sounds of surprise flowed through the room. "She spoke of many things and reveled aspects of my future to me. One of her request was that I listen to the women of Rome. She said that you have a brilliance that Rome is missing out on."

The room had grown completely silence. Women throughout the room held stunned expressions as they let his statements sink in. Glancing back, Phoebe noticed that the outspoken beauty was shocked into silence as well. Turning back towards the Julius Caesar, Phoebe felt pride in her mistaken wish that had brought them here. *These women deserve to have a voice. Everyone deserves one.*

"I have called you here today," continued Julius Caesar, "to listen and find this brilliance which Venus speaks of." Whispers of excitement began to circulate through the meeting as the women realized the Dictator was serious. It took a few minutes before anyone responded to his request.

"I do not know if I have brilliance to share," a lady on the far side of the room stood and addressed Julius Caesar. "But I would have you listen to what I have to say." The Dictator nodded for her to continue. "During our recent civil war, I lost my husband and had to return to my father's household. I lost my home and much more. My father arranged another marriage, so once again I had a home to manage and slaves to supervise. Yesterday my new husband was slain as a traitor during the Senate meeting and you confiscated all his properties. So again I return to my father's household, this time having lost everything." The woman retook her seat and hard eyes turned back to the Dictator, waiting for his reaction.

"I am sorry for your loss and glad you were willing to share your story," was Julius Caesar's response. The Dictator looked around the room. "Who else wishes to speak?"

"I will," the dark haired woman in the back spoke up. "You know my story Julius, but I will tell it anyways. My family is one of the most prestigious in Rome, yet fortune has not smiled upon me or my generation. My brothers and I were harassed in court for years by those jealous of our status and fortune. The death of my first husband gave you the providence of Gaul to conquer. When my youngest brother Clodius was murdered, Pompey took advantage of the tragedy to gain control of Rome, leading us into civil war. Now my brother and second husband are dead, slain as traitors in the heart of Rome. I am left with nothing but a famous name. Even my daughters were denied to me, exposed for not being male."

"I have gained from your loss, Clodia," Julius Caesar said. "It was never my intention."

"If you are looking for brilliance, you summoned the wrong Romans," Clodia continued. "We are oppressed, exploited and dominated. Our thoughts are considered foolish gossip and when any of us attempts to influence the course of our lives, it is considered scandalous. Remember your sisters and daughter, Julius and know how they felt."

Phoebe remembered that Caesar's daughter was given to Pompey years before, to ensure Pompey's cooperation. *He sold his own daughter for political gain*, thought Phoebe. But she still felt empathy for him. *My wish placed the Dictator here and he is trying to understand.*

The meeting continued for hours. The Roman women stood, one after another and told Julius Caesar their stories. Phoebe's heart ached as she listened to their tragedies, realizing just how tough life in Rome could be. The Dictator listened to them all. When the women were finally finished, Julius Caesar remained seated in his gilded chair silently considering the room. He looked to be in shock. Mark Anthony sat next to the Dictator looking quite uncomfortable. Phoebe was wondering what would come next when beside her, Cleopatra rose. All eyes turned to the Pharaoh.

"Ladies of Rome, I am honored to be a part of this monumental occasion," Cleopatra told the group. "Never before has the leaders of Rome listened to your stories. Your experiences reflect the widespread misfortune of women occurring throughout most of the civilized world. In my own country of Egypt, women have not yet been silenced. I am full of pride to know your Dictator has chosen to address this crisis and delighted that you will soon join me as free women."

Cries of excitement and confusion spread throughout the room. Women rose to their feet, shouting questions at the Dictator. "What does she mean? Will we have a right to vote? What freedoms will be granted?" Julius Caesar rose to his feet and held his hands up to silence the room. Gradually the women returned to their seats and the room grew silent.

"There are many decisions to be made over this issue," the Dictator addressed the room. "I do not yet know what form they will take, but I assure you that I will grant freedom to all women of Rome." In an instant, every women was on their feet cheering over the promise. Julius Caesar smiled proudly as he looked across the crowd. When finally the room settled down again, he addressed the group once more.

"There is a brilliance here that Rome had been missing. I will do my best to balance the injustice done to each of you. Return to your homes now, knowing that I will do my best." He returned to his seat amid another round of cheers.

The women began leaving in chattering groups until the room had almost emptied. Phoebe remained with Cleopatra and Calpurnia amazed at what just occurred. *My wish made this possible*, she thought feeling thrilled. Julius Caesar spoke to a troubled Mark Anthony for a moment then strolled over to where they waited.

"Julius, you were wonderful," Cleopatra commended her love. Then a request from behind them interrupted their conversation.

"Julius, I would speak to you for a moment," Clodia called out. She came forward and joined their group.

"Certainly," the Dictator responded.

"Will you truly do as you have promised and grant liberties to us?" she questioned.

"I will," came Julius Caesar's quick response.

"Then I want the Consul," Clodia said. "My name alone gives me the right to request such a position and you know the connections which I have throughout our city." Julius Caesar took a moment to contemplate the request.

"It shall be yours," he decided aloud and then turned to Calpurnia, "and you shall be our other consul. With a look of elation, Calpurnia pulled her husband into a tight embrace. Phoebe realized that these two did love each other in a way. Not the deep love Cleopatra and Caesar felt for each other or how she felt... No, why would she even think of Jaxom.

"Then when the time comes, I will grant you a divorce so you may follow your heart," Calpurnia promised as she released her spouse.

Phoebe only half heard the conversation. *Follow your heart*, tumbled again and again through her mind. Turbulent emotion twisted through her as she recognized deep feelings she felt for Jaxom. At the same time she remembered his anger, his grief and the many times he had wounded her with his careless words. *It's too hard to deal with*, she thought feeling anxiety rise within her.

Cleopatra was now embracing Julius Caesar. "Would you like to accompany me, Phoebe?" the Pharaoh suddenly asked her.

"Where?" Phoebe asked unsure of what she had missed.

"I sail today for Egypt," Cleopatra informed her. "I would love to show you my home." Phoebe saw her chance to escape the chaos she was feeling over Jaxom. *I need space and time to figure things out.*

"Yes, I will travel home with you," Phoebe told her royal friend.

Chapter 27

"Wibbly, Wobbly, Timey, Wimey Stuff"
David Tennant

Benjamin was glad that his dad had hauled him to his room. Otherwise, he would never have found it. His dad pushed him into the room and hollered something about studying. *That man can be so dramatic. Why act like that over a girl visiting?* The bedroom was larger than before, just like the house. As Benjamin looked around, his heart sunk. He didn't recognize anything in the room. *I've lost my new girlfriend and all my stuff in the same day*, he thought. *This magic is a foul thing!*

He felt sorry for Kristy. His dad had been real harsh and she wasn't handling anything well lately. But he also felt relief to be away from her. *My hand still hurts from her crushing it for days.*

He decided to put all thoughts of her out of his mind and figure out what was going on in this new timeframe. Benjamin tossed his backpack onto the bed, and sat down to unzip it. *There should be clues in here as to what my life is like.* He knew he had hit the jackpot when he pulled out a thick daily planner. There was also a pile of textbooks and a few other items.

He first glanced through the textbook titles. Advance Alchemy, the Ecology of Western Rome, History of the Viking Empire, Plant Taxonomy, and

Religious History of the Roman Empire. *That seems like a heavy load*, Benjamin thought with a sigh.

Next Benjamin flipped through the calendar. It was filled with lists of classes and homework assignments. There was even several more classes listed than he had books for. Then he noticed the date was wrong. *How can it be the year 2768?* Besides the date, it looked a lot like his old planner except that he attended a different school in the afternoon three times a week for the history classes. *That's where Kristy and I showed up earlier today*, he realized.

Then he noticed with a groan that classes were also listed on Sunday. The only thing written on Saturday was Sabbath. He wondered what his grandfather would have planned for him on that day. He had always led their family services and was very particular about the details. Overall this new life didn't seem any more enjoyable then the last one.

He picked up the History of the Viking Empire, remembering what Mrs. Branson said about a test. The thick text was earmarked in several places so Benjamin opened to the first one. It was dated 1541 and discussed a Viking attack upon the Roman providence of England. The section was entitled, The War of Viking Aggression.

Benjamin began to read through some of the text. Apparently when the Vikings began their raids, Rome already controlled both England and Ireland as well as most of Europe. The Romans had been knocked back a bit when the

Vikings first surprised them, but in the usual Roman manner, defenses were built and legions recruited to counter the attacks. Rome quickly took the upper hand and then built a navy to patrol the North Sea.

Benjamin flipped to the next dog-eared page and found the next chapter was about Erik the Red. This is who Ms. Branson had mentioned. The text claimed he was the leader of Norway and that in 1734 he met with Roman leaders to form a peace treaty between the two nations. *How will I ever learn these strange dates*, he moaned to himself?

The treaty was simple. All lands north of the Baltic and North Sea were granted to the Viking under the rule of Erik the Red and his descendants. There was to be a cease in all hostilities from both nations and traders were granted safe harbor and passage throughout both nations. There was mention about a code of Caesar that all travelers must follow to ensure their own safety. A knock at the door pulled Benjamin out of the text, and his sister, Naomi hurried in carrying a tray of dinner.

"Momma said to bring your food up," Naomi informed him. "Daddy's real mad still and she doesn't want fighting at the table."

"Thanks," Benjamin told his little sister. The tray was piled high with food and smelled delicious. *I'm glad mom is still a great cook.* Naomi stood and watched him as he sampled the squash soup. She was fidgeting with her hair obviously wanting to talk about something. "What do you want?" he asked her.

"Why is dad so mad at you, Benny?" Naomi asked. Benjamin was unsure how to answer, not really knowing why his dad had freaked out. *It has something to do with where she lived.*

"What did mom say?" Benjamin questioned back. He knew his sister usually started with mom when she didn't understand something.

"She said that girl was from the wrong sort of family," Naomi replied. "But my teacher says that all sorts of families are good." Benjamin thought about her question for a few minutes. Apparently this society was segregated and Kristy was off limits because of that. But why would saving Julius Caesar cause such division? Her sister stood, wide eyed waiting for his answer.

"On this one, I think your teacher is right," Benjamin told her. "There's all kinds of different people, but none of them are wrong for being who they are." He thought of Kristy's beautiful smile ringed by her lovely red curls. He felt terrible over the thought that he may never see her again. *This was my first chance with a girlfriend and these horrible magical changes ruined everything.*

Chapter 28

"You have to give people something to dream on"
Jimi Hendrix

This has been a bizarre week, contemplated Marcus. Chris's chaos theory had been twisting everything around like a hurricane rearranging the beaches. The always fun and cool Jaxom had become sullen and snappy. Chris had gotten so serious with his business ideas and new love that he had no time at all for Marcus. Those two had left earlier to visit the Blacksmith family Balbus had suggested. They were going to see samples of the bike parts they were working on. *I hope it all works out for him,* Marcus thought with mixed emotions. Marcus was worried about the fact that she was a slave of Caesar's, but Chris had just disregarded his concerns.

Since Cleopatra and Phoebe had left, the Dictator had become a recluse, staying in his private quarters with Calpurnia and no one was saying anything about the secret meeting. They had moved into their new home, leaving an empty wing waiting for Phoebe's return. Lepidus was now sailing towards Syria in command of a vast Roman army, accompanied by Cornelius Balbus, which left Mark Anthony to deal with.

Julius Caesar had placed the Consul in charge of translating the books from the schoolhouse as well as producing a set of regulations and protocol for a Roman Gladiatorball tournament. They had finished the maps first, so that Lepidus could use what he needed in his campaign against the Parthians. Then they had moved on to the tournament.

That was why Mark Anthony had come over today. He and Jaxom were meeting with the Consul to finalize the plans for Rome's first annual Gladiatorball Tournament. Marcus thought they had done a fairly good job putting together a set of rules for the game, but he was a little worried about the actual action. Mark Anthony had insisted the players must have weapons. It wouldn't be Roman if there wasn't some risk involved, he had declared. Now the game was a strange mixture of Roman and modern sports.

"Why should the half-time be so lengthy," Mark Anthony questioned. "The people may began to leave before the second half commences. I feel we should shorten the time to match the breaks between quarters."

"Football teams back home put on all sorts of half-time performances," Marcus explained. "Musicians and actors perform and marching bands do elaborate shows. Also they have a ton of vendors selling food to everyone."

"We could make something like that work," Mark Anthony declared with excitement. "I know of a few performers who would love a chance to appear before the whole of Rome." Marcus really didn't like the Consul that much, but as they worked together throughout the past week, he had realized Mark Anthony had an alter ego quite distinct from the tough guy Centurion he was most of the time. A few times after drinking too much, he had talked about going clubbing in Baiae, a resort town down south somewhere. *It might be interesting to see who he finds.*

"What do you think, Jaxom," Marcus asked looking over at his friend. Jaxom startled as if he was half asleep. *Why doesn't he care about any of this, Marcus wondered?*

"Sure, we need something for half-time," Jaxom mumbled. *At least he's paying some attention.*

"I think we have everything figured out," Mark Anthony declared. "I'll deliver these to Julius Caesar and let you know what else he needs from you." The Consul rose and left, leaving Marcus and Jaxom with the rest of the day free. Marcus looked at his friend. Jaxom was staring into space looking upset. *He was so excited about being in Rome, why is he now so down about everything?*

"Let's make something to eat," Marcus decided out loud getting up.

"Go ahead, I'm not hungry," Jaxom muttered.

"What is wrong with you?" Marcus snapped, feeling tired of Jaxom's depressed behavior.

"Nothing, I'm fine," Jaxom yelled. Marcus remained standing, arms crossed and stared at him. Jaxom looked down refusing to meet Marcus's eyes.

After a minute he finally responded. "I just don't know why Phoebe would leave like that," Jaxom mumbled. "She didn't even say goodbye."

"Is that what's eating you?" Marcus replied. "Remember, on our first day here, you left for Rome without telling her."

"That was different," Jaxom grumbled. Marcus wondered why Phoebe leaving would mean so much to Jaxom. *Wasn't Jaxom the last one to see Phoebe, when they went on that tour of Caesar's mansion?*

"What did you say to her the night before she left?" Marcus questioned.

"Nothing," Jaxom replied, but the look on his face told Marcus that something had happened that night. A mixture of anger and sadness was fighting for room on Jaxom's face. *Yea, he likes her.*

"If you stop being so mean to her all the time, you might have more of a chance with her," Marcus told his friend. As Jaxom looked up, Marcus could see that the anger was winning.

"You don't know what you talking about!" Jaxom screamed, rising quickly and getting in his face. Marcus regretted his comment. *I don't want to fight with him.* Luckily, Chris's voice called out, interrupting the conflict.

"Marcus, Jaxom you got to come see this," Chris rushed into the room with Miriam at his side. They both were flushed with excitement with huge smiles contrasting the tension in the room.

"What's up?" Marcus asked his best friend, happy to be interrupted.

"Caesar's in the forum announcing some kind of new laws for Rome," Chris declared.

"Everyone's saying it's divinely inspired because of the sun!" Miriam continued. Not understanding, Marcus followed the two outside. High in a clear blue sky, the sun was ringed by a spectacular rainbow. It was the most amazing sight Marcus had ever seen, though the sun was too bright to look for long.

"What new laws?" Jaxom asked joining them outside. He still looked upset but Marcus was glad to see him interested in something again.

"He's giving the women of Rome the right to vote and claim their children," Miriam announced.

"There's a bunch more. We didn't hear much," Chris answered. "The forum is crowded and I wanted to let you two know about it."

"Thanks," Marcus told his friend. "Let's see what's going on." The Via Sacra was empty but as they headed towards the forum they could see the crowd up ahead. All of Capitoline Hill was filled with Roman families and Marcus could see the Senators gathered near the top. Chris led the way into the energized crowd until he found his new blacksmith friends about half way up the hill. As they grew closer to the senators Marcus noticed several women were included in the group wearing the traditional togas of the Senate. *Something strange is going on.*

"This is Domitius and his wife Aria," Chris introduced his business partners. "This is Marcus and Jaxom." Marcus shook Domitius's hand feeling crushing strength in the huge man's grip. The blacksmith's friendly smile was as big as he was and Marcus immediately liked the man.

"Great to meet friends of Chris," Domitius told them.

"Glad to meet you too," Marcus answered. "Is Chris's crazy ideas giving you any trouble?"

"This friend of yours is a genius," Domitius boomed slapping Chris on the back. "We're loving the challenge he's brought to us."

"These bicycles will be a great success," Aria added, "but did you hear the announcement made by the Dictator?" She smiled brightly obviously trilled over the new laws.

"We only heard a little," Chris admitted, "but we saw the amazing sun!"

"I'll see if I can get a copy for you," Miriam announced then took off through the crowd.

"It is by divine will that we are here today," Domitius declared looking equally glad over Caesars announcement as Aria. "I will be glad to share all that

I have with my lovely wife. I do anyways." Domitius laughed with Aria over his own joke and gave his wife a hug. Marcus glanced at the sky again, remembering reading something about Caesar Augustus receiving such a sign. *Is this really just a weird coincidence?*

It will be easier for the Plebeians to accept," Aria commented. "We usually marry for love while the aristocrats must marry for duty."

Suddenly an unsettling voice rang out above the noise of the crowd. Marcus knew just who the troublemaker was before seeing Cicero standing before the Romans. *He has to cause problems.*

"Men of Rome, will you stand by and allow this desecration of our Roman values and traditions to occur," Cicero began. "I am unsettled to think our Dictator believes Rome will regain its strength and values by granting our women control of our property including our children. On any emotional whim, our wife's can now take half of our property, our daughters and leave. These additional laws over private life will allow the traditional Roman ideals which this city was built upon, to slide into immoral depths of depravity." *That man really likes to hear himself talk*, Marcus thought. But he noticed that the crowd was silent and listening to the old senator.

"But what I am most disturbed by is the women Julius Caesar has chosen to elevate to the top political positions of our great city," Cicero continued. "Calpurnia is a predictable choice. With his new code of law our Dictator now has cause to placate his wife's cravings and he has much to lose if he does not. I cannot fathom though, why he would choose Clodia Metelli to lead us. Her scandalous affairs are known throughout the peninsula and both her husband and brother were found last week to be traitors of Rome."

"Cicero," the voice of Julius Caesar rang out, interrupting the old senator. "We shall not hold any action against any Roman woman before today. From this day forth, they hold rights as Roman citizens and shall be held accountable to their duties to our great Republic." The crowd roared in approval, causing the Dictator to pause. He held up his hand to quiet the crowd. "As to law on Roman privacy, our law courts will no longer waste time hearing outrageous remarks over what someone eats, how they dress or with whom they are socializing. Henceforth, the law shall be decided based on the facts of the case." Cicero was obviously offended over this comment and Marcus wondered if Caesar meant it to personal.

Julius Caesar continued with a straight face. "As to my choice in Consuls, Clodia and Calpurnia belong to prestigious aristocratic families, both deserving of such position. These shall be my last imposed positions to the Senate." The Dictator looked across the crowd. "I have decided instead to hold a vote for one hundred open seats remaining in the senate." Waves of joy rose at this announcement. *The people are stoked over all this*, Marcus thought, "but why is this happening?"

"Any man or woman wishing to run must submit their name within the week," Julius Caesar continued. "Elections will be held will be held two months hence. A new style of games will be held in honor of the elections. Rules are being posted for any interested party wishing to participate." *That would be our Gladiatorball*, Marcus thought. He was troubled with these changes. They didn't seem that bad but it seemed unlikely this was occurring because they saved Caesar.

Marcus noticed that Miriam had returned with a scroll. Chris handed it to him since it was written in Latin. He was the only one who had worked at learning the language. The Code of Caesar listed dozens of new laws on the rights and duties of citizens, parents, children and travelers. What Marcus could read seemed to be fair, but also completely unexpected.

"Jaxom," Marcus called to his friend. "How many more wishes have been made?"

Jaxom looked at him with a pained expression and answered. "Two."

Chapter 29

"To love another person is to see the face of God"
Victor Hugo

"Kristy, have you seen Phoebe? I can't find her anywhere," called a voice she recognized. Kristy turned, feeling relieved to see Phoebe's mom heading towards her through the crowd. *Maybe she knows where my mom is!*

"I haven't seen her since this yesterday," Kristy answered, pulling Antonio towards the familiar face. "Have you seen my mom?"

"Yes, she and your sister went to choose their winter quarters in the temple earlier," Ms. Holland told her gesturing towards the massive building near them.

"Winter quarters?" Kristy repeated. *Were they really going to live in that incredible temple and did she say sister?!*

"Of course, silly," Ms. Holland smiled. "Last night was the Harvest festival. You and Phoebe always have fun at the festival but disappear for the work afterwards. We need to count and distribute all this food." She gestured towards the tables piled high with produce. "Phoebe promised to be back this morning to help."

Kristy didn't know how to answer. She couldn't tell Ms. Holland that Phoebe was in ancient Rome. *She would know that I'm crazy!* Luckily Ms. Holland noticed Antonio holding Kristy's hand.

"I see what you've been up to," Ms. Holland stated with a devilish grin. "I'm Sophia Holland," she introduced herself to Antonio. "Did you enjoy our Harvest Festival last night?" Kristy quickly released Antonio's hand, feeling embarrassed over her comment. *What does she think I would be doing with a guy I just met?*

"Actually, I wasn't here yesterday," Antonio told her. "Kristy and I met this morning."

"Oh, well I welcome you to our district," Ms. Holland smiled at Antonio. Then she turned back to Kristy. "Your mom left bags. You should take them with you. I expect she's trying to grab a room overlooking the river again." Kristy headed towards the tent that Ms. Holland had indicated. A pile of cloth sacks laid near the entrance.

"I'll help you with those," Antonio offered. He picked up several as Kristy did. She gave him a smile of thanks wondering how she would find her mom in the huge temple. *I guess I'm supposed to know my way around.*

"When you see Phoebe, tell her I really need her help," Ms. Holland called out to them.

"I will," Kristy answered as she headed towards her incredible winter home. The stone courtyard seemed to wrap around the entire temple complex. She noticed others carrying their belongings in through several archways on the temple side so she headed in that direction. Antonio stayed right behind her as they made their way through the clusters of carefree women still dancing. Kristy didn't know what to make of all this. *I just need to know if mom is alright, and how I have a sister.*

The inside of the temple looked like a high class museum except that no one was charging admission. Kristy looked around in wonder at the beautiful marble room they had entered. Great works of art were hung upon the walls and scattered throughout the room. The room felt as if it was spilling over with generations of love.

To Kristy's delight, she spotted a large directory map in the center of the room. Antonio seemed in awe over the space, which was good since it kept him from noticing Kristy's surprise.

"I've never been inside the temple before," Antonio commented, still looking about at the masterpieces. Kristy steered them closer to the map until she could see that living quarters were located on the second floor.

"It's amazing, isn't it?" Kristy answered. She followed a small crowd of other temple residence up a huge double staircase and turned west towards the rooms overlooking the river. They wandered down a wide hallway. Kristy hoped to catch a glimpse of her mom somewhere in the crowd. *Where is she?* Again she heard someone call her name. As she turned around, an adorable five year old girl with red pigtails leapt into her arms.

"Kristy your back! We got the same room as last year," her little sister cheered. Then to Kristy's relief, her mom's head leaned out of a doorway she had just past. Her smiling freckly face looked free of the fear and confusion, Kristy was used to seeing. Kristy felt a wave of peace wash over her, now that her mother was near.

"We're in here dear," her mom called out. Kristy swung the bag over her shoulder and carried the squirming child into the unknown room. Her mom took the girl and gave Kristy a kiss on the cheek. Kristy stared at the beautiful face of her mother. There was a twinkle in her eyes and a relaxed smile that had been missing for so long. Kristy felt a tears threaten to fill her own eyes and pushed them back, not wanting to appear silly. Her mother had not noticed for she was regarding Antonio with interest.

"Oh, and you brought muscles to help," her mom cheered and gave Antonio a similar peck. "I'm Matilda Clark, thanks for the help."

"I'm Antonio and it's not a problem, Ms. Clark," Antonio responded setting down the bags on the sofa. Kristy looked around the room and noticed it was actually a suite. The large main room had both a kitchen and family space and was filled with sunlight flowing in through huge windows. Three open doors reveled bedrooms and Kristy guessed the other door contained a bathroom. The space was brightly colored and beautiful artwork was displayed on the walls. *It feels like a high class hotel.*

"Just Matilda," her mom corrected Antonio. "Would you mind fetching the other bags?"

"Sure, Matilda," Antonio responded. He smiled at Kristy and left. Her mother turned and regarded her with a heartwarming grin.

"I love you mom," Kristy blurted out and wrapped her arms around this woman who was the most important being in her world and the small child who was apparently her little sister. Her mother enfolded them both in a tight embrace.

"Don't squish me," the young child complained laughing.

"Oh, my sweet girl, I love you too." Her mother pulled back from the hug and smiled. "Both of you," she added, giving the small child a squeeze.

"I also love this new dress and your new man," her mother continued. "He's cute, where did you find him?" her mom asked her with a knowing smile. *Everyone seemed to think that she and Antonio were a couple.*

"I met him in the Jewish district but he only works there as security," Kristy explained. Her mom's expression dropped into a concerned frown. "He's actually from the Bolivar district."

"He was sent to escort you home?" her mom asked as she setting down the little girl. "Go unpack your things, Mandy," her mom told her little sister. Mandy grabbed a bag and ran into one of the bedrooms and her mom attention came back to her. "Kristina why would you choose to visit the Jewish district?"

"I was visiting with another boy," Kristy mumbled, hoping she wouldn't be in trouble for long. *At least this will be a nice place to be grounded in.* But to Kristy's surprise, her mom shrugged it off.

"That's not the place to chase guys. There always trying to cause trouble for us. No real harm done and I remember being a teenage girl," her mother sighed. "Now Antonio is quite a catch. Be sweet and he might stick around. Come help me unpack the kitchen."

She spent the next ten minutes helping to unpack the bags Antonio had carried. It was wonderful chatting with her mom about the great room and the plentiful harvest. *Her mind is whole and strong again. Her face is divinely beautiful like it was when I was Mandy's age. I wonder, where is dad?*

They had just finished with the kitchen when Antonio returned. He was loaded down with bags but still had a big grin for Kristy. *He is a really nice guy,* she thought.

"Here's the rest, Matilda," he announced.

"Wonderful!" her mom cheered. "Here's our bags, Kristy." Her mom grabbed two of the bags and headed into a bedroom leaving her and Antonio together. She assumed the last two bags were hers and accepted them from Antonio.

"Thanks for helping," she told Antonio. "You didn't have to."

"I like to help," he answered. "I guess that's why I'm in security." She laughed at that, feeling fortunate to have met this nice guy. *I do kinda like him.*

"Would you like to stay for a while?" she asked him.

"I've got to get back to work," he answered with frustration in his voice. "I've already been away half the day."

"Well, stop by sometime," Kristy invited, feeling disappointed.

"In two days, I have a day off," he told her. "I'll come by to visit. Your home is amazing."

"It really is," Kristy beamed him a happy smile. Everything felt perfect. Then life was even better as Antonio leaned in to kiss her cheek.

Chapter 30

"I'm not afraid of storms for I'm learning to sail my ship."
Louisa May Alcott

Phoebe stared at the dark southern sky along with most of the ship's passengers and crew. They had been sailing for over a week and were coming to the end of their voyage. She watched as a faint glimmer caught her eye and slowly grew into a bright light. *There it is!*

"Praise Mother Isis," the ship's captain called. "Her lighthouse shines bright, waiting for our return." The crew cheered and danced as they celebrated their safe voyage. Phoebe understood their enthusiasm, herself feeling relieved to see Pharos and the end of their journey in sight. She had never sailed before and even though she had gained her sea legs after a couple days, the endless stretch of sea made her feel nervous.

She watched the merriment for a time, enjoying the music. Her mind kept drifting back to Rome and those she had left behind. She turned to stare back at the lighthouse beacon wishing she could find peace in the lovely glow. Instead images of Jaxom's angry hurt eyes haunted her and her newly realized feeling for him added additional chaos to her thoughts. *Should I have left without saying goodbye?*

"You are lost in thought, my young friend," Cleopatra commented, interrupting her thoughts. "Are you thinking of Jaxom?" Phoebe glanced at her royal friend who had joined her at the ships rail. *Her grandpa liked to say, if you bottle up your emotions inside, they will eventually explode like a shaken soda. It might make me feel better to talk about this.*

"Maybe I should have spoken to him before I left," Phoebe replied. "Tried to convince him it was a mistake. He was just so angry!"

"His anger will dissolve with time," the kind Queen told her, "and his feeling for you will still remain when it does. This is not the first fight you two have had."

"How do you know that?" Phoebe questioned.

"The evening you arrived you spoke of fighting," Cleopatra reminded her. "Though you never told me what the argument was about."

We were arguing about Julius Caesar," Phoebe admitted, "and whether the Senate was justified in killing him." Phoebe was concerned about how the Queen would take this admission, but Cleopatra just laughed.

"It is so easy to justified someone's behavior or scorn their choices," the Pharaoh stated. "Julius is a son of Rome and they are an aggressive but noble people. He's always tries to do what he should. I believe our intentions are just as important as the outcome. How can a history text explain anyone's true intentions?"

"I certainly didn't intend to upset Jaxom before I left," Phoebe replied, "and I wish I knew how he feels about me." The Pharaoh looked out across the sea and laughed again.

"That young man loves you," Cleopatra declared. "I can hear it in his voice and see it in his eyes. The Queen turned and looked right at her. "Remember his eyes, Phoebe."

Phoebe thought of Jaxom. This time she remembered the joy filled mischievous eyes he often portrayed. She realized his playful antics weren't really meant to be mean. Jaxom was usually just trying to get her attention, like when he switched lunches with her, knowing she would confront him about it. She thought though years of pranks, smiling with the realization. *He's like a dog who won't leave me alone, no matter how many times I shoo him away.*

Then Phoebe remembered the night in the garden. She could see right through his chocolate brown eyes into his soul. He shared his hidden grief with her, needing her help with the heavy burden. She felt fortunate to be the one he opened up to. *If only I hadn't made that wish!*

"Your right, he does care," Phoebe answered Cleopatra. "He's been through so much pain, that I hate to have caused him more."

"Because of what he's been through, your young man should be strong enough to weather a little disagreement," the Queen assured her. "He will see that your wish is good for Rome and feel your absence while you are away."

"I'm feeling his absence already," Phoebe sighed, amazed at how important Jaxom was becoming to her. "I didn't really consider how long this trip would take."

"Do not worry so," Cleopatra advised her. "Remember him fondly. Distance allows for such indulgence. Tomorrow evening we shall be in Alexandria, and I will show you my home."

"I've dreamed of visiting Egypt," Phoebe admitted to the Pharaoh, "and many of you accomplishments, like your lighthouse and libraries, don't exist in my time."

"That is a future I plan on changing," Cleopatra assured her.

Chapter 31

"The most effective way to do it, is to do it"
Amelia Earhart

Julius Caesar strolled up Capitoline Hill, followed by his lictors. Dressed in a loosely belted toga trimmed in purple, he was heading towards Pompey's Theater to meet with the Consul before meeting with the Senate. His mind was contemplating how successful these past weeks had been.

Word had just come from Syria of a stunning first victory against the Parthians. Lepidus sent word that they routed the enemy base camp and were now heading southeast down the Euphrates. The maps had proven invaluable to the campaign and Balbus was building fortifications to secure the area against further hostilities.

His popularity in Rome had soared more than he realized it would. The people cherished the fact that he had given them back the vote. Over two hundred Romans were running for a seat on the Senate, filling the forum with their politicking. His new code of law had been accepted well, though a few new divorcees were harboring grudges. *Thank you, Venus for providing your divine approval so clearly.*

Gladiatorball was looking to be a great success as well. Nine teams were already registered for the tournament and the people seemed intrigued by the sport. Mark Anthony and their young foreign friends had done an incredible job creating the regulations. *I wonder what this mysterious halftime show is all about.*

Calpurnia had filed for divorce, leaving Julius's heart free to dream of his beautiful Pharaoh. He was surprised that many Roman couples choose to remain together. He wondered what the Roman reaction would be when he announced his choice to marry Cleopatra. *That will stir up the few traditionalists we have left,* Julius chuckled thinking of Cicero.

As he entered the Senate, Julius saw Calpurnia and Clodia deep in conversation. Both women had taken to the job quickly and were to present him with several proposals today. The ladies looked up as he walked into the marble room.

"Good day ladies," Julius Caesar greeted the new consuls. "Are you ready with your proposals?"

"Yes, Julius, we are," Calpurnia assured him. "Shall we wait for Mark Anthony?"

"I am here," Mark Anthony announced as he hurried into the room. "Ambassadors from Athens have just arrived to speak with you, sir. You'll love the reason their here." Julius wondered about the strange grin Mark Anthony wore. *What could this be about?*

"Show them in," Julius decided aloud. "We can deal with them first." Mark Anthony dashed from the room and in a few minutes returned with five Greek ambassadors, one he knew quite well.

"Posidonius, welcome. I did not know you were coming to Rome." Julius Caesar gave the Greek philosopher a firm hug. "What brings you to our great Republic?"

"You're many sudden changes, Julius," the famous philosopher replied. "I hear you have spoken to a Goddess."

"I have, though you are not here for religious debate," Julius Caesar replied. Posidonius was known throughout the Mediterranean as a gifted counselor. Many Romans sought this man's advice including Pompey and Cicero.

"You are correct," he answered. "We have come to ask entry into your upcoming tournament." *Mark Anthony's right. I love it!*

"I will gladly accept your entry," the Dictator responded cheerfully. "Cleopatra has also entered a team, the Egyptian Cobras."

"Wonderful," he cheered. "We shall enter the Greek Achilles."

"I offer you and your men rooms at my estate," Julius suggested and he eagerly agreed. "We shall speak further when I have completed my duties for the day. " As Mark Anthony escorted the Greek ambassadors out, Julius reflected on the timing of their visit. *Posidonius hopes to influence the course of Rome and I may choose to let him. He is a wise man, for a Greek.*

When Mark Anthony returned, Julius Caesar announced to his Consul the successful report from Lepidus. "Our strategy worked perfectly," Julius proclaimed. "The Legions have taken control of the Euphrates River and its tributaries. This is the only viable land in the region for crops and the indigenous population cannot stand against Rome without it. Cornelius Balbus is constructing permanent Roman fortifications at key points along the river."

"I am also glad to report that Cleopatra had sent Egyptian forces to help secure the region," Julius continued. "The countries of Syria and Parthia should be under Roman direct rule very soon without a huge loss of life on either side. The Egyptian forces will help construct permanent defense between our two countries." He then added that he would be placing similar fortresses within the providence of Gaul as well. *The loss of life has been too great in that region already*, Julius thought remembering the memories that Venus had called forth during his vision.

Next, Julius Caesar asked for proposals from his Consul. First to speak up was Mark Anthony. Julius Caesar was already aware of his proposals, having spoken to Mark Anthony at length the previous evening.

"My first concern is the congestion of our city," Mark Anthony announced. "I propose we look at our boundaries and consider moving out our walls to compensate for our growing population." Julius was happy to see both ladies smiled widely over this idea. *This has been needed for some time.*

"I agree that we should deal with the crowding," Julius gave his approval. "We shall review the maps tomorrow to decide how to best to proceed."

"My other proposal today involves the vast amount of real estate recently confiscated. I believe we should auction off the countryside estates and use the sales to fund improvements within the city." Julius and Mark Anthony had actually received this idea from their new protégé, Marcus. Julius planned to give his approval when he noticed this idea caused both Clodia and Calpurnia to frown and catch each other's eye.

"How do our ladies feel about these proposals?" Julius questioned them.

"Expanding our city is an excellent idea," Calpurnia spoke up. "Before giving my support to the second proposal, I would need more specifics on which real estate would be auctioned. It may affect the proposals we shall present today."

"Then please, present your proposals," the Julius stated, intrigued as to what the women would be requesting.

"Calpurnia and I have chosen two topics of concern to focus upon for our proposals," Clodia began. "Our first area of concern is the health of the Roman people. Mark Anthony's first proposal should help with this. We feel lack of water to some areas of Rome are linked to the increase in malaria outbreaks. Most epidemics began on Aventine Hill," she advised him, directing his thoughts to the congested shanty town on the south side of the city. *That is an area of concern in our city.* He thought over what the project would entail. *The area will never improve without fresh water.*

"Rome now has numerous Aventine apartment blocks and storefronts in its possession," Julius Caesar mentioned. "The land could be used for the project. Perhaps a new aqueduct and drain would prove valuable to the population."

"Another health issue we wish to address is our infant mortality rate," Calpurnia added. "Only two out of three newborns live to their first birthday and this does not count those who are exposed at birth." Calpurnia looked to Clodia, who was quite agitated over the matter. *Her anxiety is understandable,* Julius thought remembering that Clodia had been forced twice to expose newborn daughters. *They're about to ask for something big,* Julius's instincts told him.

"We feel space should be set aside to ensure the survival of our future generations," Clodia interjected.

"Which space do you want?" the Dictator asked.

"Lucullus's estate," Clodia answered quickly. Julius Caesar was surprised at such an extravagant request but not displeased. *The proposal I bring to the table is even greater.*

"That is a ridiculous request!" Mark Anthony declared. "Lucullus's estate is the wealthiest piece of land we confiscated and you wish to give it to babies. Its sale alone could pay for the wall!"

"I wish to set the property aside for the use of midwives and healers as well as expectant mothers and their children," Clodia detailed to Mark Anthony. Her stance was defiant despite the distress Julius could read in her eyes.

"Your wall could be used to enclose the estate making it part of the city," Calpurnia suggested. Julius loved how quick witted his ex-wife could be. *This is a great way to tie their proposals together.* He knew Mark Anthony would remain stubborn in his arguments unless he intervened.

"Would you be willing to use one of your wishes to ensure our proposals today," Julius asked. He had confided in Clodia soon after she became Consul. *Calpurnia insisted, actually. Now Mark Anthony will be able to save his own wish a little longer.*

"I will gladly use my first wish for these concerns," Calpurnia agreed. Mark Anthony backed off with a resigned glare.

"Clodia, was there a second topic of concern you wanted to address today," Julius Caesar interrupted their argument. Mark Anthony sat down and allowed Clodia to continue.

"Yes," Clodia answered. "In your new code of law you added two Consul Seats each year to be filled by Roman Women, and then granted Calpurnia and myself our current positions. There is nothing in the code as to the Proconsul duties for our office."

"We would ask that for the year following her term, each Woman Consul is granted either the southern or northern half of our Italian peninsula as Proconsul Duties," Calpurnia concluded. *Another big request!* Julius was surprised that they would ask for so much. *I remember a time in which I fought against an Italian command with all the political strength I could muster. I succeeded in winning the Gallic provinces which brought me my current position.* Julius was pleased, almost amused to grant this request.

"I believe all your proposals have merit and can be accomplished," Julius assured the trio. "I have a proposal of my own to present to the Senate. If you will all back my request, I will make sure your proposals are successfully implemented."

"And what are you asking for?" Clodia quickly questioned him. He enjoyed Clodia's forward, self-assured personality. His instincts had been right in giving her the Consul seat.

"I wish to grant Egypt the status of Most Favored Friend of Rome," Julius announced to the Consuls, "and grant their kingdom right to all lands south of the Mediterranean Sea." All three Consuls were shocked by the request. "Cleopatra has agreed to grant Rome a similar title. It is in the spirit of this agreement that her armies march in aid of our own." No one answered for a few minutes, each looking uneasily at the others.

"Will you rule as Pharaoh of the Nile after your marriage to Cleopatra?" Calpurnia asked. She knew where his heart lay better than the others. He had hoped for her support over the idea but she appeared to be as reluctant as the others.

"I will be named her Royal consort during the wedding," Julius informed them. "I will not accept any other titles of Egypt. I am the Dictator of Rome and will honor my duties. This deal will end the struggle for control of the Mediterranean and allow Rome to focus on our other borders."

"You will still hold supreme positions in over half of the world," Clodia voiced her concerns. Mark Anthony and Calpurnia both had to smile at her misunderstanding.

"The world is much larger then you might imagine," Julius Caesar explained. Clodia did not seem convinced by his word, but finally his ex-wife showed him some support.

"It truly is," Calpurnia told her friend. "I have seen maps of the lands no Roman has ever seen." Then Calpurnia turned to look at him. "I will support your proposal and expect you to be true to your word."

"I will stand by you as always," Mark Anthony affirmed his loyalty. Clodia looked unsure but after a few minutes of deliberation she nodded a silent agreement.

"Excellent," Julius exclaimed. "We shall present our proposals today and Clodia will accompany me to Jaxom's estate this evening." *Everything is falling into place*, Julius felt. *With the power of the ring, I can flow the future into a world of my own choosing.*

Chapter 32
"I'm getting closer to your heart"
Paul McCartney

She is so beautiful, Chris thought as he watched Miriam bring in trays of food for dinner. He admired the simple white dress she wore. *She moves so gracefully, it's like watching the clouds float by.* Miriam had come over every day to help out with things. She was smart and sweet and Chris felt more attracted to her all the time. She always returned to Julius Caesars home in the evening. A fact that was quite frustrating.

"This looks great," Marcus complemented Miriam as he sat down near Jaxom. Chris was glad his best friend would know he wanted to sit by Miriam.

"Yea, she's an awesome chief," Chris answered, smiling at the lovely slave girl.

"The gardens are the reason it taste so good," Miriam replied. "They are doing quite well for you." Chris piled his plate high with sautéed greens and roasted roots. Then grabbed himself a large chunk of fish.

"This delicious fish didn't come from the garden," Chris responded after taking a bite. "Hey, Jaxom, since you're not using them, can I borrow your jeans."

"I think we should try to blend in while we're here," Marcus commented. Chris rolled his eyes in aggravation at Marcus.

"We saved Julius Caesar's life," Chris retorted. "He's not gonna care what we wear."

"You can have them if you want," Jaxom responded with a smile.

"Jaxom," Julius Caesar's voice boomed from the front of the house.

"In the dining room," Chris hollered back. Jaxom gave him an irritated glance.

"That's the Dictator of Rome," Jaxom began to fuss. He stopped short as Julius Caesar, Mark Anthony and Clodia Metelli entered the room.

"Ah, there you are," the Dictator continued. "Jaxom I need to speak with you for a moment."

"Sure," Jaxom replied. He stood and followed Julius Caesar and Clodia out of the room. Mark Anthony strolled over to inspect the food and Miriam quickly brought him a plate. *And she's the perfect hostess.*

"How's your bicycle building going?" the Consul asked as he filled his plate.

"Fantastic," Chris cheered. "Domitius is a very talented blacksmith. He's already made four frames. Now he's working on the gears."

"I'm going to on a trip to Baiae next week," Mark Anthony announced after he had sat down. "I know a talented musician there who would love to put together a halftime show for us. I thought you might all want to come."

"That would be great," Marcus answered, obviously thrilled at this chance to travel.

"How are we going to get there?" Chris questioned. *Not another painful ride.*

"I've horses for us," Mark Anthony chuckled, "but you can buy a carriage to use if you can't handle the ride."

"I could handle it," Chris objected as the others laughed. "I just don't want to. Do you think Julius Caesar will let Miriam come with us?" Miriam smiled as she settled herself next to him.

"I'll ask," Mark Anthony replied. "That shouldn't be a problem." *Perfect,* Chris thought. *We can finally spend time together alone.* He looked at Miriam and could tell by the twinkle in her eyes that she was also excited over the idea. Chris was about to ask her about Baiae when Jaxom returned with the Roman leaders. *Something is wrong,* Chris knew immediately when he looked at Jaxom's expression but then Miriam spoke and pulled his attention back.

"Miss Metelli," Miriam unexpectedly called out. Everyone turned to look at the servant girl who looked surprised as everyone else that she had spoken.

Miriam took a deep breath and continued. "I wanted to speak with you about your daughters."

"Miriam," Julius Caesar reprimanded, "this is very inappropriate of you."

"It is fine," Clodia assured the Dictator, but her expression was cold as ice as she turned back to hear what the slave girl had to say.

"I know where they are," Miriam announced. This got a startled reaction from every Roman in the room. Clodia gasped and her eyes grew wide. Both Julius Caesar and Mark Anthony seemed astonished by this news. Even Jaxom seemed to understand the significance in Miriam's words. *What is she talking about? Why wouldn't she know where her own children were?* Chris looked at Marcus who seemed to be as lost as he was over the situation.

"They are still alive!" Clodia exclaimed. *Oh, this is serious*, Chris realized.

"There is a midwife on the Aventine who rescues as many exposed babies as she can," Miriam disclosed to the astonished Consul. "Your infant is still with her and she would know where your older daughter is living." Clodia Metelli swiftly crossed the room and pulled Miriam into a tight embrace.

"Thank you," the Consul whispered as her tears began to flow.

"This is extraordinary news," Julius Caesar declared. "You must take us to this woman immediately. Sounds like an excellent candidate for your healer's estate." Miriam was rushed out of the room by Clodia with the Dictator following.

"What was that about?" Marcus voiced the question Chris was about to ask. He was aggravated to lose Miriam so early in the day. *I hope she returns today.*

"Clodia was forced to expose two of her daughters," Mark Anthony explained as he resumed his meal.

"What does that mean?" Chris questioned.

"When a father refused to accept a newborn, the child is left outside the city to die," Marcus clarified.

"Now that women are gaining rights," Mark Anthony said between mouthfuls, "I doubt the practice will continue. Mothers are usually quite attached to their offspring even when they have too many."

"I'm the youngest of five and I am so glad to have my mother's love," Chris declared. *And I'm so proud of Miriam for helping to reunite Clodia to her family*, he thought as his feelings for the lovely slave girl deepened another level. *Is this what it feels like to fall in love!*

Chapter 33

"The course of true love never did run smooth"
William Shakespeare

Miriam peeked through the curtains of the new carriage hoping to catch her first glimpse at the infamous Baiae. She couldn't believe that Julius Caesar was finally allowing her to visit the ultimate party town of the Republic. Miriam glanced at the blond foreigner sitting next to her. Chris sat close with one arm around her waist. He leaned towards her to see the countryside, giving her one of his bright smiles. *This has been my best job ever!*

"Can you see the city yet?" Chris asked her. He and his friends were the reason they were heading south. Mark Anthony was to introduce them to Roman performers interested in the half time celebrations for their tournament. The others went ahead on horseback but Chris wanted to try out the new carriage he had commissioned. *I hope he was looking for alone time with me too*, Miriam thought with a smile.

"Not yet," Miriam answered, "but look at the oyster beds." She held the curtain aside allowing him to see the acres of manmade ponds strung along the coast. The elite of Rome had cultivated the entire region around Baiae, sparing no cost in doing so. Miriam had never seen the area before, but she felt much more interest in the tall blond sitting at her side.

"Wow, look at that," he exclaimed, pointing towards the shore. Miriam followed his gaze and caught her first glance of the shimmering docks. "Are they really made of gold?"

"They are just plated with it," she informed him. "They sure are beautiful." Stunning villas doted the countryside they were traveling through and fancy yachts floated in the waves offshore. They pointed out the sights to each other and shared a flask of straight wine. By the time they reached the city, Miriam felt giddy and lightheaded. *Oh, this trip is so exciting!*

Their driver stopped before an upscale inn. The Wolves Den was one of the aristocratic hangouts in Baiae where the upper-class of Rome spent their holidays in luxurious extravagance. Mark Anthony reserved rooms here for their two day adventure. *This will be my first night with Chris,* Miriam thought with a mixture of anticipation and concern. *I hope I will make him happy.*

They spotted Marcus and Jaxom as soon as they entered the lodgings front room. She followed Chris as he hurried to meet his friends. The lavish front room showed the wealth of its clientele with marble walls, fine furnishings and a fountain centerpiece in the middle of the room. Most of the people were also dressed in their finest adding additional glamor to the space.

"Mark Anthony is securing our rooms," Marcus announced. "Isn't this place fantastic?" Miriam looked around the hotel recognizing faces from Rome in the crowd. Miriam noticed several faces from the Roman Senate, surprised to see some of the more traditional speakers in infamous Baiae.

"It's awesome," Chris agreed with his friends. Do you think they play any real dance music?" Miriam had been surprised to learn that Chris loved dance and gymnastics. *The more time I spend with him, the more Chris surprises me.*

"Mark Anthony thinks they do," Jaxom said. "He was talking about the talented performers he knew for most of the ride. You didn't miss much."

"Except a sore ass," Chris joked. "Here he comes." Their group turned and greeted the Roman Consul. Mark Anthony ordered someone to deal with their bags and then quickly ushered them towards the back of the hotel.

"We must hurry to speak to Cinnamon while he is on break," the Consul explained. They were led through a back hallway to the performer's dressing rooms, and for some reason Chris kept snickering. They found the entertainer sitting before a large mirror applying stage makeup. Swirls of blue and white surrounded one eye and traveled down his cheek in a wave. Miriam was in awe as the tall and tan performer gracefully rose to greet them. She had heard of some of his music from other slaves with the luck to travel this way. *My friends are so jealous over my unexpected adventure.*

"Welcome, my friends! It is fabulous to have you here tonight," Cinnamon cheered. "Our lineup tonight is a perfect mix of talent for your halftime performances. You will love what you see!"

"It's great to see you, Cinnamon," Mark Anthony greeted his friend with a hug. He introduced Chris, Marcus and Jaxom to the star musician. Cinnamon welcomed each of them and turned back to his friend.

"Will you dance again with me tonight?" the handsome entertainer joked with the Consul. Mark Anthony blushed in embarrassment but smiled at his friend.

"If the liquor is flowing freely tonight," Mark Anthony replied. Cinnamon laughed with delight as if it was a joke.

"Of course," Cinnamon countered, "for you and your friends."

"I'll dance with you too," Chris added, "and you don't even need to liquor me up." Cinnamon turned dramatically to Chris.

"Wonderful!" the entertainer shouted. "How well do you dance?"

"He's awesome," Marcus praised his friend. "While all the other guys were in little league, his mom signed him up for dance and gymnastics."

"My sisters were taking the classes. I didn't want to be left out," Chris answered back.

"It will be a fabulous evening and I must prepare now," Cinnamon suddenly ushered them from the room. "I shall see you in a few moments from the stage."

They followed Mark Anthony out of the backstage area and to the resorts dining hall. It contained clusters of couches and low tables surrounding the long stage. The Consul led their group to a seating area front and center of the stage. Miriam was thrilled. *One of the perks to being Julius Caesars slave.*

Miriam settled herself next to Chris in complete bliss as he wrapped his arm around her again. Mark Anthony ordered food and drinks for everyone. As their drinks were delivered, the lights dimmed and drums began an irregular rhythm from the dark recesses of the stage.

Lanterns were lit across the stage, revealing Cinnamon poised before the drummers. His iridescent blue costume shimmered in the low lights as he began to sing a number about Neptune, the Ruler of the Sea. Cinnamon's dance flowed with the rhythm of the drums and reminded her of the waves. The audience cheered and stomped as the song ended. The famous entertainer performed another song, with equal flourish and talent. His audience adored him. *I adore him*, Miriam thought.

While Cinnamon performed, their group ate a fine meal and consumed several rounds of drinks. When Cinnamon had completed his part in the show, he joined their group, reveling in the praise he received from the crowd.

Miriam was feeling more than tipsy now. *I'm not usually allowed to drink like this.*

"Another round for my friends," Cinnamon called out. "How was I, tonight?" Cinnamon asked Mark Anthony, clearly looking for complements.

"Wonderful, as usual," Mark Anthony praised his friend.

"You're so amazing!" Miriam announced unable to stop herself. She felt in awe by the celebrity in their mist and the alcohol had loosened her tongue. As soon as she had spoken, Miriam regretted it. Cinnamon gazed over at her with a twinkle of desire.

"We have not been introduced, my dear," Cinnamon responded sensuously.

"I am Miriam," she answered, realizing her mistake in speaking up. *A slave should be silent and observant until spoken to*, she thought regretfully.

"She's here with me," Chris stated possessively.

"Yet she may decide to leave with me tonight," Cinnamon responded with a smile.

"She belongs to the Dictator," Mark Anthony informed his friend.

"I'll step back for that," the entertainer stated, losing all interest in her. She hoped her forwardness did not cause any problems but when she glanced at Chris he gave her a look of concern. *I hope I didn't upset him. Caesar would be angry.* She smiled sweetly at him and Chris smiled back. *Maybe everything's ok.*

A trio of ladies began to sing an exquisite song about deep peace accompanied by a wooden flute. Miriam snuggled closer to Chris and listened to the music. She missed out on the men's conversation and was startled when Chris pulled his arm away to stand up.

"I'll be back after I show this old man how it's done," Chris goaded the entertainer.

"My years of experience will stand against your classes," Cinnamon taunted back. "Show us your moves." Cinnamon snapped towards the stage and the drummers began pounding out a dance rhythm. Chris did some fancy footwork and a spin. Cinnamon laughed and repeated the moves exactly. Chris grinned and hopped onto the stage.

"Bring it up here," Chris chuckled as he baited the Roman star back onto the stage. Cinnamon gladly followed Chris on stage and again repeated his fancy maneuverings. The crowd in the room was cheering widely over the dance off. Miriam was impressed by this fine foreigner. Chris was smart, fun and apparently talented as well. *He's always so sweet to me, unlike some of the men I've had to accompany.*

Miriam watched in amazement as Chris added flips and acrobatics that she had never seen before. Cinnamon duplicated the gymnastics but was off a little this time around. Chris laughed and performed another round of complex moves. He concluded his dance with flip off the stage. Cinnamon tried one more time, but lost his balance when he attempted the last flip. As the entertainer fell onto the floor, he laughed cheerfully.

"You are very talented, my boy," Cinnamon complemented Chris, who helped him to his feet. Cinnamon wrapped his arm around Chris and hollered to the servants standing near, "Anything this man needs is on the house." This caused a very drunk Mark Anthony to leap onto the low dining table to perform his own footwork. This dance was terrible, but what the Consul lacked in talent, he made up for in enthusiasm. Chris dropped back onto the couch next to her laughing wildly. Miriam laughed with her date, feeling almost like part of the group.

"How was that?" Chris asked her with a twinkle of amusement still in his eye.

"Even more amazing," she answered. He gave her a sweet kiss and she felt delighted.

"That's enough for me," Jaxom commented chuckling over Mark Anthony's antics. "It's been a long day. Which way to our rooms?"

"The night's just begun!" Mark Anthony hollered from the table top.

"I'm about ready for bed too," Chris added.

"Yea, because you bought a hot slave along," the drunken Consul cackled. "What about the rest of us, Cinnamon. Where are the women?" Miriam smiled over the compliment but Chris again looked bothered. *What is wrong? Does he not like it when someone compliments my beauty?*

"When has Dionysus needed help with his women?" Cinnamon teased his friend. Then calling over a slave, he gave instructions to escort his new friends to their rooms. As they rose to leave, Mark Anthony was beginning a slurred monologue about the God who needed his nymphs.

She followed along with Chris, holding his hand. His grip was tighter than usual and his usual wide grin was reduced to a weak smile. Miriam felt frustrated that she didn't know what was wrong.

As they found their room, Chris called good night to Jaxom and quickly pulled her inside. He let go of her hand and looked around the lavish guest quarters. Miriam wondered if she should say something. *He will tell me what he wants*, she decided as she watched him sit down on the edge of the bed.

"Why are you here?" Chris asked her suddenly. She didn't understand his question.

"Because you invited me," she answered meekly.

"No, I mean are you with me because you want to be or because Julius Caesar told you to be?" Chris asked her. Again she was confused. *Doesn't he understand that it isn't my choice?*

"Both," she answered. His face dropped into a scowl and Miriam felt fear rise within her. *If he is displeased with me, Julius Caesar will never give me such freedom again.* "I really love spending time with you," she told Chris kneeling before him.

"I love being with you too," he answered running his hand through her golden hair. She smiled and rose to kiss him. He responded for a moment than pushed her back. "What are your orders from Caesar?" *Why is he being so difficult?*

"He said to keep you happy," she responded then kissed Chris's neck, "which is what I'm trying to do." He pulled her onto the bed next to him and kissed her forehead.

"Then it's not really your choice," he replied. "I don't want it like that." He curled up around her, holding her close. "Let's get some sleep." The first rule in being a slave was to never fall in love. *He's making it really difficult.*

Chapter 34

"How to remember, how to be good, how to continue when I feel I really shouldn't"
Vic Chesnutt

Jaxom stared at the image of Jessica one last time as low battery flashed in the corner. She was sitting at the top of her little slide with Jaxom at the bottom, ready to catch her. Then the screen went black. The tablet was the last of his electronics to run down. There was no way to charge anything here in Baiae or anywhere else in the ancient Mediterranean.

Jaxom leaned back and closed his eyes holding the photograph in his mind for a time. Then, for some reason his mind pictured Phoebe, pushing away the old memories for newer ones. *I really miss her.* After talking things out with Chris and Marcus, he no longer felt angry at her. He knew how passionate she could be over issues. *That was one of the things I love about her.* Jaxom realized it was just a mistake and one that was actually pretty great for Rome. *I hope she comes home soon so I can tell her.*

Now Lepidus's wish still bothered him considerably. Every time he heard anyone talk about the successful campaign, he felt like the blood was on his hands. Before he left with the legions, Lepidus had wished on Jaxom's silver ring that every objective of the campaign was successful. He fiddled with the silver band and wondered, *how many more objectives? How far do they plan on pushing this war?*

Last week, Clodia had asked for the Consul's proposals to be passed. Jaxom didn't even know what were in these proposals. *I've got myself stuck in the middle of something here, and I'm in over my head. I just need to get some rest. Tomorrow there would be more performers to meet and hear. At least this trip is providing an amusing distraction.*

Jaxom tossed and turned for a time wishing that sleep would come. *But I have no more wishes*, he laid in bed thinking. A knock at the door startled him and he jump up to answer, glad to have something to do. Chris stood in the doorway, looking just as miserable as Jaxom felt.

"Come on in," Jaxom invited. "Thought you were spending time with Miriam. What's wrong?"

"That's what's wrong, man," Chris answered as he entered. His friend flopped onto the sofa and gave Jaxom a look of sheer agony. *He's more miserable then I am*, Jaxom thought, kind of glad for the distraction. Then he corrected himself. *I don't want him to feel this bad.*

"Well, how far did you get?" Jaxom asked, not sure what the problem was yet.

"I didn't even try," Chris responded miserably. "She's a slave, Jaxom. I don't even know if she wants me. She said that Julius Caesar told her to keep me happy."

"That's rough," Jaxom declared. He wasn't surprised though. "I feel like the house and money are supposed to keep us all happy too," Jaxom told his friend.

"What do you mean?" Chris questioned him.

"I think Julius Caesar plans to use the ring over and over," Jaxom explained his concerns. "He commanded me to let Lepidus and Clodia make wishes like I was one of his soldiers. He can do that anytime he wants. What if all that he's giving us, including your slave girl, is to keep us content enough to stay here and give him access to the magic?" Chris leaned back to considered what Jaxom had said.

"Why doesn't he just take the ring?" Chris asked.

"I don't know," Jaxom answered back. "I've been worried that he might try." They sat in silent agony for a few minutes. Jaxom considered all the events that had transpired during this trip to ancient Rome. Nothing had turned out like he wanted. *Phoebe was right. There are always unintentional consequences. Oh, I really miss her.* "If Phoebe was here, we could just go home," he remarked to Chris.

"I can't leave Miriam to spend her life as a slave!" Chris exclaimed. "I care about her too much. Hey, maybe she can come with us."

"No, we need to put everything back the way it should be," Jaxom argued.

"Why?" Chris questioned. "We've made lots of things better already. I could wish to free all the slaves. Wouldn't that be awesome?" Jaxom stepped away from his friend. *Even Chris wants to use the ring now!*

"No more wishes, Chris," Jaxom yelled at his friend, "until we're all together again and going home." He felt bad for shouting but he was tired of everyone using his magic to get what they want. Chris looked hurt and angry. He didn't say another word. Instead Chris just got up and left, slamming the door as he went.

Jaxom felt like he was drowning in his many mistakes. *Now Chris hates me. Things just keep getting worse,* Jaxom moaned to himself. He laid back down and fiddled with the silver ring, hoping that sleep would come soon.

Kristy awoke feeling refreshed and happy. Everything about this new life was better. Her mom was healthy, she had a beautiful little sister and tomorrow Antonio was coming back. Kristy crawled out of bed and looked through her clothes for something to wear. She now owned a dozen lovely dresses to choose from. *Even my wardrobe had improved.*

As she ran a brush through her hair, Kristy could hear her mom and sister moving about in the front room. She couldn't wait to spend the day with her improved family. A knock at their door caused Mandy to squeal and shout daddy. *I was right! My dad is back.* Kristy hurried out to see how her father looked and found her sister in the arms of a total stranger. Even worse, her mom gave this man a big hug.

"Where are you two going today?" her mom asked.

"I brought the bikes," the stranger told Mandy. "I thought we might take a ride somewhere." Mandy cheered and jumped out of his arms.

"Let me get my helmet," Mandy yelled as she ran to her room. "Can we ride to the lake again?"

"Of course we can, Amanda," the strange dad laughed, "that's why I packed a lunch." Her little sister ran back into the room in great excitement.

"Bye Kristy," Amanda called, gave their mother a hug, and left with the man who was apparently her father. Kristy felt heartbroken. Her mom looked at her and could tell.

"Kristy, what wrong?" her mother asked.

"Where is my father?" she gave voice to her sadness. Her mom gave her a look of pity. Kristy could tell that the news was not good.

"I don't know," her mom answered. "I didn't realize you even thought about him anymore. I guess with Bruce being such a great dad to Mandy, you feel left out."

"Yea," she didn't know how to answer. Her dad was the same dead-beat in this life as he was before. "I guess I was wishing he would show up and take me for a bike ride." Her mom came and gave her a big hug. *At least I have you,* Kristy thought.

"I don't know why your dad didn't claim you," her mom expressed kindly, "but he's really missing out." Kristy smiled at her mom and gave her another hug. A knock at the door pulled them apart. "I wonder who that is?" her mom questioned as she headed towards the door. She opened it to find Phoebe's mom who was quite distressed.

"Sophia, what is the matter?" her mom asked as she quickly pulled her friend into the room and escorted her to a chair.

"I cannot find Phoebe anywhere," Ms. Holland cried. "She never showed up yesterday and no one has seen her!" Both her mom and Ms. Holland looked to her for help. *I don't know what to tell them!*

"I haven't seen her since the festival," Kristy lied.

"Is that where you met the Jewish boy?" her mom questioned her and she nodded.

"Do you know who she was hanging around with?" Ms. Holland asked frantically. "She never stays out for this long."

"I really don't know." Kristy answered. How could she tell them that she left Phoebe behind in ancient Rome? *Maybe there is another Phoebe in this world.*

"Did you check with the healing circle?" her mom asked.

"Yes, nobody there has seen her either," Ms. Holland replied. "I guess I need to report this."

"I'll come with you, Sophia," her mom kindly offered. "Those legionnaires can be tough to deal with. Be back soon, Kristy." The two lady's rose and left, leaving Kristy alone. *So much for a wonderful day with my family.*

Kristy made herself some eggs and sat in the cozy window seat to eat. The incredible view lifted Kristy's spirits. The riverside was bustling with activity. Drummers were setting up as children played tag among the trees. Colorful boats filled the river and several teens were diving into the water off the docks. The day was so bright and inviting, Kristy decided it was time to go outside. *This looks like a great place to explore.*

She left her room and made her way down the long hall to the huge set of stairs. The view from the top was beautiful. She was looking into a huge two story marble room filled with century's worth of the fine artwork. *I could spend all day in here*, she thought. She still wanted to go down to the river first, so she headed towards the west door.

Outside, a light breeze ruffled her hair. Kristy took a deep breath and felt refreshed by its coolness. The drummers began to play down by the river so she headed in that direction, feeling their rhythm flow through her. She noticed that much of the food was gone, stored away for the winter, she supposed.

Kristy was surprised when several of the dancers called her name and waved. She waved back even though she didn't recognize them. She casually turned away from them, taking a stone path which followed along the riverbank. *It's weird to have strangers recognize me as if we were friends. Everyone thinks that I belong here, but I really don't.*

She thought about what it would have been like to grow up in this community. *It would have been wonderful.* Antonio had mentioned that her district didn't have to attend school like others did. *I would have spent a lot of time out here by the river. These kids would probably be my friends. Phoebe would love it also,* her thoughts turned towards her missing friend. *This is the same river we played near as kids, just better cared for.*

What if something had happened to the Phoebe of this world? It seems like we're still close in this place, like we used to be when we were young. Kristy sat on a large stone near the bank and wondered which Phoebe they were looking for. The pleasant breeze and the murmur of the water helped to calm her thoughts. *I'll find out soon enough. Everything's already so mixed up and muddled.*

She stayed by the water for a while, enjoying the view and the day. *This is the first time I have felt so relaxed in a long while.* Kristy's thoughts were interrupted by her mother's voice calling for her. She rose and looked around, spotting her mom heading her way.

"I knew I would find you out here," Her mom gasped, out of breath from running. "You need to come with me quickly." She took her mom's offered hand and found herself being pulled into a quick jog.

"What's wrong?" Kristy asked feeling panic rise within herself again. "Did something happen to Phoebe?"

"She is still missing," her mom panted. "When Sophia listed you as Phoebe's friend, the computer cross referenced your name to a complaint made this morning against you. The legionnaires think it might be linked to Phoebe's disappearance." Her mom stop for a moment to catch her breath. "They were going to send men after you but I promised to bring you in. They ordered you to appear in one hour and the times half up. Kristy, do you know anything?"

"No, mom, I don't," Kristy puffed felling winded and fearful. *A Roman legionnaire had ordered her to be brought in. I thought I was done with the Romans!* Kristy knew she would never hold up against any interrogation.

"OK, we better get going," her mom declared and they began to run, leaving behind the joy of the Serpent District. Kristy didn't recognize any of the area they sped through and she really didn't care. Her mind was in turmoil, wondering what story she should give to the legionnaires. *The truth will get me locked up for sure!*

Chapter 36

"We all go a little mad sometimes"

Alfred Hitchcock

Chris watched as Miriam rushed about the kitchen. She had decided to make a celebration feast to honor today's success. Domitius and Aria had brought the last pieces to the store and together they all assembled the first four bikes. They had a great time riding around in the store. He loved to see Miriam so happy. *She has such a beautiful smile.*

During their fun, Miriam had the fun idea for the celebration feast tonight. His blacksmith friends said they would love to come. Domitius was also going to pass an invitation to the leatherworker who had created the tires, seats and handle grips for them. *I have a few things I want to talk to him about. It will be nice for us all to just relax together. Maybe Jaxom will calm down enough to enjoy himself.*

Miriam moved gracefully around the room. She was kneading dough for bread and cooking a huge pot of something that smelled wonderful. *She's beautiful, smart and talented. I really love this slave girl.* He wanted to help her cook, but Chris was afraid he would mess something up. So instead he watched as she tenderly folded the dough and formed the loaves. Then lots of noise in the front of the house pulled at his attention.

"I'll see who here?" Chris announced and heading to the front room. There he was surprised to find Cinnamon and his troop of entertainers. Chris was delighted to see the musician again and gave Cinnamon a friendly hug.

"I didn't know you were coming into Rome so soon," Chris exclaimed to his new friend. "The tournament isn't for a couple weeks." He noticed the troupe was burdened by piles of luggage and realized they must have just arrived.

"We need time for practice, my boy," Cinnamon announced, "and we had to see your new accommodations. Very nice for a newcomer. Plenty of space." Chris smiled as he caught the hint.

"Would you like to stay with us while you're in town?" Chris offered. "There's room for everyone." The performers all cheered and thank him. As he found rooms for his guests, Chris and Cinnamon chatted about the upcoming performances. "Have you figured out all you're routines for halftime yet?"

"We have chosen all our pieces," Cinnamon informed him, "but I need your help with our dance numbers."

"Sure, I can give suggestions and maybe even teach you a thing or two," he joked with the star. Cinnamon laughed and clasped his shoulders.

"No, Chris," Cinnamon corrected him. "I need you to perform with us."

Chris felt surprised and trilled by the offer. *What an awesome opportunity-to perform before all of Rome!*

"I would love to," he replied filled with excitement, "but don't tell Marcus and Jaxom. It will be a great surprise." *And I don't have to hear any complaints about the idea if I keep it secret,* he thought.

Chris left his friends to unpack and hurried to tell Miriam about the visitors. As always, she smiled and responded sweetly over the news but Chris noticed the strain in her eyes. As she rushed to prepare more food, Chris realized the extra work he had laid on her shoulders. *Why should she always have to cook for everyone?*

"Can I help with anything," he offered. This time he received a real smile, one that made Chris melt into a smirking idiot.

"If you would put the bread in the oven, I'll see what else we can make for your feast," Miriam responded happily. He did as she asked and then remained in the kitchen to help, letting her order him around for a while. Chris was having a wonderful time assisting Miriam when Marcus showed up.

"Chris, did you just tell sixteen performers they could stay for the next two weeks?" his best friend asked.

"Yea, it's Cinnamon's troop from Baiae," Chris answered as he continued to chop a bundle of leeks for Miriam. "They needed a place to stay while their rehearsing."

"Jaxom's not too happy about this," Marcus informed him. "You really should have talked to us first."

"It was a spontaneous kind of thing," Chris shrugged, "and Jaxom's not happy about anything lately. Do you have a problem with our friends staying?" He turned to look at Marcus. Marcus sighed and shook his head.

"No, it's fine," Marcus consented. "We've got plenty of space, but you need to talk to Jaxom. You two hardly even speak to each other anymore." Chris hadn't told Marcus about the argument in Baiae. *It would just cause more tension.*

"Don't worry, I'll talk to him," Chris promised. *Sometime next year.*

"What are you to doing back here?" boomed Domitius's voice as he and Aria entered the kitchen. "You have a houseful of guests looking for you."

"I was helping Miriam with the food," Chris answered returning to his task.

"I'll help finish in here," Aria offered. Then she took the knife from Chris and shooed them out of the kitchen. As they entered the front room, Chris spied Jaxom across the room in conversation with several dancers. When

Jaxom saw him, he rolled his eyes and looked away. *Now's probably not a great time to bug him.*

It wasn't long until dinner was ready. Chris spent the time conversing with his many guests and keeping a safe distance from Jaxom. As everyone headed towards the dining room, Domitius approached him with another visitor.

"Chris, let me introduce you to Verrius," Domitius presented his friend.

"Oh, our leatherworker," Chris remembered shaking the man's hand. "It's great to meet you. You did a fantastic job on the bike parts."

"I am excited to see the final product," Verrius responded as they followed the crowd towards the food. "Usually I work on saddles, so this has been an exciting change for me." Miriam had produced an incredible feast as always and everyone crowded the buffet table to fill their plates.

"I have some other ideas I wanted to talk to you about," Chris commented to the leatherworker as he filled his plate. "It's some improvement to the saddles and harnesses you make."

"This man is a genius with his ideas," Domitius boasted. Verrius seemed intrigued as they found an empty couch and settled themselves down to eat. Miriam brought him a wine flask and Chris gave her a kiss on the hand as a thank you. She smiled and blushed beautifully, as she always did. He watched as she circulated through the room filling empty wine glasses. *She is so graceful.* As she left to refill the buffet table he turned back to the craftsmen.

"I've drawn this out for you," Chris told Verrius as he pulled a folded paper from his jeans pocket. "These are called stirrups and they will make it a lot easier to stay in the saddle." He unfolded the paper and handed it to the leatherworker. Verrius smiled brightly over the idea.

"This is intriguing," Verrius commented. "I am interested if you want to produce a few. Where did you come up with this?"

"They use those back home," Marcus informed them. Chris grinned at his best friend who was sitting across from them. "Chris isn't much of a rider. He needs all the help he can get staying in the saddle."

"I rode all the way from Caesar's country house to Rome without falling," Chris argued back, then laughed. "I don't know how I made it though. This other one is called a trace harness. It allows your horses to breath while their pulling. You'll get more horsepower out of your horses," Chris joked. Marcus chuckled, the only one who got the joke.

"Where are you guys from?" Verrius asked.

"North America," Chris stated. Marcus gave him a look and Chris nodded back. He knew better than to talk about time travel.

"Where is North America?" Cinnamon questioned. All eyes in the room had turned towards him.

"It's far across the ocean to the west," Chris told his interested guests. "No one from Rome has made it there yet."

"Then how do you know the Dictator?" one of the dancers asked. *That's a tougher question to answer*, Chris thought.

"When we arrived, we heard of the assassination plot and informed Julius Caesar," Marcus answered for him. "He was so grateful, that he gave us the house."

"He probably has other plans for you," Domitius warned them. "Julius Caesar knows how to take advantage of every situation. "

"That's why he's our Dictator," someone across the room commented. As, Chris looked toward the voice he noticed Jaxom heading his way.

"Chris, Marcus, I need to speak with you in private," Jaxom called out. Chris noticed the tension building in Jaxom's eyes as he rose from his seat. *He's looks disagreeable.*

"We'll be right back," Chris told their guests and followed Jaxom and Marcus into the kitchen.

"What are you two doing?" Jaxom crossly asked them.

"We're trying to relax with our friend," Chris irritably answered. "Why can't you do the same?"

"You're telling them way too much," Jaxom snapped back. "Do you know what they could do with that trace harness?"

"Not have to exploit Egypt," Marcus offered. Jaxom glared at him for a moment then looked back to Chris.

"How do you even know what a trace harness is?" Jaxom questioned.

"We looked it up in our textbooks," Chris admitted.

"Don't you realize that better harnesses and stirrups will give them an even greater advantage against everyone their conquering?" Jaxom barked. "No one here should even know about America for over a thousand years and I had to stop you before you told them about the magic."

"We weren't going to say anything about the ring," Marcus stated trying to stay calm. Chris didn't want to stay calm. He was sick of Jaxom bad-tempered attitude.

"What is wrong with you?" Chris yelled at Jaxom. "You were fine with us saving Caesar. That was a lot bigger than some stirrups."

"Remember what Phoebe said about making changes to the future," Jaxom griped back. "We've changed too much!"

"Is this about your liking Phoebe?" Marcus asked. Chris was shocked by his friend's question. Jaxom didn't answer the question but Chris could tell by Jaxom's expression that it was true.

"If you have it that bad for Phoebe," Chris growled, "take it up with her instead of taking it out on us."

"She's in Egypt and the last thing I did was yell at her," Jaxom admitted. Chris noticed Miriam standing in the doorway, trying to get his attention. Chris beckoned to her to join him.

"Caesar sends messages to Cleopatra all the time," Marcus mentioned. Miriam seemed agitated and Chris wondered how much of the conversation she had heard. *I didn't mean to stress her out.* But what she had to say was much worse.

"Everyone can hear you," Miriam revealed to Chris and his friends.

"Did they here about the ring?" Jaxom asked frantically.

"I didn't hear the ring mentioned," Miriam answered, "but I heard you mention the magic."

Chapter 37

*"I love the things you say and do. I can't
get over how much I love you"*
Paul McCartney

Egypt is incredible!   Phoebe loved the ancient architecture and sculptures of the region. She really loved the people of Egypt. They were friendly and intelligent and Phoebe was being treated like a royal guest. *I could get used to this life.*

The day they arrived had been a celebration like she had never seen. Crowds filled the streets to welcome home their Pharaoh. The Egyptians had danced to wild upbeat music and sang praises to Cleopatra. Phoebe had accompanied the Pharaoh as she was carried through each district to hear the cheers of her adoring people. Phoebe had noticed the party did not extend much into the Greek district. The smaller crowds simply wave them a greeting. *I wonder if that is because of the trouble with her brother or something to do with her relationship to Julius.*

Cleopatra's palace in Alexandria was unbelievably huge and the most exquisite place she had ever seen. It was also filled with more flowers and cats then she had seen in her entire life. But what amazed her the most was the level of technological and scientific advancement the citizens of Alexandria possessed.

The first technology to amaze Phoebe upon her arrival in Egypt was the presence of electricity. Apparently, Egyptians had developed electric batteries centuries before. Phoebe had seen clay examples small enough to fit in her hand as well as the huge hydroelectric generators which powered the palace. These operated electric doors, warmed the bath water and gave light to every room. Phoebe was baffled at why the modern world didn't know about this. She had asked the Queen about them, but was told it was a National secret that could not be discussed with outsiders. *That only partially explains the loss of knowledge.*

She had spent a great deal of time in the Royal library explaining movable type to the brilliant scholars who managed the place. *If I can share my secrets, they should be happy to share theirs*, Phoebe had thought at the time. It took the Egyptian scholars less than a week to have a working printer. *This is a change for the better*, Phoebe had decided. *Printed books will allow knowledge to spread faster throughout the world, giving everyone the chance to learn.*

Today she was visiting Alexandria's Museum for the first time. Her guide, Imhotep, had given her a tour through the zoological and botanical gardens this morning. After a quick lunch in the dining hall, he guided her towards the laboratories and observatory. As Phoebe followed her guide around a corner, she was stunned by a huge mural on the wall before her. A solar system almost as accurate as what she studied back home covered the entire wall. All eight planets with an asteroid belt separating the outer and inner planets was portrayed, arranged in elliptical orbit around the sun. *Amazing!*

"I didn't realize you knew the solar system," Phoebe gasped.

"This was done several generations ago by Hipparchus of Nicea," Imhotep informed her. "Every great scholar from each generation studies here at the Museum."

"I've heard of him," Phoebe recalled, "I read he studied the stars."

"He was an incredible astronomer," her guide praised. "Hipparchus created many of the star maps which our students still use."

"How many students are here at the Museum?" Phoebe questioned.

"There are currently over 14,000 students here," Imhotep told her. "Another 3,000 students are involved in religious studies at the Serapeum. Come and I will show you our chemistry labs." Phoebe followed her guide, amazed that this ancient Museum felt so much like a modern college. She spent much of the day being overwhelmed by the sophistication of these ancient scholars.

When the tour was complete, Phoebe was escorted back to the Royal Palace by several Eunuchs. She was shown to the royal dining hall, where she found Cleopatra waiting for her. Little Caesarion was playing on the floor. When he saw Phoebe, he jumped up and ran to her.

"Phoebe, you're back," the young prince cheered. Phoebe scooped the sweet boy into her arms and settled in the seat beside his mother. Phoebe had really grown to love the little prince. He stood up on her lap to pet the Egyptian Meow perched on the back of her chair. "Roar is happy you're back too," Caesarion told her. Phoebe gave the cat a quick stroke wondering how the boy could tell which feline it was. *All these cats look exactly the same.*

"How was your tour?" the Queen asked as a score of Eunuchs brought out trays piled high with more food than the three of them could ever eat.

"Amazing!" Phoebe declared. "Egypt is much more advanced then I was taught."

"I knew you would be impressed," Cleopatra boasted. "Did you find your way back easily?"

"This place is so huge, I usually can't find my room," Phoebe laughed. As they chatted she shared her bites of fish with Caesarion and he in turn fed most of it to the cats. "Some of the Eunuchs escorted me back."

"Ironically, they are the reason the palace is so large," Cleopatra chuckled. "We keep having to add space for their growing numbers."

"Why do you need so many?" Phoebe questioned. She had not brought up the subject yet for fear of offending her host.

"No one who wishes to serve is ever turned away," the Pharaoh explained.

"Do you mean they choose this life?" Phoebe asked perplexed.

"Of course," Cleopatra replied. "They each chose to dedicate their lives to the service of Mother Isis." Phoebe found herself relieved to hear this. Religious devotees was much better then mutilated slaves. *I still think it's creepy*, Phoebe thought.

"A ship arrived from Rome today," Cleopatra casually mentioned. "Julius sent news of your friends." Phoebe reminded herself to breath. She had spent weeks pushing down her regrets over how she left. Jaxom's tearful confession and fiery anger felt as if they were wrapped around her heart. *I don't want the Queen to know that part of me wishes that I never left Rome.*

"What did he say?" Phoebe asked trying to seem calm.

"Julius mentioned them several times," Cleopatra answered, pulling out a long scroll. "First he mentions their help in his Gladiatorball tournament. He then speaks of expecting great success from Chris's business venture. He also says that Jaxom was cooperative in gaining advantage in the Parthian War."

"That sounds like a wish," Phoebe point out and the Pharaoh nodded. Phoebe thought about the way Jaxom jumps into things without thinking. *How could he think it's alright to help Caesar with his military conquests?*

"Maybe he will tell you," Cleopatra said as she pulled out another scroll. "A letter was included for you." Phoebe couldn't keep her shock from showing. She accepted the scroll and the Pharaoh took her child from Phoebe's lap. "We will leave you to your reading."

For a few minutes after Cleopatra left, Phoebe just stared at the letter in her hand. She had longed to know what Jaxom was thinking. It was wrapped with a thin purple cord and on the side of the scroll her name was scribbled. Phoebe recognized Jaxom's messy handwriting. She took three deep breaths and untied the cord. Several dry lavender blossoms fell into her lap from the scroll as she unrolled it. Phoebe picked them up and breathed in deep their calming fragrance as she began to read.

Dear Phoebe,

Marcus told me that Caesar was sending letters to Cleopatra, so I decided to write to you. I don't write many letters so I'm sorry if it's not a very good one. What I'm really sorry about is what I said to you the last time we spoke. I know what you said was an accident and I overreacted. I tend to do that sometimes. Your passion to right all wrongs is beautiful and you did make things better for a lot of Romans with your slip-up.

I hope you come back soon. I need your help with Chris and Marcus. They're acting like we're here to stay and I don't want that. I miss our real life back in the modern world. I feel like things could be better between us when we get back home. I miss you, but I hope you're having a good time in Egypt. I kind of wish I was there with you instead of here in Rome. I hope you like the lavender. I remembered you saying you loved it so I sent some for you. Please come back to us soon so we can go home.

Truly, Jaxom

Phoebe smiled with joyful excitement. Jaxom missed her and needed her. She tenderly caressed the lavender sprigs. Cleopatra's palace was filled with lovely blooms, but nothing else had ever smelled so wonderful. *I need to go back!* She jumped up and hurried into the hallway.

"Where is the Pharaoh?" she called to a passing eunuch.

"She is in the Prince's chambers," he informed her. Phoebe rushed down the hallway towards Caesarion's room. She knew the way since the boy always wanted her to come play after dinnertime. She found Cleopatra helping Caesarion change for bed.

"Did you receive good news?" the Queen asked when she saw Phoebe enter.

"He says that he misses me and needs my help," Phoebe revealed, "and he says my passion is beautiful."

"See, I knew that young man loves you," Cleopatra stated, losing Caesarian to the cats again.

"I need to get back to Rome," Phoebe declared to her Pharaoh friend. "Can you grant me passage on one of your ships?"

"I shall also be returning with you," Cleopatra told her. "I have entered a team into this tournament our men have concocted. We will leave for Rome tomorrow."

"Can Kitty come too, mama?" Caesarion questioned as he snuggled another of his furry friends.

"No, my child," Cleopatra answered as she slipped his night shirt over his head. "Remember Julius does not appreciate our feline friends."

"He's scared of them," the little boy laughed. Phoebe laughed with the prince as her heart soared. She would be with Jaxom again soon and they could finally return home.

Chapter 38

"Love means never having to say you're sorry"
Erich Segal

Jaxom sat in the garden chewing on a chive. It was a beautiful spring morning and he kept feeling drawn out the back door into the lovely space. The extensive grounds of their new home was marvelously cultivated. Miriam and Chris had been harvesting all kinds of food from the property, providing them with great meals. What Jaxom loved most though, was the peace he could find among the flowers and herbs. *There's been too much chaos with all these people staying here.*

Jaxom felt better about things in ancient Rome. He had apologized to Chris for being so cross. Chris promised in return to be careful about changing things. They weren't speaking much but at least they weren't fighting. Actually, Chris was hardly ever around. Since Jaxom revealed his magic to a houseful of people, he didn't feel so angry at Chris anymore.

Their new friends had been really cool about the fight, not mentioning it at all. It had actually been kind of fun having all these entertainers staying with them. There was always someone around singing and dancing. The music was different, but Jaxom was impressed at how talented Cinnamon and his group were.

Writing to Phoebe had been a great idea. He received news last night that Cleopatra's ship had arrived in Ostia, the port where the Tiber River meets the Mediterranean. Jaxom felt both excited and nervous that they would be arriving sometime today. *I hope she received my letter. Does Phoebe know how much I care about her?*

Phoebe was showing up just in time for the tournament. In a few hours, the first teams would take the field. Jaxom hoped the regulations worked out. *I really didn't pay much attention to what Marcus and Mark Anthony were deciding.* He knew that he wasn't thrilled about the players having weapons, but it should be less gory then the gladiator games that the Romans normally watched. *I hope it's not a bloody massacre in the field.*

"Jaxom, you ready yet?" Marcus called from the house. "Chris already left and I want good seats."

"Caesar said he would reserve us a space," Jaxom called to his friend as he got up. He headed into the house and found his friend in the kitchen. "We still have time. I was hoping Phoebe would show up."

"She'll find us at the tournament if she does," Marcus answered him. "I've got our tickets. Let's go."

"Alright," Jaxom agreed. The two headed out of the house and around Palatine Hill. The streets were crowded and Jaxom overheard animated conversations about the upcoming game. It seemed that everyone in Rome was excited about game but more so about the monumental elections taking place simultaneously. This was the first Roman election where womyn could vote as well as run for office.

The street heading down to the Circus Maximus was packed. Jaxom was glad they left early for it took a while to make their way into the tournament arena. Julius Caesar had ordered the construction of the Gladiatorball field in the center of the Circus Maximus. Jaxom looked around at the sports grounds and was impressed. *It looks like a real field. Just a little too long and a bit too skinny.*

He followed Marcus through the crowd. They were heading toward a shaded wooden pavilion elevated a little above the rest of the spectators. Upon this dais, Julius Caesar and the Consul sat on display. The aristocrats of Rome were finding their seats around this area as well. Mounted on the front of the pavilion was a strange looking contraption. As they got closer, Jaxom realized it was a water clock. *Interesting way to keep time.*

Jaxom spotted Chris and Miriam. They were situated near the Senators, looking out of place amongst all the white togas. As they headed towards Chris, Jaxom was glad to see two empty spaces waiting for them. *But what if Phoebe shows up?*

"Isn't the Circus Maximus amazing?" Chris cheered as they arrived. Marcus took the seat next to Chris so Jaxom took the remainder.

"Yea, Julius Caesar did an awesome job setting everything up," Marcus praised the Dictator.

"I doubt he was doing the work," Jaxom commented as he took a closer look at the field. It was definitely longer and skinnier then back home. It looked like the floor had been covered with dirt then topped with grass seed. Lines were drawn across a fine layer of young grass poked its way through the loam. *That's gonna get torn up quickly*, Jaxom thought. A scoreboard was set up across the field from them. At each end of the field golden goal posts had been erected and behind them wooden buildings had been constructed. *Those must be locker rooms.*

"Why is the field shaped like that?" Jaxom had to ask.

"There isn't room to make it any wider," Marcus answered, "and Romans don't measure things in yards. They use the pes which is a just little shorter than a foot so I had to work with that."

"Wouldn't that make the field a little shorter," Chris commented.

"Yea, but I didn't want to go shorter, so I made a yard four pes instead of three," Marcus revealed. Chris chuckled over Marcus' maneuvering of facts, but Jaxom just saw it as another change. *We're messing too much with history.*

Jaxom jumped as the loud ring of chimes suddenly echoed throughout the stadium. The startled fans grew silent and quickly took their seats. He looked up at the podium and saw Calpurnia striking a hanging set of metal pipes set up near her chair. Jaxom gave Marcus a stern look.

"That was Chris's idea," Marcus pointed to his friend.

"It's a great way to get everyone's attention," Chris commented. "Now be quiet." Jaxom's aggravation with his friends was overshadowed by the excitement of the game. *I won't let it spoil my day.* He watched as Julius Caesar rose to address the eager crowd.

"I welcome you, citizens and friends of Rome, to the first ever Gladiatorball Tournament," the Dictator called out. The crowd began to cheer, but quieted as the Julius Caesar held up his hand. "Fourteen teams are here in our great city to compete for a chance to triumph in the end. Only one team will stand victorious. The champions will receive the grand prize of 500 Denarii each as well as our championship trophy." Next to Julius Caesar, Mark Anthony held up an incredible golden trophy. "Our first two competitors will be the Palatine Wolves and the Ostia StingRays. *That's where Phoebe's traveling from,* Jaxom thoughts wandered back to his heart as the crowd applauded.

From the end zones, the two teams ran onto the field. Both were clad in lightweight armor and each player carried their weapons with them. Numbered on their backs as well as their shields, the Palatine Wolves were dressed in Silver and black while the StingRays wore all blue. The crowd cheered wildly for the players who quickly took their places on either side of the field. Jaxom glanced back at the podium and noticed Julius Caesar had returned to his golden chair. Mark Anthony and Claudia Metelli rose to address the crowd.

"Welcome to game one of our tournament," Claudia Metelli began. "A coin toss has determined that the Ostia StingRays will be receiving the kickoff. May Fortuna shine on those most worthy!"

"As the players ran into position, Jaxom wondered at how well the announcers could be heard. Their voices seemed to be amplified and as he looked at the Consuls he noticed the flared roof above them had been fashioned with acoustical understanding in mind.

"Kicking for the Wolves will be #5 Cornelius Porcius," Clodia announced. Calpurnia rang the chimes and the game began. The punt went left but long and a StingRay dived to catch it on the thirty yard line. Two referees dressed in black and white signaled the ball was dead. *Marcus really thought of everything.* The chimes rang ended the play before the two lines even touched swords.

"Throwing for the StingRays will be #17, Maximus Aetius," Mark Anthony declared. Jaxom felt every nerve tense as the offense and defense slammed into each other on the next play. But these men were experts and while their metal rang loud throughout the stadium, not a player was hurt. *These men aren't out for blood*, Jaxom realized with relief. The StingRay's quarterback connected to # 26 at the thirty-seven and ran another ten yards before being forced out of bounds by #20 of the Wolves. *This feels like being at a game back home*, Jaxom thought as the stress began to drain out of him.

"That was #26, Atilius Paula of the StingRay's advancing the ball seventeen yards," Mark Anthony revealed. Jaxom noticed the Consul's each held scrolls listing the teams information. *They need to make copies for everyone else too.*

On the next play, the pass went wide and was missed. The crowd groaned beginning to get into the game. The StingRays then tried to run the ball but only gained three yards.

"Third down and seven yards remaining," Mark Anthony declared. Maximus Aetius tried another pass but the ball caught the edge of a raised shield and ricocheted to the right. A Wolf defender snatched the ball out of the air and ran towards his end zone.

"Interception by # 35, Quintus Marcellus of the Palatine Wolves," Clodia yelled, "and touchdown!" The Roman fans went wild in the stands as the player ran into the end zone to score. Jaxom jumped up to cheer, caught up in the excitement with everyone else. "Six points for the Wolves who now will attempt an extra point." Cornelius Porcius sailed the ball straight through the goal post and the crowd cheered madly again.

"That guy's was a great find," Marcus commented as Roman numerals were added to the scoreboard.

"Yea, I met him the other day," Chris said. "He's actually a pig farmer."

"When did you get to meet the players?" Marcus asked his best friend.

"I was in here with Cinnamon," Chris answered. "Look the kicking teams back." As they turned their attention back to the game, Jaxom had wondered about Chris's activities. He was always out with Miriam. *At least it kept us away from each other. This love affair may help keep him out of trouble.*

This time an Ostia StingRay caught the punt and ran it back for fifteen yards. Their Quarterback connected twice in a row moving them to their twenty yard line. Then a missed throw and blocked run put the StingRays at third and nine. Maximus Aetius threw a quick pass to the left, but the ball sailed passed Atillius Paula and out of bounds.

The chimes rang out higher and longer and as Jaxom turned he understood the change. Calpurnia was signaling a timeout for on the field laid a StingRay bleeding profusely from a leg wound. Team mates grabbed the injured player and carried him off the field. Jaxom grimaced at the sight but remembered seeing bad injuries at games back home. *There's usually not so much blood.*

The StingRays succeeded in kicked a field goal making the score VII to III. Jaxom brushed aside his worry for the injured player as the StingRay kicked to the Wolves giving the Palatine offense its first chance on the field.

"Throwing for the Palatine Wolves will be #14, Marius Nerva," Clodia announced to the crowd. The teams lined up and clashed together. The quarterback handed the ball to #31 who found a hole and ran for twelve yards before being flattened by a huge StingRay.

"#31, Otho Longinus with a gain of twelve," Clodia declared for the cheering crowd. The Wolves repeated the run on the other side and made a gain of eight. A long bomb to a wide open receiver and the Wolves were in the end zone again.

"Touchdown by #22, Germanus Septimus," Clodia proclaimed. Another perfect kick and the Wolves extended their lead XIV to III.

"The Wolves got this game," Marcus uttered then turned to Chris. "If you've been here before, do you know where the bathrooms are?"

"That's almost it for the first quarter. I'd like to find something to drink," Jaxom expressed feeling the discomfort of the stone bench. He needed to move around a bit.

"Follow me," Chris said as he and Miriam started through the crowd towards the entrance. They found bathrooms at the entrance and food vendors just outside. Jaxom lost track of the others while he bought himself a drink. It took forever to make his way through the crowds but when he heard the fans shouting their approval, he pushed through to see what he had missed. He arrived in time to see the Wolves kick another extra point. XXI to III, *what a lead!*

"Where's Chris?" Jaxom asked Marcus when he made it back to his seat and noticed Miriam sitting alone.

"He said he had something to do," Marcus answered. "Can you believe the Wolves scored again? I wish there was an instant replay we could watch."

"I guess Chris couldn't figure that one out for them," Jaxom said sarcastically.

"Give him a break," Marcus scolded him. "He promised you he wouldn't give them anything else."

"I was joking," Jaxom protested and turned back to the game. The two minute warning had stopped the clock and the StingRays offense was lining up on their thirty-six. *I missed most of the second quarter,* Jaxom grumbled to himself. A perfect pass to # 24 brought the StingRays to the twenty-eight. *They might make it this time.*

Maximus Aetius threw for a short four yard gain. On the next snap, the StingRay Quarterback dropped back for a pass but couldn't find an open receiver. A Defensive end broke through the line tackling Maximus Aetius on the thirty-five yard line. The stands roared with a mixture of cheers and groans. *I guess the fans are choosing sides*, Jaxom thought.

"With a loss of eleven, the StingRays are now third and seven," Mark Anthony announced. On the next snap as Maximus Aetius surveyed the field, Atillus Paula shot past the defenders into the open. The Quarterback lobbed the ball high into the air. *There's no way!* The receiver sprinted for the ball, snatching it out of the air on the two. As he ran it in, the crowd screamed wildly.

"How could inexperienced players connect so easily?" Jaxom questioned aloud, amazed by the catch.

"They're fishermen," Miriam unexpectedly answered him. "They toss fish all the time." *What kind of explanation is that?* The extra point was too wide and the score was adjusted XXI to IX. With only a few seconds left on the clock, the StingRays punted the ball and the Wolves let it bounce out of bounds.

The chimes sounded ending the first half. As soon as the players cleared the field, wooden platforms were brought on, fitting together to create a huge stage. *Now we can see what Cinnamon has come up with*, Jaxom thought. *But where is Chris?*

"Where is Chris?" Marcus echoed Jaxom's thoughts aloud.

"He'll be back soon," Miriam said, not really answering the question. Huge drums began to sound from the field as the halftime performance began. *Why would Chris miss the show? He's been so into Cinnamon and his group.* Jaxom felt suspicion tug at his mind.

"Fire, fire, burning bright," began Cinnamon's lady vocalists. Gymnasts flipped across the stage between them. That's when he saw Chris, bare chested and crimson red pants to match the other tumblers. Jaxom turned to Marcus who seemed amused by Chris's performance.

"I didn't know," Marcus shrugged, "but look at him. He's really good." Jaxom watched as Chris did a back handspring in time to the music. Jaxom had to agree that Chris was talented. *It doesn't really change anything if he performs.*

Then Jaxom felt himself go numb as colorful explosives flamed up on either side to the stage. The fans roared with approval of the display but Jaxom fumed with anger. *The Romans don't have pyrotechnics!* Looking at Marcus, Jaxom could tell his friend was just as surprised. He turned back to watch as Chris danced to the fire song, wishing he could somehow stop the performance. *It's too late*, he thought as he rose and pushed his way through the crowd. He wanted to get away from all of this, including his own thoughts over what Rome would do with this dangerous new gift.

When Jaxom finally got away from the crowds he began to run, charging up the side of Palatine Hill. He tried to let the stress drain from him as he ran, but still felt horrible when he arrive at the house. An Egyptian carriage pulling away from the front door caused his pounding heart to skip a beat. He rushed inside to find Phoebe.

"Jaxom, what wrong?" Phoebe asked looking worried over the sight of him. She was standing in the front room surrounded by luggage. *Exactly who I needed to talk to!*

"Everything," he panted trying to catch his breath. "You won't believe... what Chris has done now.., that stupid fool. He's freely giving them everything... he can think of and I'm being forced to help. I hate this ring!" Jaxom glared at the ring circling his finger for a moment. Then he looked back to Phoebe. "I missed you so much. I'm so sorry about our fight. I need you here with me." Without thinking, Jaxom grabbed Phoebe and wrapped her in a tight embrace. . "I'm so glad your back!" He needed her comfort and help to figure everything out. To his relief, Phoebe hugged him back.

"You don't have to say you're sorry," she whispered in his ear. "I'm glad to be back." Locking eyes for one moment, Jaxom felt a rush of emotion for this beautiful womon. Then to his surprise and pleasure, Phoebe leaned in and grazed his lips with the softest of kisses. For a moment, all other cares slipped away...

Chapter 39

"Courage is grace under pressure"
Ernest Hemingway

Benjamin leaned over his test and read the next question. *In what year did the Battle of Bornhohn occur? How should I know?* Benjamin remembered reading about this battle while studying last night. Some tiny island was wiped out by the Roman fleet sent to bring an end the Viking raids. He looked through the multiple choice answers. *It can't be 1525 since that's before the raids began, and 1709 is too close to the treaty with Erik the Red.* Benjamin chose one of the two remaining dates. *50/50 chance at least.* He was about to read the next question when Ms. Branson tapped Benjamin's shoulder.

"There are men here to speak with you," his teacher informed him. Benjamin looked towards the door and was shocked to see two Roman Legionnaires waiting. *Why would they need to talk to me,* Benjamin wondered as he rose and headed towards the men?

"Benjamin Ezra," the tall legionnaire asked. Benjamin nodded, too nervous to speak. "You are to come with us for questioning in the disappearance of Phoebe Holland."

"Yes, sir," Benjamin stammered. *Phoebe's in ancient Rome. Why would they be looking for her here?* Benjamin followed the guard out of the school house and towards the center of town. The second took position behind him as if they were afraid he would run. As they walked, he wondered why the guards were still wearing breastplates and leather lappets. *Shouldn't their uniforms have evolved in two thousand years?*

Tall stone building of the business district soon surrounded them. Benjamin speculated about where he was being taken and why. *Is this just for questioning or am I being incarcerated*? Benjamin wondered with concern. He was led towards a large stone fortress in the center of town.

Benjamin surveyed the stronghold as he was brought in and told to sit on a bench with several others. The room he was in looked like a modern military basecamp except for the tall stone walls and strange outfits. Rows of desks filled part of the room, most containing soldiers working on flat screen computers. The far end of the room held racks of weapons and a large table filled the remaining space where legionnaires stood deep in conversation. A row of closed wooden doors across the back wall blocked most of the fortress from his view.

Benjamin was surprised to see Kristy emerged from one of the doors, accompanied by her mom. She looked distressed and confused as she followed an officer his direction. Kristy was ordered to wait on the bench where he was sitting. *Maybe she knows what's going on.* He gave her an anxious smile but she didn't respond to the gesture. Instead she slumped onto the bench with a sigh.

"Hey Kristy," Benjamin called and he caught her distraught eyes. "What wrong?" She stared at him for an anxious moment before she answered.

"No one has seen Phoebe since you came to the harvest festival two nights ago," Kristy mumbled. "Do you remember meeting her that night while we were hanging out?"

"Yea, I think so," Benjamin responded unsure of what Kristy meant. He had known Phoebe for years, but maybe not in this reality. *She just gave me my alibi*, he realized.

"Benjamin," his father's voice rang out. *Of course they had to call him.* "I knew your inappropriate behavior would lead to more trouble. What accusations are these Serpent womyn making against you?"

"We haven't made any accusations against your son," Kristy's mom retorted. The two parent stood face to face for a moment.

"Mr. Ezra," called a legionnaire, and his father turned. "Your son has been called as witness to a missing person's report. Please follow me." The soldier gestured for him as well, so Benjamin reluctantly rose and trailed behind his father into the depths of the stronghold. They were escorted down a long dim hallway into a small square room. Chairs surrounded a table in the otherwise empty stone room. *Time to be interrogated,* Benjamin shuddered, trying to remember everything that Kristy had said.

The soldier indicated where they were to sit and left them alone. Benjamin settled into his chair and contemplated Kristy's words. *What was this harvest festival where I supposedly met Phoebe?* He had read that the Serpent district was where the Earth pagans lived. Thinking back to a show he had seen about Native Americans, Benjamin figured he knew enough it pretend to have been there. The real problem was his dad sitting beside him. *He's going to flip if I say I snuck out to some pagan party.*

Benjamin was still considering the dilemma when two officers entered and sat down across the table. Their red cloaks were trimmed in purple and they wore golden armor. His father seemed startled and straightened his spine like he was a soldier standing at attention. *These guys must be important.*

"Mr. Ezra, good to see you again," one of the officers stated, "though the circumstance of today's meeting is misfortunate."

"Centurion Lopez," his father responded, "it is an honor. I assure you that my son has no part in this business. Our family has always been honorable citizens of Rome."

"I am well aware of your respectable family history, but we must do a thorough investigation of every incident," the Centurion replied, then turned to

Benjamin. "I am 1st Centurion Brutus Lopez and this is 3rd Centurion Publius Rufus. You are here to give testimony over your whereabouts and actions on the evening of September 21st. You were seen that evening outside your own district. Tell us where you went."

"Yes sir," Benjamin answered. "I went to the Serpent district to see their celebration." Benjamin was careful to avoid his father's eye and looked straight at the head Centurion. *I'll deal with that problem later, after I get out of this one.*

"Did you attend the festival with anyone?" Centurion Lopez asked.

"No, I went by myself," Benjamin answered. He needed his story to match hers and she didn't say anything about the others.

"Who did you meet while at the festival?" the officer questioned.

"Lots of people," Benjamin lied. "The place was packed. I spent most of my time with Kristy, a girl I met there."

"We have spoken to a Kristy Clark whose testimony concurs," Centurion Lopez informed him of what he already knew. *But what is going on with Phoebe?* "What did you and Kristy do during the evening?"

"We danced and ate," Benjamin said knowing these were things everyone did at a party. "We just hung out with everyone."

"Do you recognize this girl?" Centurion Rufus asked as he placed a picture on the table.

"That's Kristy's friend, Phoebe," Benjamin answered. "She's the girl you are looking for. I met her at the festival but we didn't really spend much time with her."

"Do you know the names of anyone who Phoebe was with that evening?" Centurion Lopez questioned.

"No, I don't," Benjamin continued to lie. "I only remember her name because everyone keeps mentioning her. I hope you find her, but I really don't know anything."

"Where did you and Kristy spend the night?" the Centurion continued his questioning. That was something Kristy hadn't mentioned. *We were seen at the school together*, he remembered.

"It was very late when we left the festival and went to the school," Benjamin replied. "We wanted to get away from all the noise." The Centurions expression didn't change but something in about eyes did. Benjamin knew he had said something wrong.

"Which school are you referring to?" Centurion Lopez inquired. *Kristy didn't mention the school*, Benjamin realized.

"The history academy," Benjamin answered reluctantly.

"Did you go anywhere else between the festival and the school?" the Centurion asked.

"No," Benjamin responded. The head Centurion leaned back and studied him for a moment. *I don't think I convinced him of my innocence,* Benjamin thought trying to keep a straight face.

"Bring the other one in," Centurion Lopez ordered. Centurion Rufus jumped at the command and rushed from the room. Kristy and her mom appeared a few minutes later, ushered in quickly to the remaining chairs. Kristy glanced at him with such sad eyes, his heart felt heavy for her.

"It will be alright, Kristy," Benjamin tried to comfort her.

"You were not told to speak," Centurion Lopez snapped and then turned to Kristy. "Young lady, where did you spend the night of September 21st?"

"By the river," Kristy answered, directly contradicting his testimony.

"At any point that night did you leave your district?" he continued to question.

"No, I don't think so," Kristy responded looking uncertainly at Benjamin. The soldier looked at each of them, knowing he had caught them in a lie. *How do we get out of this?*

"How do you explain the inconsistencies in your testimonies?" Centurion Lopez asked looking straight at him.

"We did rest by the river for a while," Benjamin scrambled for an answer, "but we got up and left to get away from the noise. That's when we went to the school. Don't you remember Kristy?"

"I will ask the questions," the officer barked at him and again turned to Kristy. "Do you remember leaving your district that night?"

"Maybe we did," Kristy fumbled. "I don't remember when we went to the school." She looked as if she was about to cry. Centurion Lopez was obviously bothered by her unclear answer but stopped the interrogation. Both officers left to converse in the hallway. Benjamin wanted to say something to Kristy but was afraid he would cause more trouble. His father sat scowling next to him and he knew more trouble would come when they left. *Everything has just gotten worse and worse since Jaxom made that wish.*

"We don't have enough evidence to hold either of you," Centurion Lopez announced as he returned to the room, "but you are both under restriction until this case is resolved. You are to remain within your own district unless I send for you. Is that clear?" He and Kristy both quickly agreed and they all were escorted out of the stone fortress.

Kristy and her mom hurried towards waiting friends without even a word. Benjamin was sad to see her go. *If I can't leave my district then I will never see her.* His father turned and glared at him, interrupting his thoughts of Kristy.

"You have brought a great deal of trouble upon yourself," his father griped as they headed towards home. "Sneaking out to go to some Serpent party, messing around with one of those girls and now this trouble with the law. I hope you are ashamed of your actions." Benjamin felt his anger rise within chest, bringing him to a standstill. His father stopped and turned around to face him.

"No, you should be ashamed," Benjamin yelled. "You treated Kristy like you hated her, but she's kind and beautiful. I would be lucky to have a girl like her." He didn't care if he got in more trouble. Benjamin had to tell his dad how ridiculous his prejudices were at least once. "Why should it matter where she grew up, if I truly love her?!" His father's eyes flashed in anger, matching his own.

"You won't be feeling lucky for a long time," his father growled, "and you will marry who I choose." His father grabbed him by the arm and dragged him down the street. Benjamin stumbled to keep up, glad that he had at least stood up for Kristy. *I only wish I could have another chance with her.*

Chapter 40

"All the world's a stage, and all the men and women

merely players"

William Shakespeare

Marcus laid in bed unable to move. His head ached and he felt exhausted. After the games yesterday, he and Chris were invited to Clodia Metelli's estate for the wildest party he had ever attended. It turned out that Cinnamon and Clodia had been friends for years. The Consul's mansion at the top of the Palatine was packed with partyers and Marcus had danced and drank late into the night. *I wonder if anyone would notice if I stayed in bed today.*

Someone screaming forced Marcus to roll out of bed. *That sounds like Jaxom and Chris.* He grabbed a clean tunic and threw it over his head. Marcus wished his head would stop pounding as he headed towards the quarrel. Following the noise, he found everyone gathered in the dining room and Chris face to face in argument with Jaxom.

"It won't take them long to turn those pyrotechnics into weapons," Jaxom yelled.

"China had fireworks for centuries before guns were developed," Chris argued back. "Why can't you lighten up? Everyone else said the half-time shows were amazing!" Marcus dragged his aching head into the room and sat down beside Phoebe.

"Hey, good to see you, Marcus," Phoebe told him.

"You too," Marcus answered, "but my head is killing me. Can you two keep it down?" Chris turned, noticing Marcus for the first time."

"Sorry man," Chris apologized. "Miriam can fix your hangover." Miriam brought Marcus a cup of warm tea. He took a sip and grimaced. *That's really bitter.*

"It's gross, but you'll feel great in ten minutes," Chris informed him. So Marcus took another drink.

"You went way overboard with the explosives," Jaxom fussed, trying to resume the argument.

"What's done is done," Phoebe said and Jaxom deflated. "We need to decide where we go from here."

"Home!" Jaxom declared with less forcefulness as he sat down on the other side of Phoebe.

"Not yet," Chris argued. "I haven't even sold a bike yet, and I want to see how the tournament turns out. Don't you want to see it, Phoebe?" Miriam arriving with food, gazed in worried at Chris and Jaxom.

"I want to see who wins," Marcus added, already feeling a little better.

"I told Cleopatra that I would watch the Cobras play later today," Phoebe stated. "It's an all women team and they're up against the Greek Achilles. I'd like to see who wins, but I also don't want to stay here forever."

"None of us do," Marcus assured her. He turned the subject back to the games. "They're not the only all women team to play. Yesterday the Artemis Amazons played and won. They were awesome to watch."

"The kicker for the Sicilian Volcanos is a women," Chris commented, "and a few of their other players. Yesterday, they creamed the Baiae Pearls." Marcus noticed his best friend looked relaxed again, standing with his arms wrapped around Miriam. *He drops his stress so easily*, Marcus thought.

"Who else won yesterday?" Jaxom asked, still looking distressed.

"The Wolves beat the StingRays thirty-one to twelve," Marcus answered. "They were the highest scoring team. You should have watched the whole game."

"That means they'll be exempt from round two, if no other team beats their score," Chris explained. "The other winner was the Ravennian Wild Boars. They're from up North somewhere."

"After the tournament, we're all going home," Jaxom stated. Everyone looked at Chris.

"That's fine," Chris replied. "Just don't ruin what's left of our time with your issues."

"What are you all doing here," boomed the voice of Domitius. "You don't realize what you have missed." The big blacksmith rushed into the room straight to Chris. "After announcing the election results, Julius Caesar did the unthinkable. He declared slavery a crime against the Republic!" Chris grabbed Miriam and spun her around.

"That means you are free!" he cheered, and pulled her into a tight embrace. Miriam looked like she was in complete shock. *What if she doesn't want to stay with Chris*, Marcus thought with concern. Everyone congratulated Miriam on gaining her freedom. Her smile grew until she was beaming widely.

"I never thought I would be free," Miriam exclaimed. "I don't know what it feels like."

"It feels like choosing your own path," Phoebe stated giving Miriam a hug.

"What do you want to do right now," Chris asked her. "That's what we'll do." Miriam gazed into Chris's eyes with love. Marcus realized that Chris had really found his partner before she even spoke.

"I want to eat and then ride our bikes to the games, right after you kiss me," Miriam said smugly. So Chris did and everyone laughed as they filled plates with the fruit and bread that Miriam had prepared. They ate quickly and soon headed out towards the stadium.

Chris and Miriam rolled down the Palatine on their new bicycles and were quickly out of sight. *They won't have such an easy ride on the way home,* Marcus thought with a grin. When Marcus and the others reached the stadium they found Chris and Miriam waiting outside to show off the first Roman bike locks. Marcus wondered how he could ever make Chris leave. *He really loves her. Maybe we could take her home with us.*

The Circus Maximus was packed again and Marcus was surprised at the changes made since the prior afternoon. Julius Caesar's dais had been extended and now took up almost half of one side. Senators and others were mingling about there as they watched the game. The field had been covered with strips of green sod to replace the destroyed grass from yesterday. *Someone worked late to do all this.*

Phoebe and Jaxom headed towards the Pharaoh and Dictator. Marcus wasn't surprised as Chris headed in a different direction, towards a group of Patricians they had met the night before.

"There's our young star," Cornelia Metelli called out. The distant cousin of the Consul stood with Servillius Casca and an aristocratic lady he had not met.

"Will you be performing today, Chris?" Servillius asked. He was a friendly middle-aged Senator they had met at Clodia's place.

"Yes," Chris answered with excitement. "We're doing an Egyptian piece in honor of the Pharaoh's return. So how's the game going?" Marcus glanced at the scoreboard. XI to III in the fourth quarter.

"Pompey's Warriors are a sure win," Cornelia shrugged. "All experienced war veterans verses a bunch of grape pickers. It was so obvious that no one even took bets on the game. Let me introduce you to Atia Caesonia." As Chris kissed the lady's hand, Marcus contemplated her name.

"Any relation to the Dictator?" he asked and Atia smiled brightly.

"Julius is my Uncle," Atia revealed. "I hear you performed magic to save him in the Senate attack."

"Where did you hear that?" Marcus asked, taken back.

"Rumors flow easily through Rome," she responded. "I am grateful if you did. Look at all that Julius has accomplished."

"We heard about his announcement today," Chris exclaimed. Marcus was glad about his friends' interruption. *Such a rumor already flowing through Rome?* He felt unsettled by the idea.

"That will be too much for the traditionalist to handle,' Servillius commented looking almost insulted over the change. "He can't decide to free all the slaves. The vineyards and granaries depend on their labor."

"Yet he has," Atia glowed with pride at her Uncles actions. "He has the might of the legions to enforce it too." Chris pulled Miriam close, looking bothered by the conversation.

"You will not be so proud when Rome is starving," Servillius countered.

"I will always be proud of Julius," Atia responded forcefully.

"You must be proud of Octavian as well," Cornelia changed the subject. "Her son is returning from Syria today," she informed them.

"I am and I will be very glad to have him home," Atia answered.

"More slaves are being captured during this war," Servillius said, renewing the argument.

"Actually, Lepidus has orders to only detain political prisoners," another Senator nearby informed them. "I am Dolabella. You must be Chris and Marcus." *Why does everyone know us*, Marcus wondered as he shook the man's hand?

The Chimes announced the end of the game, sending Pompey's Warriors to round two. The crowded stands began to empty a bit, but no one seemed to be leaving the raised elite platform. If fact it seemed to be getting more crowded. Marcus looked around and saw Cicero leading a group of Senators towards Julius Caesar. *He's planning to cause more trouble.*

The crowd began parting to let the faction of traditionalist past. The Dictator stood, surrounded by his consuls and Cleopatra and watched them approach.

"We shall discuss your complaints at the next Senate meeting," Julius Caesar remarked as they drew near him. "This does not seem like the proper time or place for such rhetoric." Cicero stepped forward to speak for the faction of disgruntled men.

"You announced the election results in this arena, as well as your newest proposal to free all slaves of the Republic," Cicero countered. "That seems a fitting precedent to continue the discussion here. Your many changes are shaking Rome to its very foundation. The prosperity and excellence of our great Republic depends upon following the traditions and wisdom of our ancestors. These alterations to our law completely disregard our customs which were passed down by the very men who secured our freedom from tyranny."

"Our Roman Republic was founded upon the principles of freedom and duty," Julius Caesar interrupted. "I have strived to expand what our forefathers began centuries ago to include everyone under the care of our noble Republic."

"You have stripped the power of the paternal father, effeminated the Senate with women and now you would crumble our economy to free those whose place was chosen by the Gods," Cicero accused. The other Senators in his faction grumbled in agreement.

"I have six hundred slaves on my plantation," one Senator complained. "How am I to continue my business without their labor?"

"I give my slaves food and shelter," another exclaimed. "They'll starve or become thieves to survive."

"What's going on?" asked a voice behind him. Marcus turned and was startled to see two legionnaires standing next them.

"Octavian!" Aria squealed and pulled one of the soldiers into a tight embrace. Marcus realized this young soldier was destined to become the famous Caesar Augustus. *Except we changed everything.*

"Mother, it's great to see you," Octavian said, returning the hug. "This is my friend, Marcus Agrippa." Aria greeted the other soldier. "What's Cicero issue?" Octavian asked.

"Your Uncle announced this morning that all slaves in the Republic are to be freed," Aria informed her son. "While you've been away, much has occurred. Women now hold seats in the Senate and we held true elections again yesterday. The traditionalist are not happy over all the changes."

"What are we doing in the Circus Maximus?" Octavian questioned, looking intrigued by the changes.

"This is Gladiatorball," Cornelia announced. "You should meet Chris and Marcus. They are travelers from across the Western ocean. This game is from their homeland." Marcus shook the hand of the possible future Emporer not knowing what to say.

"They saved Julius in an attack last month and he had declared them family friends." Aria told her son.

"Then I shall consider you friends as well," Octavian announced shaking Chris's hand. "Let's give Uncle Julius some support." There group made its way to the Dictator to stand with a growing crowd of allies. Jaxom and Phoebe were also there, standing behind the Pharaoh.

"As Dictator of Rome, it is my duty to look to the future of this great Republic," Julius Caesar roared out over the voices of Cicero's faction. "My ancestral Goddess told me that I should look for the divine in each one of her children. I declare that all slaves within Rome and her many providences will be set free!" A loud rumble from high overhead caused every eye to raise. Marcus caught his breath as he saw a huge meteor blazing across the blue sky. *It is a sign from Venus* was his first thought. Then he corrected himself. *Didn't a meteor fly over Rome at about this time? They saw it as a sign for Octavian.*

Marcus looked around at the crowd. Everyone in the Circus Maximus was in complete shock. Even the Dictator seemed at a loss for words. Strangely, the first to move was Marcus Brutus. He stepped forward next to Julius Caesar, his alleged father, to defend the great leader of Rome.

"By this divine sign, Venus shows her approval," Marcus Brutus announced. "Julius Caesar's word shall be followed." The crowd in the stadium roared with approval, calling out praise to their Dictator. When the noise decreased, Cicero, still looking stunned, conceded.

"Venus has made her decree known and I cannot stand against it," Cicero acknowledged. "I withdraw my protest." His faction of Senators had already begun to quickly disperse when Cicero turned around dejectedly and left.

"I feel kind of sorry for him," Atia disclosed. "He has nothing left now."

"What do you mean," Chris asked?

"Six months ago, his daughter, Tullia died in childbirth, Atia revealed. "She was the light of his world. All he had left was his political career and now that is in ruins."

"Perhaps a position as head librarian of Rome will provide him with something new," Julius Caesar suggested giving Aria a squeeze. "I don't want my favorite niece to be saddened." Then the Dictator focus moved to Marcus

Brutus. "I am honored to stand beside you, my son. I should have acknowledged you many years ago." The Dictator embraced Brutus then turned to Cleopatra. "My love, I also wish to claim Caesarion as my own and to make you my wife."

The crowd, which had been silently watching the exchange, burst into roaring applause. The noise drowned out the Pharaoh's answer though it was obvious as the two embraced. Marcus was amazed at how the people of Rome adored Julius Caesar. *It was the right thing, saving him like we did. When we leave, will everything return to normal?* Marcus remembered the civil war that should be ripping Rome apart right now, ending this great Republic, and shuddered.

The Dictator gave a signal to Calpurnia who rang the chimes, beginning the next game and stepped back to give the announcers space. Marcus had almost forgotten the purpose for being here, caught up in the incredible changes going on around him.

Octavian moved forward to greet his Uncle. Julius Caesar embraced the teen, glad to have him home safe. The crowd cheered for the players now entering the field, but Marcus leaned in close enough to hear the exchange between the two famous Romans.

"Welcome back to Rome, nephew. It is wonderful to see you return victorious and whole," Julius Caesar declared. "Have you brought Lepidus's report?"

"I have, sir," Octavian handed the Dictator a thick scroll with the somber feel of a legionnaire. Then Octavian's face opened into an easy going grin. "I am so glad to be home. This is my friend, Marcus Agrippa." Caesar shook Agrippa's hand as he continued to chat with Octavian.

"You must have many deeds to share from your travels," Caesar continued. "You and your friend will dine with me tonight so we can catch up. Much has occurred in Rome since your departure." Julius Caesar then turned looking for someone behind him. Marcus leaned back, not wanting to be caught eavesdropping, but the Dictator looked right passed him. "Miriam, tomorrow I shall need you to clean the Subura estate for Octavian." Marcus's surprise was nothing compared to Chris's shocked expression.

"Yes sir," Miriam responded automatically. Marcus could read the disappointment in her eyes, while Chris's eyes were transitioning to anger.

"Sir, by your command, Miriam is free now to do as she chooses," Chris stood up to the Dictator. Julius Caesar looked at him with a calculating glare. The look gave Marcus a sudden fear for his best friend's safety. *I hope Chris doesn't take this too far. It seems unjust, but still this is the Dictator of Rome.*

"You do not understand her situation," Julius Caesar told Chris. "Miriam will remain in my household and abide by my decisions. You are welcome to join her if you wish." Marcus knew Chris would not accept this.

"What if she wishes to live with me?" Chris continued.

"She does not have that right," the Dictator snapped. "Miriam is not a slave. She is the daughter of leaders from both sides of the Rhine. She is a prisoner of War and will remain in my custody."

Chapter 41

"Of course it's happening in your head,
but who's to say it's not real"
J.K. Rowling

Kristy hurried toward the Serpent district surrounded by anxious chattering women. Several other friends of Ms. Holland had shown up to offer their support while Kristy was inside. She only heard part of their conversation, their worries over Phoebe and the relief that the interrogation was over so quickly. Her own thoughts kept interrupting, pulling her away from this reality. *Why am I here when Phoebe is not? What is really happening to Phoebe and the others?*

Kristy wondered if her time in Rome had ever actually happened. *Maybe Phoebe and the others are still back home, working on their Julius Caesar project. Maybe I was never at that afterschool meeting.* She began analyzing the events of that day. Everything had been perfect. The arrival of child support had yielded an excellent new outfit. Then Benjamin was at her locker, wanting to talk about their group project.

It was strange that Benjamin asked me out right before the trip to Rome. I was hoping for a date to the dance in a few weeks, or what would have been a few weeks. *I wonder what day it really is. Maybe my mind has been dreaming this all up while I'm lying in some mental ward.*

They soon reached the Serpent District which still seemed to be in the midst of a celebration. The sounds of the river and music lifted her mood, but only a little. This new reality was amazing, but not real. Kristy knew she had not grown up here. She felt torn by her desire to live in this world, where her mother was whole and she had a perfect little sister. Antonio's face flashed through her thoughts, adding another perk to this world. She looked at the joy and beauty all around her and even though she loved it, she knew it for what it was, an illusion. *None of this can be real!*

She followed her mom into the too fancy temple she supposedly lived in. This time Kristy didn't even notice the incredible artwork as they headed up the marble stairs to their too perfect apartment. She continued into her new bedroom hoping that everyone would leave her be.

"Kristy, are you alright?" her mom asked from the doorway. *My fantasy won't leave me alone!*

"No, everything is wrong," Kristy answered with a sigh.

"This will all work out," her mom assured her as she entered the room. "We will find Phoebe soon and our life will go back to normal."

"But none of this is normal," Kristy exploded. "We don't live in a temple, these aren't my clothes and you… are different." Kristy didn't know how to tell her mom how mentally sick she should be. "I've never even had a little sister!" A confused look crossed her mom's face and was then replaced by pity. It was the same look she had seen everyone give her mom for years.

"I don't know what's wrong, dear, but we will figure this out," her mom consoled her. Kristy was swept into a tight embrace by this womon she loved so much. She was glad her mind had made her mom so healthy and happy. *I hope I can always remember her like this.*

Her mom pulled her over towards the bed and sat down on the soft green quilt. "Come sit down and tell me what you remember." Kristy sank onto the bed next to her mom and tried to explain.

"I live in another world, where there are no Goddess Temples or Roman Empire anymore," Kristy began. "I was at school with other students studying Julius Caesar and we were pulled back to ancient Rome. My friends stopped Julius Caesar's assassination and then I was in this world. Benjamin was there with me in the other worlds too." Kristy watched her mom's expression switch from concern to surprise. Then unexpectedly, her mom looked excited. With a bright smile, she hopped of the bed and offered Kristy her hand.

"We need to visit High Priestess," her mom said. Kristy reluctantly stood and took her mom's hand. She found herself again being pulled along to a new destination. They quickly descended the marble steps and then turned towards small wooden door behind the stairs. Kristy had never noticed it before.

They entered into a huge room which resembled the waiting room of a fancy hotel. The walls were covered in more beautiful artwork and plush couches were clustered throughout the room. *This reminds me of Julius Caesar's fancy front room.* Several ladies in long flowing dresses lounged on the comfy sofas chatting about the harvest. Kristy's mom pulled her toward the group who fell silent as they approached.

"Kristy has had a vision," her mom announced to the women. Everyone reacted with great elation. *But it's not a vision*, she thought, as the women rose with abundant chatter. *This is the hallucination!*

"That is wonderful," one lady exclaimed.

"It must be her psychic opening," another cry out.

"Tell us about it, Kristy," a third called to her.

"We should find High Priestess first," her mom said. The women all followed as Kristy was led deeper into the temple. They rushed down a long, wide hallway and into another chamber. This room was more elegant than the last with flowing white cloth draped along the walls and lovely statues displayed throughout the space. An altar was set with candles illuminating the space and the scent of incense filled the air.

A huge statue on one wall caught Kristy's eye. It was made up of three life-sized figures of dancers splashing in water, one a laughing young girl, the middle one a beautiful lady and the third, an old woman. *They resemble the people outside, always smiling and enjoying life. I wish I could find that, but in my own world instead of this fantasy.*

Their group paused here as an old woman, wrinkled but smiling, just like the third statue, arrived to join their group. She was dressed in a long blue robe and leaned upon a gnarled staff as she moved slowly toward them. *This must be the High Priestess mom is bringing me to see.* Kristy could feel a knot forming in her stomach as she realized everyone would soon know how crazy she really was. *But they aren't real so why am I so worried about what they think?*

"Ladies, welcome," the High Priestess called out. Kristy was surprised at the strength and authority in the voice of one so old. Several ladies rushed to help the High Priestess. She accepted their assistance kindly and was soon settled into one of several soft chairs lining one wall.

"High Priestess," Kristy's mom exclaimed. "Kristy received a vision at our Harvest festival. She is still confused over the experience and is in need of your counsel."

"Of course, Matilda," she responded, then turned to Kristy. "Sit with me, Kristy and we shall find understanding in what you have seen." Kristy sank into the chair next to the High Priestess. The old woman turned to those who had followed them. "Please give us peace for a time so we may talk."

The women quickly agreed and turned to depart. Kristy watched their disappointed faces as they left, glad for the privacy. Only one older priestess lingered in the opposite end of the room and busied herself in a small kitchenette located there.

"Would you like some tea, my dear?" the old lady asked but Kristy shook her head. "Would you tell me what you remember of the festival?" Kristy took a deep breath, unsure of how to answer. The High Priestess waited patiently, still beaming her sweet grandmotherly smile.

"I don't remember anything about it," Kristy announced, "because I wasn't there."

"Where were you then," the High Priestess asked.

"I was in ancient Rome with my classmates who were trying to stop Julius Caesar's assassination," she told the old womon.

"Were they successful in this quest?" the High Priestess questioned as she received a cup of tea from the remaining lady.

"Yes, but that's not important," Kristy declared wondering why this holy woman didn't seem the least bit concerned.

"Everything that happens to each of us is important," the High Priestess corrected her. "We can sometimes find meaning in even the smallest details of our lives, if we understand how to look. To succeed in preventing a wrongdoing can bring confidence and personal power into our lives."

"But it didn't really happen," Kristy exclaimed.

"We do not live in only a physical world," the High Priestess answered patiently. "Our mental and spiritual experiences are just as real as our mundane experiences. That is where we create this world that we live in.

"This is not the world I live in," Kristy grumbled wondering if the old lady had heard anything she had said.

"Tell me of the world you remember," the High Priestess continued her questioning. "Perhaps we can find out why this other world feels so real to you." Kristy was beginning to feel frustrated by the miscommunication. *Why can't they understand that I don't belong here?* She thought about her real life and the troubles of the modern world. She felt nervous looking into the deep eyes of the High Priestess, so instead Kristy focused on the water in the stone pool accompanying the statues as she tried to explain.

"My world is very different," Kristy began. "There is no Serpent district there or anyplace where everyone shares their harvest or temple. Most pagans hide their beliefs so they don't lose their jobs or have their children taken away.

Almost everyone is scraping by for a living while a handful of super-rich control things." Kristy took another breath and glanced at the High Priestess. Her smile had not disappeared yet, giving Kristy confidence to continue.

"Children have to spend most of their time away from their parents in government controlled schools," Kristy explained. "That's where I was when my study group was magically pulled into ancient Rome. In my world, Julius Caesar really was assassinated and the Roman Empire collapsed about 500 years later. New Empires have taken control, though. There's always news about wars happening and the natural disasters that are increasing, since they cut down most of the forests." Finally the old lady's smile dropped and was replaced with shock.

"Why would anyone chose to destroy the forests?" the High Priestess questioned so quietly that Kristy wasn't sure if the old woman was even speaking to her.

"To make money selling the wood or because they want to profit from the land underneath," Kristy answered. "There are no laws protecting the forests. Most laws in my world protect big companies and their profits."

"It's a harsh reality that you are remembering," the High Priestess commented. She sat pondering Kristy's words, her expression settling into a contemplative winkled mask. Kristy glanced at her mom who sat on her other side. She received a smile of encouragement, her mom's eyes still sparkling with excitement. Kristy felt confused. *Why is no one taking my delusions seriously? Maybe because they are all part of my fantasy,* Kristy decided.

"I believe you should meet Lepios," the old womon decided aloud. "Your multifaceted visions seems to be trapping you within their grasp. Lepios should help you find comprehension and clarify your sense of perception." The old woman rose from her seat, so Kristy did the same. Her mom also stood, looking more thrilled than before. *Who is Lepios?*

Kristy and her mom followed the High Priestess, slowly traveling through a small door at the back of room and down a set of steps. Kristy wondered how far underground this temple went, but she was too nervous to talk. The stairs ended in a small stone room with a pool of water located in the center.

"Remove your clothes and wash," the old woman ordered her. "You must not bring the smells of the outside world into Lepios's chamber." Kristy slowly removed her clothes, confused by the request. *Why would this Lepios care how I smell?* She slowly entered the water, finding it warm and soothing to her tense muscles. She laid back into the calming water and accepted a bar of soap from her mom. She quickly washed and then submerged herself to rinse. When finished, Kristy rose from the water and accepted a thick warm towel from the High Priestess. She looked around for something to wear but her own clothes were gone and nothing had replaced them. Her mom noticed her confusion.

"You must not wear anything when you enter into his chamber," her mom told her. "This is a great honor," she added as Kristy began to protest. *How can it be honorable to visit some strange guy naked?* Then Kristy remembered this was all an illusion. *Maybe nothing here really matters at all.*

Kristy numbly allowed them to take the towel and usher her through another door. This time they did not follow her. Instead the stone door closed loudly behind her. She instinctively turned and tried the door, finding it locked. There was no turning back, so Kristy slowly walked down a small flight of steps, finding herself in a dimly lit stone chamber. The room seemed to be unoccupied but then Kristy heard strange scrapping sounds from the corner.

She took a few cautious steps into the room feeling the hairs on her arms rise in apprehension. *Something's not right*, Kristy thought as she looked around the room for another exit. *Where is the man I'm supposed to meet?* At the far end of the room she saw a round hole in the wall emitting low light into the room. It was at least four feet in diameter, so Kristy headed towards it to see where it led. *Maybe I'm supposed to crawl through that*, she considered with dread.

She was almost to the back wall when the circular exit disappeared and the room was plunged into complete darkness. Kristy froze in fear and listened as the scrapping sound increased and flowed around her. She realized in horror something was coming through the hole, blocking the light. After a minute, the circle reappeared, but only the edges of it. She could see glimmers of blue scales as a round serpentine body continued to slither through the opening.

You are filled with terror, child, a voice echoed in her head. She turned in panic to flee and found herself face to face with the largest snake she had ever seen. The beast's round head was larger than her own, covered in iridescent blue and silver scales with pointed horns above its large dark eyes. *Why do fear me? It is you who has come to my home.* Kristy suddenly realized with alarm, it was the serpent speaking into her mind.

"I was told to come by the High Priestess," Kristy stammered. She took a step back and bumped into the serpent's huge twisting body. Kristy realized she was surrounded. *There is nowhere to run!*

High Priestess was right to send you to me, the snake spoke telepathically with her. *Your mind is chaotic. I can give you the peace that you long for.*

"I just want to go home," Kristy sobbed as her tears began to flow again. *Why am I talking to a giant snake? Wake up! I have to wake up!*

Kristy heard the snakes voice laughing as she watched its head rise above her flicking its forked tongue. She felt its scaly body tighten around her. Then with the speed of a waterfall, its fangs dropped and sank into her shoulder. Kristy screamed.

Jaxom's embrace was unexpected, thrilling and confusing all at the same time. Phoebe had just returned from her impromptu trip to Egypt and she felt travel worn from the long journey. Cleopatra had delivered her and her greatly expanded luggage to their new estate in Rome. She found the unknown house empty and was considering what to do next when Jaxom rushed in, sweaty and ranting. Then he threw his arms around her and pulled her close apologizing again for their fight. *Wow!*

"You don't have to say you're sorry," she whispered in his ear. "I'm glad to be back." Phoebe looked into Jaxom's troubled brown eyes. She was concerned with the stress she felt pouring through them towards her. His breath was slowing down but seemed too short and shallow. His brow and jaw were tight as if the weight of the world was upon him. Yet mingled into the stress, fear and sadness of his eyes, she could see his love for her. *He didn't mean what he said*, Phoebe mused. *And it doesn't even matter. I love him.* She leaned in and grazed his lips with the softest of kisses.

Phoebe felt the stress melt out of Jaxom's jaw. His eyes first showed his surprise at the kiss, then joy. He kissed her back. It was a gentle kiss, not like how all those cheesy romance movies described it. There weren't any fireworks, time didn't stand still and she was still aware of their surroundings. But there was a feeling of depth, as she could feel her own stress melting, relaxing into his arms. *Yes, I choose him.*

After the kiss, Jaxom smiled an almost embarrassed sort of grin and dropped his arms. Phoebe stepped back, almost tripping over one of her bags piled around them.

"Let me help you with these," Jaxom offered noticing for the first time the pile of bags. Without waiting for an answer, Jaxom began gathering her possessions and hauling them to her apartments. "You've done some shopping while you were gone." Phoebe grabbed some of her things and followed.

"Everyone just kept giving me stuff," Phoebe answered. "The Egyptians are a fun, friendly people and you'll be amazed when you see some of the treasures I was given."

"I'm glad you had a good time," Jaxom answered giving her a slight smile. Phoebe looked around the sitting room delighted to have space of her own. The room was spacious and furnished well with an open door in the side wall showing her a glimpse of a large bedroom. Looking back at Jaxom, Phoebes smile dropped. He stared at her with those brown puppy dog eyes and Phoebe felt such concern for him.

"Sit down and tell me what going on," Phoebe suggested and settled herself onto a soft green sofa. Jaxom slumped down right next to her, so close that their legs and arms were touching. She reached out and entangled her fingers into his.

"Everything's been going wrong," Jaxom scowled. "Chris and Marcus are being ridiculous. Chris just gave the Romans pyrotechnics just to make his performance cooler. They're both acting like they want to stay. I tried to talk with them but instead I let a houseful of people know about the magic. I'm so stupid! "

"It's not your fault," Phoebe replied. "Chris and Marcus are the ones who aren't acting smart," Phoebe replied, worried that Chris and Marcus weren't even thinking about what they're changing.

"Julius Caesar is even worse," Jaxom told her, squeezing her hand. A wave of emotion washed over her with the connection. "He's using me for the power of the ring. I didn't know what to do. But now that your back, we can wish ourselves home and be finished with this crazy trip." Phoebe hesitated for a moment before answering.

When Phoebe left Egypt she had thought she would want to go straight home when she got back to Rome. On the ship she had thought through the choice more deeply. *I want to be with Jaxom and help him with these problems but I'm not ready to leave Cleopatra and Caesarion yet.* She knew what their fate would be when she tried to put everything back the way it was. *Except for Jaxom*, she thought. *I don't want to lose this relationship we're beginning.*

"We will go home soon," Phoebe assured Jaxom, who was looking worried over her silence. "But I just got back here. Let me have a little time." Jaxom looked like he was sinking back into his despair. "Everything will be fine now that we're together," she told him. This seemed to reassure him a little.

"If that's what you want," he answered quietly. "I'll get the rest of your bags." Jaxom stood quickly, pulling away from her and rushing from the room. Phoebe sighed. *Jaxom's a mess. He looks like he's putting his cool kid mask back on.* Phoebe was glad he was again trusting her enough to be his true self. *This time I won't mess things up with him.*

"This bag feels like it's filled with rocks,' Jaxom commented as he returned carrying the rest of her luggage. He set the offending sack down near her.

"It does have rocks in it," Phoebe laughed. She untied the slip knot and pulled out one of many cloth bundle. Jaxom watched her as she carefully unrolled the material until one of her new treasure was revealed.

"Looks like a hippo," Jaxom remarked, "except for the weird tail." He obviously wasn't very impressed by the little statue.

"It's a crocodile tail," Phoebe explained. "She's an Egyptian River Goddess Taweret. She protects childbearing womyn. The Egyptians have so many deities they revere. I was given a dozen little statues like this." Jaxom's eyes told her that his mind was already wandering. "Here something you might like more." Phoebe pulled out the long flat parcel and unwrapped the soft linens.

"Oh, I recognize this," Jaxom exclaimed. "It's a Senet board. King Tut had a bunch of them in his tomb. But no one in our time knows how to play."

"I do," Phoebe told him with a glimmer in her eye. "I can show you how to play."

"Cool," Jaxom answered. "Teach me the rules."

"These are your markers," Phoebe handed him a bag as she began to explain the complex rules. They played the ancient board game for hours. Phoebe was glad to watch the stress drain from Jaxom's as the conversed. They shared with each other many tales about their adventures throughout the past few months. Phoebe realized that Jaxom was right. *Chris and Marcus are interfering too much with this past.*

It was late when Phoebe ran Jaxom out of her quarters. Exhausted, she fell asleep immediately. It felt like only minutes had past when she was awoken by a knock at the door. Phoebe stumbled to the door and was surprised to see Jaxom waiting to escort her to breakfast.

"Give me a few minutes," Phoebe grumbled as she let him into the sitting room. Leaving him there, Phoebe rushed into the bedroom and changed as quickly as she could. She grabbed her shoulder bag and took a deep breath. *Why do I feel nervous now, when we were fine last night? I'm just going to eat breakfast with him,* she told herself as she ran her brush through her hair.

"All ready," Phoebe announced as she returned to the sitting room. Jaxom's eyes quickly surveyed the dress then rose to meet her gaze. His lips twisted into a smirk. "What's wrong?" Phoebe questioned looking down at the pale green gown.

"If you keep dressing up like this when we get back home, I'm going to have a lot more competition," Jaxom laughed, "but I still hope you do anyways." Phoebe felt her cheeks flush at the compliment. She picked up a pillow and threw it at his head. He caught it and laughed again.

"You better behave yourself, if want me to eat breakfast with you," Phoebe threatened. Jaxom jumped to her side and slip his arm through hers.

"Shall we go then, my fair lady," Jaxom responded with a terrible English accent. "Your breakfast awaits." Phoebe allowed herself to be escorted through their lovely new home to the dining room. *He's so goofy when he's in a good mood,* Phoebe thought, loving every minute of it.

Unfortunately, the dining room was occupied by the one person Jaxom didn't need to see. Chris, who was lounging on one of the couches, sat up quickly when he noticed them enter, almost spilling the cup he held. Phoebe felt Jaxom tense and she squeezed his arm hoping to reassure him. He looked towards her with mixed emotions.

"Hey Phoebe, glad your home," Chris called out. "How was Egypt?"

"Great," Phoebe replied. "How have you been?"

"I'll be fantastic as soon as Miriam's tea heals this hangover," Chris chuckled, then glanced at Jaxom's face. Chris gave him a sarcastic sneer. "As long as Jaxom doesn't whine." Jaxom snapped and begun to scream. Phoebe let go of him arm and signed. *Why did Chris bait him like that?* Phoebe sat down on the closest couch to wait out the fight. Miriam stepped into the room, wringing her hand as she watched the two.

It didn't take long before Marcus stumbled into the room. He looked awful as he threw himself down next to her. His painful expression glared at the two arguing.

"Hey, good to see you, Marcus," Phoebe quietly said.

"You too," Marcus grimaced, "but my head is killing me. Can you two keep it down?" Chris turned his back on Jaxom's anger to console his friend and Miriam quickly moved to the table to pour a cup of tea. Jaxom grounded his teeth in anxiety.

"Sorry man," Chris apologized. "Miriam can fix your hangover." Taking the cup from Miriam, Marcus slipped the liquid and grimaced. "It gross, but you'll feel great in ten minutes." Phoebe watched as Jaxom debated with himself on what to say next. Marcus's interruption has deflated him a little and Phoebe hoped he would drop the issue. But he wouldn't catch her eye.

"You went way overboard with the explosives," Jaxom gripped. *At least he's not screaming*, Phoebe thought.

"What's done is done," Phoebe announced to him, using a phrase her grandpa liked. "We need to decide where we go from here." Jaxom looked straight into her eyes this time.

"Home," Jaxom said to her and he sat quickly by her side. She reached out and held his hand hoping the contact would help soften the fact that she wasn't ready to go.

"Not yet," Chris argued. "I haven't even sold a bike yet, and I want to see how the tournament turns out." Then Chris turned to her. "Don't you want to see it, Phoebe?" *Why is he pulling me into the middle*? Phoebe didn't want to seem like she was siding with Chris. *I'm not ready to leave Cleopatra and Caesarian yet.*

"I want to see who wins," Marcus added. *Of course he would support Chris.*

"I told Cleopatra that I would watch the Cobras play later, today," Phoebe stated. "It's an all women team and they're up against the Greek Achilles. I'd like to see who wins, but I also don't want to stay here forever." As Marcus assured her they also wished to go home, Phoebe watched Jaxom's reaction to her words. First he looked hurt and then his face settled into a resigned mask. The others discussed the teams they watched yesterday and Jaxom even relaxed enough to join in their conversation. Phoebe was glad the fight was over for now. She should have known Jaxom wasn't going to let the issue drop.

"After the tournament, we're all going home," Jaxom suddenly insisted. Chris stared at him for a moment then caved.

"That's fine, just don't ruin what's left of our time with your issues," Chris snapped. Jaxom was about to respond when Domitius burst into the room and announced that Julius Caesar had declared slavery a crime. Their petty argument was forgotten as everyone congratulated Miriam on her new found freedom.

Chris and Miriam quickly ate, then took off on their bikes towards the Circus Maximus. *Jaxom is breathing easier again, now that Chris is gone,* Phoebe thought as they headed out on foot with Marcus and Domitius. She was glad for Miriam and all of Rome over the change, but the realization that they would soon wish this all away dampened her joy. Chris and Miriam looked quite serious about each other. *I can't imagine how much it will tear him up to leave her.*

"Remember last night when I told you about our trip to Baiae," Jaxom interrupted her thoughts. Phoebe nodded. "Chris made a wish about freeing the slaves, but he wasn't actually touching me when he did."

"Maybe someone only has to be in your presence to receive their wishes," Phoebe suggested. "I don't think Benjamin was touching you when he made his wish."

"Chris made a wish in Baiae?" Marcus jumped into the conversation. "He never told me that."

"The rumors are right then," boomed Domitius. "You do have magic." Jaxom spun around and stared wide eyed at Domitius. *I forgot the he was with us.*

"Please don't add to those rumors," Jaxom begged. The big man chuckled in delight at being in on their secret.

"You have my word," Domitius promised. Jaxom remained quiet the rest of the walk. *He's condemning himself again*, Phoebe thought but she wasn't sure how to break the silence. When they reached the stadium, Chris and Miriam were waiting for them. She followed Jaxom towards a raised platform constructed for the aristocrats of Rome. They separated from the others as they headed towards Cleopatra and Julius Caesar.

"Welcome Jaxom," Julius Caesar called out as they approached them. "It is wonderful day when our women returned to us safely."

"Yes sir," Jaxom answered.

"Our tournament is quite successful," the Dictator praised. "The betting has doubled and there was only two deaths yesterday." Phoebe could believe Julius Caesar thought two deaths were inconsequential. *He's got a lot of blood on his hands already*, she thought.

The Dictator turned to speak to others and little Caesarian wiggled from his mother's arms to greet Phoebe. Cleopatra gave her a wide smile before she moved to follow her love.

"Up, up," the Egyptian Prince called and Phoebe raised him to her shoulders so he could watch the game. The first game of the day was almost complete and next would be the Egyptian team. Phoebe didn't really care about the games but was glad to spend more time with her new friends. She introduced Jaxom to Caesarian and listened with amusement as the young child explained Gladiatorball to them. Jaxom listened attentively and Phoebe was glad to know he could easily bond with kids.

As the game ended, problems arose. Cicero and his faction of traditionalist confronted Julius Caesar over his many changes to Roman law. *It must be hard for these men to accept everything the Dictator accomplishing*, she thought as she listened to the rhetoric. *These wishes keep making new ripples of change in every direction.* Then she noticed that Marcus and Chris had joined them accompanied by several Roman legionnaires. *How do they have so many connections already?*

"As Dictator of Rome, it is my duty to look to the future of this great Republic," Julius Caesar roared out over the voices of Cicero's faction. "My ancestral Goddess told me that I should look for the divine in each one of her children. I declare that all slaves within Rome and her many providences will be set free!" A loud rumble from high overhead caused every eye to raise. Directly above them, a huge meteor blazed across the blue sky. Caesarian scurried down from her shoulders, trembling, and rushed to his mother's arms. *Poor thing's never seen a comet*, Phoebe guessed feeling a little shocked herself.

Complete silence filled the stadium. Everyone was stunned over the magnificent aerial display. Then a man stepped up beside the Dictator in support.

"By this divine sign, Venus shows her approval," the Roman announced. "Julius Caesar's word shall be followed." The stadium flooded with cheers and praise for Julius Caesar. Phoebe wasn't surprised when Cicero and his faction yielded to the Dictator and his overwhelming support, but Julius Caesar's next actions astounded her. Not only did the Dictator give Cicero a prestigious new position as the head librarian of Rome, he than claimed Caesarian and Marcus Brutus as his legitimate children. *This has nothing to do with anyone's wish. Given the chance, Julius Caesar is proving he isn't such a tyrant.*

Julius Caesar signaled his ex-wife to begin the next game and moved back towards his gilded chair. A purple divan was situated next to him for Cleopatra, who settled herself down as Caesarian returned to Phoebe. Calpurnia rang a set of hanging chimes to start the next Gladiatorball Game. This time, Jaxom swooped Caesarian onto his shoulders to see the game. They watched as the two teams raced onto the field.

Phoebe thought the Egyptian Cobras were beautiful. Their tight fitting armor was banded in gold and black and completed with a Nemes-style helmets. They made the Greek Achilles look plain in standard Greek hoplite uniforms with blue helmets and lappets. Phoebe watched a Cobra caught the kick off and ran it back about twenty yards. Then Chris's raised voice caught her attention.

"What if she wishes to live with me?" Chris asked, as Phoebe spun around to see him face to face with the Dictator.

"She does not have that right, the Dictator snapped. "Miriam is not actually a slave. She is the daughter of leaders from both sides of the Rhine. She is a prisoner of War and will remain in my custody." Julius turned away, considering the matter closed yet Phoebe could tell by Chris's expression that he would not accept the Dictators decision.

Phoebe felt wretched for Chris, even though she was aggravated at him. *Falling in love with Miriam was such a bad idea.* She couldn't believe how wrong Julius Caesar was in not allowing Miriam her freedom. *I guess Caesar still needs his power-over someone to justify his self-worth.* Chris was seething in anger over the injustice, but Phoebe's heart went out to Miriam who seemed crushed. *Will she remember anything when we leave,* Phoebe wondered sadly, watching as the slave girl led Chris away.

"Look Phoebe, Kia's got the ball," young Caesarian broke into her thoughts, tugging on her hair and reminding Phoebe of her own sorrow. *How can I leave him and Cleopatra behind knowing the tragedy they must endure?* Jaxom's worried look told her that he had not missed the conflict.

"Caesarian, let's go visit your momma," Jaxom suggested as he set the boy down. The little Prince grabbed each of their hands and pulled them towards Cleopatra who was settled on her divan. Julius Caesar stood a ways away, chatting with the legionnaires she had noticed before.

"Are you enjoying the game?" Cleopatra asked her son. His jumping cheer clearly demonstrated the answer and Phoebe couldn't help but laugh at the little Prince's antics. *Oh, I will miss him when we go,* she thought, wondering how long it would be until she had a child of her own. The thought of a child with Jaxom made her blush and she looked at him to see if he noticed.

Jaxom was staring over her shoulder so Phoebe turned to assess the situation. Chris was leaning towards Marcus, speaking quickly and quietly to his best friend. He held Miriam close. *He's afraid he's going to lose her.*

Then Chris quickly walked away, taking Miriam with him. Marcus looked in their direction and as he caught Phoebe's eye, he gestured to her. She looked at Jaxom and knew he also was watching Marcus. Phoebe glanced at Cleopatra, finding her occupied with her son. Julius Caesar was also oblivious to their departure. Jaxom grabbed Phoebe's hand and headed towards their friend.

"We're leaving Rome," Marcus whispered to them when they reached his side. "If you want to come, that's fine. But don't stop us unless you're willing to take Miriam back with us." Marcus shrugged his shoulders. "His words, you know. But I think you should get that ring out of town." Jaxom looked at the silver ring and then to Phoebe. *We need to stay together*, she thought as she nodded to Jaxom.

"Ok, let's go," Jaxom agreed.

"Where are you going?" Caesarian's voice asked. They turned around quickly to face the child. Phoebe noticed the Pharaoh watching them, looking concerned. Jaxom leaned down to speak to the young child.

"Our friend is upset. We need to see if he is alright," Jaxom explained to Caesarian. "Tell your mother, we will see her soon." Caesarian raced back to Cleopatra and Phoebe tried to look cheerful as she waved to the pair.

They followed Marcus quickly to the stadium exit. The bikes were missing, evidence of a clean escape. They pushed through the crowd which began to lessen as they got farther away from the Circus Maximus. Phoebe looked towards the Palatine rising before them and spotted Chris and Miriam pedaling across the side of the hill. *Why are they riding the bikes up the hill?* Phoebe wondered, watching as their speed decreased.

"Jaxom, Marcus," an unknown voice called out. They turned quickly and found one of the same legionnaires Caesar was speaking with only minutes before. *Had Cleopatra told Julius Caesar we were leaving?* Just then the other legionnaire galloped past them towards the Palatine.

"Octavian," Marcus called out, "we need to speak with our friend. He is distraught and we are unsure as to what he will do." *This is the first Emperor of Rome,* Phoebe realized not happy at all to meet the famous Roman.

"You may go, Marcus," the soldier replied. "But I have orders to detain Jaxom, Chris and Miriam." Phoebe gasped knowing this was what Jaxom had been dreading. *Julius Caesar will surly take the ring if he is unsure of our loyalty.* He gazed at the Palatine, seeing the horse and rider closing in on the bicyclists. Phoebe looked from Jaxom to Marcus, hoping they could read her thoughts. She suddenly grabbed Jaxom's arm and ran, pulling him into motion. Phoebe could here Marcus behind them, attempting to detain the legionnaire. She only needed a minute of time.

"I wish that without losing what we've gained, we all returned to our proper time and place," Phoebe cried out. She had thought carefully how she would word her last wish, after carelessly using her second. For one last moment, Phoebe could make out Chris and Miriam on the Palatine with the legionnaire's horse right behind them. Then the air was swirling around them blurring out any vision. Phoebe clung tightly to Jaxom within the center of a vortex, like the eye of a hurricane.

Then suddenly, they were home. The schoolroom was exactly as it was before their adventure. Phoebe found herself taking a deep breath, watching as Jaxom caught his silver ring.

"No, you left her behind!" Chris cried, startling everyone. Phoebe felt Chris's pain wash through her. *Jaxom has to help him.*

"What's wrong with you?" Kristy asked as she snuggled against Benjamin. "I thought we were debating whether Julius Caesar was one of the good guys or one of the bad." Phoebe thought about that for a moment.

"I think," Phoebe told her friend, "that like everyone else, Julius Caesar was just trying to do the best he could."

"Jaxom, Marcus, I'd like to talk to your group before you go," Ms. Branson called out as the bell rang. Hand in hand with Phoebe, Jaxom headed toward their teachers desk. Marcus, Chris, Miriam and Benjamin met them there, eager to know what Ms. Branson would say.

"That was the best presentation I have ever seen," Ms. Branson praised them as she passed out the grading sheets. "You are all receiving A's, and I'm so proud of you for welcoming Miriam into your group so kindly. It can be hard being a foreign exchange student."

"She grew up in Italy," Chris commented, "so it makes sense for her to join us." He stood close to her, and Miriam smiled brightly.

"We love having her with us," Phoebe remarked.

"It's too bad about Kristy," Ms. Branson said. "Do you know how she's doing?"

"I've been visiting her at the hospital every day," Benjamin revealed. "She's doing well most of the time, but keeps having these episodes."

"Like when she flipped out in the hallway, screaming about snakes," Chris said grinning until Miriam frowned at him. He dropped his grin but Jaxom could tell that Chris was still amused by the incident.

"Yea, a lot like that," Benjamin agreed without a trace of humor. Jaxom was impressed that Benjamin was sticking with Kristy even after she was institutionalized. Neither of them seemed to have any memory of the trip to ancient Rome, unless Kristy's fits had something to do with it. *I hope not*, Jaxom thought, *but why would snakes have anything to do with the trip?*

"Well, I do hope she gets better," Ms. Branson replied then turned to deal with other students.

"We rocked that project," Chris cheered as they walked into the hallway.

"Now you can skate the rest of the semester and still pass," Marcus joked.

"I'm so sick of studying Julius Caesar," Benjamin commented, "I've even been dreaming about being in Rome. I got to go, you guys." Benjamin waved and hurried down the hallway.

"'He's not bad a guy," Chris remarked.

"I kinda like him," Jaxom agreed. "Let's get out of here." Their group headed out of the school building and towards Phoebe's house. Miriam was living with Phoebe, so they had all been hanging out there. It was a nice little place near the river and Phoebe's mom was cool.

"I can't believe no one's questioning those papers you had made for Miriam," Chris declared to Jaxom. "The school's totally oblivious."

"I told you, I know the right people," Jaxom boasted with a smile.

"Thanks again for letting Chris wish me here," Miriam said, "and for the awesome language ability. I aced both of my foreign language classes." Chris had used two wishes right after the returned from Rome, one bringing Miriam forward and another to let her understand everyone.

"I knew he couldn't live without you," Jaxom replied. "I kinda wish we didn't leave so quickly. I'd like to know who won the tournament."

"The Sicilian Volcano's did," Miriam announced and everyone turned to look at her. "I didn't leave Rome for several weeks after you left, so I was there for the entire tournament."

"I was hoping the Cobra's won," Phoebe sighed. Jaxom knew she missed her friends.

"They made it into round three where the Palatine Wolves beat them," Miriam told them. "Then when the Wolves were beaten by the Volcanoes, Julius Caesar granted citizenship to every Sicilian. The people loved him for that."

"Wow, Caesar really wasn't such a tyrant," Marcus expressed.

"He was just a man," Miriam responded."

"It's strange that bringing Miriam forward didn't change anything about our world," Chris wondered aloud

"My life in Rome as a slave was insignificant," Miriam replied. "Here in America I'm free to make whatever impact I choose!"

Thinking of wishes caused Jaxom's mood to drop. Phoebe instinctively wrapped her arm around his waist. *How does she read me so easily now*, he wondered. They were almost at her place but Jaxom wanted some time alone with her. *I need to ask her.*

"Let's take a walk by the river," Jaxom suggested. Phoebe smiled and agreed. "We'll catch up in a bit," he called to the others. They turned off the road onto a dirt trail that led to the water. They walked along the bank in silence for a few minutes. It was a beautiful early spring afternoon and Jaxom felt the soothing spirit of the river calm his nerves. He had something he wanted to ask Phoebe, but he didn't know how to begin.

"What's bothering you," Phoebe asked. Jaxom looked into her concerned eyes and felt so glad to have someone who worried about him. Jaxom sat down on boulder overhanging the river and pulled out the silver ring. Phoebe was surprised to see it as she settled beside him. "It might be dangerous to carry that thing around," she commented. Jaxom took a deep breath and looked deep into Phoebe's eyes, hoping she would understand.

"Remember in Rome, that night in the garden," Jaxom began. "I told you I wanted to wish my family back." Jaxom gazed at the silver ring as it shone in the sunlight.

"Yes," Phoebe answered quietly.

"I thought that since your wish brought us back to before my wishes, I might be able to use it again," Jaxom admitted to her. "But it won't work for me. I've wished aloud a dozen times to have my mom and sister back without breaking us apart but nothing happens. Will you try?" Phoebe slowly raised her hands and wrapped them around his own.

"I wish for you to have your mom and sister back without breaking us apart," Phoebe said. Jaxom caught his breath and waiting. Nothing changed. He dropped his head onto his knees and moaned. He yearned to change his past mistakes but some things just can't be undone. The song of the flowing water sang to his sorrow and Phoebe's arms wrapped around him. Her love helped to fill the hole in his heart as she tenderly kissed him.

"Stay in the present with me, Jaxom," Phoebe told him. A small smile found its way to his lips.

"That is a wonderful place to be," he replied and he kissed her back.

www.ingramcontent.com/pod-product-compliance
Lightning Source LLC
Chambersburg PA
CBHW080951020726
47505CB00009B/2162